KINGDOM OF

SIRENS AND

MONSTERS

By

PAGAN ALEXANDRIA

Copyright © 2021 Pagan Malcolm
Printed by P. S. Malcolm
Kingdom of Sirens and Monsters
Cover design by Bianca Bordianu
ISBN: 978-0-9756203-2-8
Second Edition (Published 2024)

Find out more about the author and upcoming books online on Instagram: @PaganAlexandriaCreative

For Sam

It has been said since ancient times that one rule shall remain true,

From the furthest reach of the underworld to the seashore, clear and blue,

That the kingdoms united in harmony shall thrive upon one thing,

From Atlantis to Coronis to Veranis—through sorrow, life shall sing.

For no being of the underworld can survive without a soul,

And no remorse can be felt from a being who is not whole,

And so, upon the world's shores, the kingdoms laid their claim,

For stealing the souls of Humans would allow their continued reign.

PROLOGUE

Her hair was suspended in the green-blue water; she was lifeless, still, and *stunning*. The rays of light from the surface were just enough to make out the light freckles on her sunkissed olive skin and the highlights in her blonde waves. He gazed, watching the way her eyelids had fallen shut in protest, the way her lips were slightly parted and turning blue.

She was dying.

Maybe he should help her. But why would he do that if it would prevent him from gazing upon her features just a few seconds longer? He'd never been this close to someone like her before. He'd never *dreamed* he'd be this captivated, but here he was, frozen, almost as still and timeless as she was.

He knew she was the one. He knew in that moment, with every fiber of his being, only she would do—that *nobody* else could compare.

Now, there was another figure swimming down to help her: a girl with a dark complexion and wavy afro curls stringing along behind her in the water. Beautiful in her own way, but there was something about the blonde that made him shiver in longing. He watched as the second girl took hold of the blonde and dragged her up, up, to the surface.

It was then that the male turned his back. Behind him were two other figures, both waiting stiff and prim for a response. The male nodded, knowing he'd finally made a decision, and they raised their spears in response as he spoke:

"Her."

PART ONE

CHAPTER ONE

Coral

The waves lapped at my feet as if beckoning me—and my
stomach turned.

Heavy black storm clouds hid the starry night above us.
But beyond the shore, the moonlight peeked out, hanging just
low enough to cast a sliver of silver light on the dark waves.
The ocean roared in my ears, and warm, salty wind blew on
my skin. I swallowed hard, remembering the last time I'd set
foot in the waves... the last time I'd tasted the ocean.

I blinked the memory away before the tears formed, and I
clung tighter to my surfboard tucked under my arm. A fond
part of my soul missed those waves, the way they used to
carry me, guide me, *free* me. But I hadn't been able to surf in
almost a year.

My stomach turned in knots as Matt came up behind me,
dragging his surfboard to the edge of the sloshing shoreline.
We looked at each other, and I could see the resolve in his
brown eyes.

I'd been through enough storms to know this was a bad
idea.

"Matt," I breathed warily, eyeing the waves with a frown.
"This is dangerous."

"You can't stop me," he said gravelly. His voice was deep
and thick, laced with the same hurt that had come crashing
back into me. And in that moment, I understood—probably

better than anyone else did—why he felt he needed to do this. But I also knew that *she* wouldn't have agreed with this.

Matt held out a hand, gesturing for me to join him, and I hesitated. I couldn't help it—I no longer trusted the sea the way I used to. I knew he wouldn't force me to come with him, that he would understand... but I couldn't ignore the pain in his eyes. And I couldn't risk losing another person.

I took his hand in mine, and we both took our first step into the shallow water.

This is crazy, I thought, as I waded through broken shells and tangly seaweed, feeling the smooth sand under the soles of my feet.

We waded into the water, surfboards in tow, until we were deep enough that we could mount. I lay on the board, the movements as familiar as ever—as if I'd never stopped surfing.

Together, we paddled farther through the sloshing waves. They were growing larger and larger—another warning sign. With no lifeguard on duty and practically no moonlight shining down on us, no one would know we were out here. Nobody would hear us screaming if something went wrong.

My heart hammered in my chest, and I felt like I couldn't breathe properly as the ocean waves caressed my skin. It wasn't cold, but it wasn't warm either. A slight shiver ran down my spine as I pushed deeper into the water.

My instincts helped me navigate the roaring, rolling waves. I knew which ones I could handle and which ones would take me under. I had to time this right. It was a shame, what with the weather warning and all, that we weren't able to do this during the day. But we'd have definitely gotten caught... and I, of all people, should have known better.

This was the only way.

When we were far enough out, we waited in the warm water until the right sized wave approached us.

"Ready?" Matt asked, eyeing the upcoming wave. The ends of his long rolled locks were sodden from the water.

"Yes," I replied firmly. My gut turned with nerves, half anticipating the wave and the sensation of surfing it that I'd missed so much. The other half of me couldn't wait to get back to shore where I'd be safe again.

Matt kicked into action first, paddling along the curve of the water. I followed, watching as he jumped up first to ride it. I was out of practice and barely stood in time to balance as the force of it came onto me.

Roaring water filled my ears as we glided along the water with our boards, the wave curving over and around us like a tunnel. I let out a laugh of delight, my stomach feeling as if I'd just rode over the edge of a rollercoaster. But suddenly, my foot slipped, and in an instant, all control was lost.

I hit the water. The salty sea sucked me under, and panic seized my chest. I saw her—a flashback—and I was paralyzed, remembering that day, remembering what had happened. Instinctively, I gasped for breath, but only water filled my lungs. Salt was in my nose, my hair, on my lips...

I couldn't breathe the way my therapist had instructed me to when these panic attacks happened. I couldn't *breathe.*

Desperately, I clawed at the water, fighting the current, which my dad had always instructed me not to do. But the panic was controlling me, urging me to get out of there. I had to *escape.*

I couldn't see anything in the murky, dark water. I couldn't see Matt, and I doubted he could see me. We were going to *drown.*

Why did I listen to him? Why did we *do* this?

Bubbles escaped my lips, carrying precious pockets of air with them. All the while, I was losing air, losing strength, losing consciousness.

Strong hands wrapped around me, startling me, and carried me through the fierce current holding me under. The frail moonlight glimmered above us, and suddenly, I shot up above the water's surface.

I coughed and spluttered, rasping to get air into my lungs. The hands left my waist quickly, and I kicked to stay afloat.

"Matt?" I spluttered, heart hammering as I tried to get my bearings. Someone had saved me, and it *had* to have been Matt. Who else could it have been?

I heard someone screaming, but the sound was distant, and when I looked toward the shoreline, I saw Matt standing in the shallow water, waves lapping at his wetsuit. His eyes were locked onto me, wide with fear and panic. But it instantly subsided when he realized I was okay and began to wade quickly toward me.

My stomach turned.

If Matt was there, then who was...

I looked down into the water, looking for whoever had saved me, but nobody was there. At least, not that I could see—it was too dark. Still, my stomach tightened in fear, and confusion settled over me. I could have *sworn* someone had pulled me up... but they had never surfaced.

"Oh my God, Coral!" Matt cried, as he paddled out to me. "Are you okay?"

I simply floated there, in the water, trying to make sense of what had happened. Had it been the lack of air? Had I imagined it? Perhaps nobody had saved me. Maybe it was all in my head.

"I'm fine," I breathed finally. "I just... I want to get to shore."

"Of course," Matt said quickly and helped me back to the beach. He offered me his arm for support as I waded out of the water. Exhaustion came on fast from the stress of nearly drowning, and I collapsed in the sand. Matt knelt beside me.

"Coral, I am so sorry. That was so *stupid* of me!" he said quickly, brown eyes filled with regret. I grimaced, examining the water droplets dripping from his brown skin and locks.

"It was... but it's okay," I said finally. "I understand. And Maya would appreciate the tribute."

Matt swallowed hard and nodded.

We'd both sworn a few days after Maya's death to surf every year on the anniversary of the day she died, to pay tribute to her and to remember her. She'd been his girlfriend and my best friend, and she'd died last year in a surfing competition.

Saving *me.*

Guilt wracked me as the memory surfaced once more, and I shoved it down as hot tears filled my eyes.

We'd grown up surfing together. It was our passion, the sport that formed our friendship. I'd been lucky that day—a lifeguard had found me after Maya had helped me surface. But by the time he'd hoisted me onto the life raft and gone back under for her, she'd disappeared.

They never recovered her body and said the exhaustion must have taken her.

The water lapped gently at us from where we sat, covered in wet sand, now. I stared at it bitterly. Sometimes I had nightmares about her body drifting to shore.

"Come on, I'll take you home," Matt said gently, helping me to my feet. But I shook my head.

"No, you can't—I have to sneak back in," I replied, and his eyes lightened with recognition.

"Curfew's on again, huh?" he asked, raising an eyebrow. I rolled my eyes and wiped a few stray tears from my eyes as I forced a smile.

"When is it ever not?" I replied wearily. "Anyway, she'll sense you coming a mile away. She's *very* intuitive like that. It's better if I just go alone."

Matt offered me an apologetic smile, and I looked around to see if my board had drifted to shore.

It hadn't.

I bit back a frustrated sigh as I studied the gloomy water. Yet another thing it had taken from me. I'd have to look for it during the day—preferably before another local found it. I'd have so much explaining to do if that happened.

And if I didn't find it...

Good riddance, I decided. *It's not like I use it anymore anyway.*

"Okay then. Well... I'm glad you're okay, Coral. And thanks for doing this with me. I really appreciate it, and I know Maya would have too."

I nodded, grimacing at him.

"I know," I replied shortly. "Anyway... I'll see you later, Matt."

We parted ways—him heading for the carpark up on the slope, and I heading toward a mass of rocks and palm trees on the far side of the beach. There was a trail, which would lead me back to my house. The storm clouds rumbled overhead as if warning me to hurry before a downpour drenched me further.

I hiked the dirt trail, and when I'd made it halfway up, I stopped to take in the view of the island. I could see the marina, speckled with anchored yachts and catamarans, their night lights twinkling peacefully. My gaze then drifted to the boardwalk where the markets usually took place every weekend, and I eyed the strip of touristy shops and cafés.

Farther out was the center of the village, which was only small and, from here, I could only make out the roofs of most buildings. But during the day, the sun would bear down on vibrant, colorful buildings, abundant tropical gardens, and spruce trees lining the main street.

I continued up the path until I reached a large bed of cliffside rock. Hoisting myself up, I climbed the final yard and finally reached the back gate of my house. Towering stone walls protected it, and the gate required a code, which I punched in from memory. Once inside, I was greeted by the back garden. I snuck past the tropical shrubs, the thick, vibrant lemon trees that our father had planted beside the stone terrace, and the trellis with the bougainvillea that climbed up to our bedroom windows—all while being as quiet as possible. The wooden staircase creaked as I tiptoed my way up, pressing my hand against the white stone walls for balance before easing the painted blue backdoor open.

Our house was rather large and built on a cliffside. One of the perks of being Christopher Klassan's daughter was living away from the village, which could get busy with all the tourism. Such surrounds made it easy to sneak in and out undetected, so long as you knew which paths to take—and I'd had years to perfect that craft.

I'd only taken a few steps past the living room and down the hall when a dark figure rounded a corner. I froze, heart skipping a beat as they folded their arms.

"There you are." Kendra scowled at me, shadows covering the left side of her face in the darkness.

I suppressed a groan. *Not now*—I was shivering from the cold, still soaked and sodden from seawater.

"Ken, go back to bed," I whispered, trying to slip past her. "We can talk about this in the morning."

"Where have you been?" she demanded lowly, as she stuck out her arm to block me from passing her. I sighed.

"I was out with Matt. We went for a swim," I lied, meeting her inquisitive gaze. Her almond shaped eyes narrowed at me.

"In the ocean, I presume?" she pressed, looking me up and down. She sniffed as if to confirm her suspicions, no doubt scenting the salt. "In the middle of a *weather warning*, no less?"

"We stayed close to shore," I lied again, pushing against her arm. "Come on, move—I'm freezing."

I finally got past her, but she followed me to my bedroom as I flicked on the lights and began rummaging for dry, clean clothes in my dresser.

"I should tell Melody on you," she said finally, leaning in the doorway. Melody was our unhinged stepmother-to-be who was just six short months away from marrying into our family.

"You would, wouldn't you?" I grumbled all knowingly, turning to look at her again. She had a lithe figure—like me, being my twin. We were *almost* the spitting image of each other—except I wore my blonde beach waves long, and she wore hers short and layered. And she'd gotten our mother's thin eyebrows, while mine were rather thick.

"And Dad would be furious," she added.

"All the more reason *not* to upset him," I replied, moving past her with my clothes in tow and walking down the hall to the bathroom so that I could shower. She followed me there too, perching on the edge of the bathtub before I could close the door on her. I was freezing, my body shivering, and I craved the feeling of hot water running down my body.

I slapped the clothes down on the vanity and gave Kendra a pointed look—one that said *get out.* But she didn't, and I bit back a sigh, folding my arms.

"Why do you even care so much for Melody anyway? She's *horrible*," I asked finally.

"You haven't even given her a chance, Coral," Kendra replied, shaking her head. Before I could protest, she came to stand next to me and took my hands in hers. "Look, I won't say anything, but *please* don't do that again. It was reckless, and if anything had happened..."

21

She trailed off, but she didn't need to finish. I nodded, swallowing hard.

"I know. I'm sorry," I replied, and pulled her into a hug. "You should head back to bed. We can talk more tomorrow."

She nodded and bid me goodnight before exiting the bathroom at long last. I stripped off my wet clothes in a matter of seconds and jumped in the shower. The hot water was bliss, and I stood there for far longer than I should have, relishing it.

I was lost in my own thoughts, only vaguely aware of the hot water racing down my back as my mind replayed over and over what had happened in the sea earlier.

The feeling of hands on my hips pushing me back up to the surface... it felt too real to be imagined.

But it *had* to have been.

All of a sudden, the shower water went ice cold, and I swore loudly.

Melody.

She was the only person who would bother meddling with our hot water system at this time of night out of pure spite. Either she knew I'd snuck in, or she simply didn't care for my long late-night shower activities.

Grumbling, I quickly rinsed the remaining shampoo from my hair and stomped out of the shower. My teeth were chattering from the cold water by the time I'd finished, and I hastily pulled my dry tank top and silk shorts on, rubbing my arms for warmth. They felt so much better against my skin than the wetsuit, and I sighed in relief.

I half expected Melody to be waiting for me in the hallway, much like Kendra had been. But when I crept out, she was nowhere to be seen.

Not wanting to risk it, I crossed the hall in three long strides and shot into my bedroom, locking the door behind me, then breathed a sigh of relief as I slumped against the door.

The clock on my painted, rustic side table read 2 a.m., and my eyes were beginning to feel heavy. I crossed to my vanity to brush the tangles out of my hair before bed, and my eyes caught the picture that was tucked into the frame of my mirror.

It was a picture of our mother.

Gently, I reached out to dislodge it and held it close. She'd been so beautiful—with long, sleek brown hair and upturned brown eyes. She had a sort of timeless elegance to her. We shared the same triangular face, but Kendra and I took more after our father. I smiled, remembering how our father would talk about her. He'd often tell us how much he loved her dimples and how they would show all the time, for she was always laughing.

I wish I hadn't been so young when she'd died. I wish I could remember her.

Tucking the photograph back into the frame, I quickly brushed my hair, then made my way to my bed. Exhaustion came over me quickly once my head hit the pillow, and I inhaled the fresh, tropical lily scent of the sheets as I drifted off to sleep.

The next morning, I didn't wake until 10 a.m.

When I opened my eyes to find mid-morning sunshine pouring through the window, I frowned. It was unusual that

Melody would let me sleep in. Perhaps she'd planned a better way to spend her Sunday morning other than tormenting me, and I certainly wasn't complaining.

I got up, got dressed, then reached for the clam necklace on my dresser. It usually lived around my neck, but I'd taken it off last night, not wanting to lose it. It had been a gift from my mother.

I quickly put it on, tucking it under my flounce-sleeved top, then headed downstairs.

The foyer, which our housekeeper kept impeccably clean at all times, was made of stone, and potted red geraniums lined the entryway. There was still no sign of Melody yet, which was a relief. I took comfort in that small moment of peace as I went to the kitchen.

Light spilled through wide, arched windows that could open out to let in fresh air. I was surprised to see the heavy storm had somewhat cleared since last night, giving me an almost clear view of blue skies and a sparkling green-blue ocean.

The kitchen countertops were white marble, and the splash back was white brick. Fresh irises sat in a vase on the kitchen island, along with a bowl of handpicked lemons from the garden. I crossed to the fridge and fetched a fresh mango, kale, and some frozen banana for a smoothie.

I was halfway through chopping the sticky fruit and wondering how I'd spend my Sunday when my dad walked into the kitchen. His beard was thick and rugged and his crinkled eyes weary. I'd gotten used to the age lines on his forehead from years of hard work. But he beamed at the sight of me, and I couldn't help but beam back. I felt like I rarely ever saw him anymore.

"Do you have the day off?" I asked him, coming around to hug him. He wrapped his arms around me and chuckled lowly.

"Did you forget?" he asked, and I stepped back with a frown. He shook his head at me. "The lunch? I'm taking your sister and you to the marina like we talked about last week."

My eyes nearly bulged out of my head. I hadn't forgotten—I'd just expected it to fall through, like most of his recent plans had.

It wasn't his fault. I knew Melody was constantly interfering, making plans over his plans so he simply couldn't refuse, or adding to his workload so that he'd have to cancel. I was shocked that this lunch was even happening because I'd dismissed it as soon as it came up.

"We're really going?" I asked, my eyes wide, and he beamed.

"Get ready. We'll be leaving in a few minutes," he promised, and turned for the door.

"Wait—is Melody coming?" I asked, and I barely dared to breathe. A lunch with our dad was rare, but a lunch with *just* our dad was even rarer.

"She had an appointment this morning, but she'll be joining us later," he said. I nodded, swallowing hard, and tried not to let my disappointment show. I suppose it was fine—at least we'd get *some* time alone with him. And we'd be in public, so perhaps Melody would be on her best behavior...

At least, I hoped.

CHAPTER TWO

Coral

Dad, Kendra, and I used to come to the marina all the time before he met Melody. We would do anything that got us out and about on the island as it had been my dad's life work—his heart and soul.

He'd been on a solo expedition across the ocean when he'd discovered the island, our home. He'd come back with ships and crews and built the island resort that stood here today: Odyssey Bay. It was now a famous tourist destination, and we had thousands of tourists visit every year.

Unfortunately, all of this had attracted the likes of Melody Pryor just last year. They'd only been together for six months when Dad proposed. It had all happened so quickly, and ever since, Melody had slowly been taking control of everything. It had started with small things—like deciding when she could ground us. I think my dad saw it as her taking initiative as our new stepmother, but I saw it as crossing a boundary.

After that, she'd started controlling the finances, helping to manage the island resort, and now she was breaking our family traditions and replacing them with her own activities. I believed she was after wealth and power because she certainly didn't act like she was in love with my dad when he was absent. I still didn't understand what my dad saw in her, and I missed the days before she'd turned up in our lives.

That's why today—*this lunch*—was especially special. It had been so long since we'd gone out to lunch with our dad, and the marina held particular fond memories for us.

The marina had a long strip of cafes and restaurants lined with tropical gardens and overlooking a harbor filled with yachts and catamarans. On most days, the water was sparkling blue, but today a few clouds lingered in the distance from the storm, casting dull shadows over the water.

Our favorite restaurant was right down the end of the strip; an Italian place that made the *best* pesto chicken pizza, topped with seasoned chicken, dried tomatoes, brie cheese, and fresh arugula. We used to order one to share, as well as a variety of pasta, then finish up with gelato.

That's where Dad led us this time too, and as we were walking past the other cafes, I inhaled the scent of fish and nearly gagged. Mom had never eaten fish her entire life. She was so against it that Dad had raised us to not eat fish to honor her memory. It was what she would have wanted.

Reflecting on the tradition throughout my life, I hadn't always understood why. But something about the way Mom had felt against it... it had carried through Dad when he raised us. I understood Mom's resistance through that alone, and so I had never—*never*—eaten fish in my life. Just the thought of it made me feel nauseated.

We finally reached the Italian restaurant, and we were shown to a reserved table on the exterior terrace overlooking the waters below. Dad sat so that he had a view of the boats in the harbor—he *loved* sailing and when he wasn't sailing, he enjoyed admiring other people's boats.

"How has work been, Coral?" Dad asked after we'd ordered, turning his attention to me as I poured myself some more water.

"It's been fine. A little busy," I replied.

"Are you still enjoying it?" he pressed, raising an eyebrow curiously. "Because if not, I can talk to Melody—"

"No, it's great," I cut in quickly, and smiled reassuringly at him. "It's an easy job. And I get free food on my lunch break, so it's awesome."

That seemed to satisfy Dad, whose eyes shifted from uncertain to pleased. He leaned back in his chair, and I noticed his shoulders relax.

Kendra, on the other hand, was eyeing me with her lips pulled thin, and I knew she was seeing right through me.

I hoped she wouldn't start arguing about this again. Not *here...*

"What about you Kendra? How's school going?" Dad asked her, and she leaned back in her chair and folded her arms.

"It's fine," she said, almost mimicking my response as her eyes bore into mine. "A little *lonely* without Coral around."

I sighed.

"Kendra, *please—*"

"Complimentary bread?" a voice cut in, and our gazes whipped to the waitress who was standing beside our table, offering a basket of bread and butter.

"Yes, please," Dad said gruffly, taking it from her and setting it down in the center of the table. We were all silent for a moment as we helped ourselves to the soft pieces, but it didn't take long for Dad to speak up again.

"You know, Kendra, I think Coral is right," he said, looking up as he buttered his bread. "School is the best thing for you right now."

"So it's fine for me to be in school, but *not* for Coral?" Kendra pressed. She hadn't even bothered to butter her bread or to eat it. I tore at mine, taking small bites. Maybe if I ignored her, she would drop the subject...

"Now, you know that's not what happened," Dad insisted, and I could see the tension knitting in his brow now. "Melody just thought it would be good for one of you girls to have some work experience—"

"As her personal assistant," I drawled, unable to take it anymore. I let my bread drop back onto my plate. "Because *apparently*, it was more important that Melody had someone who could fetch her lattes and run other petty errands than it was for Kendra to stay in school. And it *had* to be Kendra, didn't it?"

Dad was shrinking back in his chair now, guilt plastered all over his face.

"I know. I'm sorry, Coral. I should have talked her out of it."

Should have. But it was too late now.

"You didn't have to do it, Coral," Kendra added quietly. "I would have done it—"

"Well, one of us had to drop out and appease her, and I wasn't going to let you throw your life away!" I spat bluntly, and my raised tone sent everyone around us silent. My cheeks heated, and I dropped my gaze and busied myself eating my bread once more.

My sister wanted to become a marine biologist—she'd known it ever since she was ten years old. But if she dropped out, she'd never get to study the career path further. Somehow, Melody had convinced my dad it was a good idea for her to gain work experience as her assistant, and she'd refused to back down. So I'd dropped out in Kendra's place... but Melody hadn't wanted *me*.

Now, I worked at Snack Shack, which was a little smoothie shop on the island. It was too late for me to go back to school now. I'd have to restart the year. And if it kept Kendra in school, I was prepared to work there as long as I needed to.

"Well, how about this bread, huh?" Dad said finally, trying to change the subject, and I felt a tightness in my chest. The *one* time we were having a nice lunch with our dad, and we'd ruined it, bickering.

"I'm sorry, Dad," I said finally, and Kendra nodded in agreement.

"Yeah, thanks for taking us here. The food is delicious," she added, and bit into her bread with a grateful smile.

Our pizza and pasta arrived not long after that, and before long, we were conversing normally again. Dad shared his sailing plans after the wedding and resort developments he was working on. Kendra told us about her friend Janice and the awful date she went on last Saturday. I told a funny story about a weird customer we'd gotten the other day. We laughed and sank our teeth into the mouthwatering pizza, and I was so caught up in it that I nearly didn't hear the familiar click-clack of Christian Louboutin heels coming our way.

Dad's gaze turned, and his eyes lit up immediately.

"Honey! There you are," he beamed.

A pit formed in my stomach, and my lips pulled thin. Slowly, I glanced over my shoulder and spotted Melody walking toward our table. Her honey-blonde hair spilled over her shoulders, and her cream-colored designer dress hugged every inch of her body in a way that showcased her curves. She tilted her head innocently with a smile, but her emerald-green eyes bore into ours as her gaze flickered between the three of us.

She walked around me, stopping behind me, and I tensed as her hands touched lightly on my shoulders.

"Why, this looks wonderful," she mused, her voice slow and whimsical. Her hands were still on my shoulders as she surveyed the food.

"Sit down, my dear," Dad gestured. When her nails began to dig into my shoulder blades, I shrugged her off and cast her an icy glare. She smiled sweetly at me before moving past me and gracefully sitting in the empty chair to my right.

I wondered where she'd been all morning. Dad said she had an appointment, but Melody did absolutely *nothing* but meddle in Dad's affairs—so unless it was wedding planning or cake tasting, it was probably nothing important. In fact, she'd probably been getting her nails done for the third time this week.

It wasn't exactly a secret that I disliked Melody. The resentment practically radiated off of me. But Melody's presence didn't seem to bother Kendra so much—though it *had* in the very beginning, which I found odd. Somewhere in the past six months, Kendra had taken a liking to her, and I couldn't help but feel as if I was the only one who saw Melody for who she really was.

I'd noticed when she dug her nails into my shoulder. I noticed when she commanded control over family matters. I noticed how she could sweet-talk our dad into almost any decision, no matter how foolish it might be. And despite all her innocent smiles, I knew there was something fake about her. Somewhere underneath the façade was a woman I didn't trust.

Yet, all anybody saw in *me* was a teenager unwilling to accept a new motherly figure in her life. I *hated* it—because that wasn't what this was about at all!

"I need to use the restroom, I'll be back," Dad said, and excused himself. Once he was gone, Melody's bright manner dulled, and she glanced lazily at Kendra.

"Sweetheart, will you go ask the waitstaff to bring us a bottle of wine?" she ordered, and Kendra practically jumped to her feet to go find one. I frowned at Melody.

"She's not your personal servant, you know," I said, and Melody raised her eyebrows at me.

"She was more than happy to oblige," she replied, feigning confusion before helping herself to a serving of gnocchi. "She really *would* have made a wonderful personal assistant. It was quite selfish of you to take that opportunity away from her, Coral."

"You don't need an assistant, Melody," I pressed, and she smirked at me.

"Perhaps not. But she *is* my favorite daughter, and I wanted to spend more time with her," she mused, as she delicately ate her pasta.

"You mean *step*daughter," I replied lowly, not even bothering to address the *favoritism* part, and she let out a single laugh.

"Of course, do forgive me. I'm just so excited to finally become a... *step*mother to you both."

A chill went down my spine.

"Do your worst, Melody, but whatever happens, I will *not* let you destroy my sister's future," I replied lowly. A scowl crossed her blood red lips, and I reached for my glass of water defiantly.

As soon as my fingers had grasped it, Melody's hand clamped around my wrist. A sick twist of fear filled my gut as she yanked hard, and the glass flew out of my hand.

It fell to the floor and shattered, the sound splintering through the restaurant and causing every head in the restaurant to turn our way. I was frozen with shock, but Melody had already let go, and she was feigning horror as she stared at me, her mouth wide open.

"What happened?" Kendra cried, as she approached our table with a waiter. Melody shook her head, disappointment in her gaze as she said, "I think your sister is upset with me. We were having a disagreement and she threw a glass at me."

Kendra gasped, then growled.

"Coral, what the *hell?*"

I could feel every eye in the restaurant on me, and the back of my neck was on fire. I wanted to disappear into the floor. But at the same time, my palms were sweating and shaking under the table, and it took all of my resolve not to defend myself. I knew how that would look right now if I started yelling in protest.

Instead, I merely glared back at Melody, and when Kendra turned to apologize to the waiter, a brief smile played on Melody's lips.

"You didn't have to *break* it," I hissed at her, referring to the glass that now lay in fragments all around us.

Eyes shining with triumph, she mused, "Of course I did. After all, my dear Coral, *everything* breaks in the end."

CHAPTER THREE

Coral

Kendra and I had been very fortunate that Dad had bought us a car for our sixteenth birthday last year. We were meant to share it, and mostly we did, but an understanding had formed between us that on weekdays, I could use it for work and drop Kendra off at school first. After that, she could use it as much as she liked, but I tended to need it during the day to pick up deliveries and whatnot.

There weren't many cars on the island—most people preferred walking, and the village was small enough to walk from one end to the other in under twenty minutes.

The year we turned sixteen was the same year Melody had shown up in our lives. Everything had changed so quickly after that. Only six months ago, we'd envisioned spending our seventeenth birthday on Dad's yacht, or inviting our friends to the sailing club. Instead, we'd been stuck celebrating Melody and our dad's engagement with an extravagant surprise party Melody had thrown last minute.

I didn't think it could get any worse than it had. But I was wrong.

After dropping Kendra off at school, I headed to the Snack Shack for my shift. It was one of the shops along the board-walk—we did smoothies and juices mostly—and it's where Melody had ordered me to work once she realized Kendra wouldn't be dropping out of school to be her "personal assistant". Because apparently, I didn't have what it takes to tend to Melody's every need—and quite frankly, I think the job would drive me insane.

I first noticed something was different when I drove past the beach—the same one Matt and I had been at on Saturday night. Now that the sun had risen, it was crowded with people.

I parked behind Snack Shack, then headed through the back door into a storeroom littered with cardboard boxes—some empty, some still packed with supplies. I could hear Beverly, my manager, out front talking to customers, and when I walked through the doors, I spotted crowds of people walking up and down the boardwalk outside.

I was in shock. It was never this busy unless the annual surfing competition was on—and I'd thought it had been cancelled due to the storm warning.

Once the customers that Beverly was serving left, I pulled her aside.

"What's going on?" I asked, eyeing the crowds. She shrugged and folded her slender arms as she raised a perfectly drawn eyebrow at me.

"What's it look like? Competition's on."

I scowled at her.

"But the weather warning..."

She gestured to the sky through the windows and flashed her pearly whites at me, adding, "Does it look rainy to you?"

She was right—the sun was out, the skies were blue, and not a single cloud was in sight. Still, with Melody controlling more and more of the island through Dad, I didn't think she'd allow the event to resume with such short notice. More work for Dad meant less time for her to coddle him.

I didn't get a chance to ponder it further; the bell tinkled, signaling yet another customer, and before long, I had to get to work blending smoothies and juices. Most had come to watch the competition, but we still had a few regulars who stopped by on their morning run, bringing the stench of post-workout sweat with them.

I missed that smell—I hadn't been to the gym in ages. And I'd stopped doing laps at the school pool when I'd dropped out. Maybe it was time to start swimming again...

My thoughts were lost as I was swept into the whirlwind of serving customers. Time seemed to fly by, and before long, I was scrubbing sticky ice cream residue off my arms and washing the juice of oranges off of my chopping board. It was enough to keep me occupied right up until lunchtime when I was finally allowed a break.

I checked my phone as I was preparing to head out and noticed I had a text message from Melody. Grimacing, I opened it.

I'm throwing a surprise party tonight for your father. Be there by 5 p.m. I'll text you the address later.

Ugh. *Fine.* It wasn't like I had a choice anyway.

Shoving my phone back into my pocket, I made a mental note to cancel my plans of binging TV all evening and tried to bury the thought of Melody's party to the back of my mind.

"I'll be back," I grumbled at Beverly, grabbing a nectarine from the fruit bowl behind the counter and heading for the door. "I need to go down to the beach."

"You checking out the competition?" she asked, raising an eyebrow. "Are you sure you'll be okay?"

"I'll be fine," I promised, forcing my tone to soften, knowing that she was referring to what had happened last year. Besides, it wasn't just the competition I was going down there for. I still needed to find my surfboard—though my chances of finding it now were even slimmer than I'd hoped.

I stepped out into the warm sunshine, the weathered boards creaking under my feet, and bit into the juicy, sweet nectarine. I loved the sweeter ones, and Kendra preferred them bitter. Unfortunately, the only way to tell if a nectarine was sweet was by its aroma, and they always smelled sweet around here.

I'd finished the nectarine by the time I reached the end of the boardwalk. Salt stained the air, and the sound of waves sloshed against the rocks. I threaded through hordes of people, squinting in the glare of the sun as I made my way down to the beach—and sure enough, it was packed.

A large section of beach had been roped off for contestants, and there were two lifeguards on duty. Dylan O'Connell, a local radio presenter, was acting as the announcer for the day, and his commentary kept the crowd informed on who was competing—as well as who was winning.

"Ladies and gentlemen," Dylan boomed, as two surfer girls waded back to shore. "That was Laura and Camille. Let's give them a big round of applause!"

The crowd clapped and cheered, and I stared at the two girls. They smiled at each other, as if they were friends, and the sight rooted me to the spot. The applause around me seemed to drown out all sense of reality. My vision swam, and the people faded away. Suddenly, those cheers turned to screams.

"Coral!"

That was my sister's voice, and the memory of me waking up to a gathering of frantic faces flashed through my mind. *"Coral, wake up!"*

There was my dad, with his rugged beard and his crinkled eyes. There was Matt in his wetsuit. There was my sister, crying and clinging to a lifeguard. And I remember thinking that the sky was so blue above them... that the day was so beautiful... so, why was everyone crying?

"And now," came Dylan's voice, and just like that, I snapped back to reality, the memory fading away. The surfer girls had gone now.

I clasped my hands together quickly, trying to still my trembling fingers. *I need to focus*, I decided, and kept moving. My break would be over quickly, and I didn't have a lot of time.

I crossed the beach until I stood in a less populated area on the far side. It was a little way away from the competition, but there wasn't enough room between the flags marking the safe zone and the jagged rocks lining the curve of the bay for my board to have floated to shore. I pursed my lips in frustration.

I spent a few minutes pacing the shoreline, trying to think of another way to search. I'd hoped that my surfboard might be drifting somewhere nearby. But with all this activity and the fact that I'd lost it more than a day ago, perhaps it was long gone by now, floating out at sea. I hoped, at the very

39

least, it wouldn't wash up on the shore in a few days where a local might recognize it. My father would have my head if he knew what I'd done that night.

Finally, I couldn't stand it, and I climbed up onto the granite outcrops fringing the shoreline—the heat from the sun stinging my fingertips as I climbed—and followed them around the sloping hillside toward the cliffs. The rocks were all different shapes—some sharper than others—but that didn't make them harder to climb. I'd been doing this since I was a kid, climbing these rocks with Kendra as we looked for crabs and shells. The only difference is that she wasn't here to help me balance as I leaped from one rock to the other.

I walked for some time, ducking under and over the fractured and weathered rocks until I was out near the sloshing waves that hit up against them. The crystal-clear waters were turquoise-blue out here, and you could see deeper hues of green and blue the further out you looked. The smell of salt hung heavy in the air.

I scanned the shoreline, hoping to catch sight of my board but saw no sign of it. I could only hope it had drifted far, far away at this point, and I tried not to feel disappointed that I'd never see it again.

Sighing, I accepted defeat. The board was gone—and there was nothing else I could do at present to find it anyway. There wasn't enough time before my lunch break ended, and I was due back at the shop.

I turned and gasped as I came face to face with a stranger in a wetsuit. He was deeply tanned, with shoulder-length black hair and sea-green eyes that seemed to study me intently.

"Ah," he said quickly, taking a step back. "I didn't mean to startle you."

My throat went dry as I stared at him. He was *handsome*, with hollow cheeks that made his cheekbones seem more defined, his chin more pointed, and his somewhat warm gaze more penetrating.

"You didn't," I said finally, getting my bearings. I hadn't even heard him approach.

"I'm glad," he mused, the corners of his lips curving up slightly. "I, uh, may have followed you out here. I... wasn't sure what you were doing and thought that perhaps you might need help."

I raised an eyebrow at him, feeling my shoulders tense.

"Do you often follow women when they're all alone?" I asked, and he let out a single laugh, shaking his head.

"Not usually. You appeared to be looking for someone though, and it had me concerned. These waters are known to have strong currents from time to time."

Understanding came over me, and my doubts about him disappeared. *Of course* it would seem like I was searching for someone, not some*thing*, and that was natural cause for concern when it came to the ocean.

"I was actually looking for my surfboard," I confessed, relaxing my shoulders. "I lost it and was hoping it might have washed up here."

"I see. Well, I've been here all morning, and I haven't seen any surfboards floating around," he replied apologetically. "But if I do see it, I'll be sure to let you know."

I nodded, offering him a smile.

"That would be wonderful—the sooner I find it, the better."

He quirked an eyebrow at me.

"Why? Are you competing today?" he asked, gesturing to the competition back on the beach. I let out an awkward laugh, and shook my head.

"No. I... I used to compete. But not anymore."

He tilted his head. "Why not?" he asked. I hesitated, not wanting to bring up the terrible memory again. If he didn't know, he mustn't be a local. Everyone knew what happened to Maya... and to me.

"It's complicated," I said finally, and left it at that. I shifted uncomfortably before checking my watch. "I need to get going," I added, noticing my break was almost over. I slipped past him, but our eyes never left each other as he turned with me.

"I hope you find your board," he called, and I offered him a wave before turning my back on him, and made my way back to the shore. I'd left him there on the rocks and hadn't dared look back. Partly because he was so handsome it was intimidating, and partly because I didn't want him to catch me looking.

But by the time my feet touched the sand once more, and I'd made it back to the competition crowd, the most peculiar thing had happened.

I spotted him.

He was standing next to another surfer, and the sound of the proceedings echoed in my ears once more. I noticed he had a board now and that his dark tresses were now wet.

I frowned at him. How had he made it back before me? And without me noticing? He couldn't possibly have slipped past me without me seeing... unless he'd swam back, which would explain his wet hair. But even then, it had been too fast...

At that moment, under the direction of Dylan, the two men headed for the waves. The blond seemed tense—I think he was nervous, and he looked young too. But the other was confident in his movements, mounting his board with ease, as if it were an extension of his body. He seemed to be able to predict the waves...

I was transfixed watching him: he was mesmerizing. Possibly the best surfer I'd ever seen in my life. He was only lean, but he had broad shoulders and made easy work of the waves as he paddled. He was the kind of person you couldn't help but admire when watching him—he made it look so effortless.

That easy smile, the way he rode the water... I was nowhere near as good as him. And probably never would be now, after the incident. But I felt inspired, regardless, as I watched him.

There was never any competition between the two—the blond had never stood a chance. He knew it too. It was written all over his face when they came back to shore, dripping from the water, and the crowd cheered loudly for the amazing surfer.

"Well, wasn't that quite a show," Dylan said, clearly impressed. "Let's give a round of applause to Lysander."

I swallowed the name, stored it in my brain, and melded it there with seaweed restraints.

Lysander.

43

My watch beeped, warning me that my break was ending, and I turned to go back. But before I did, I caught Lysander's eye as he scanned the crowd, and our gazes met. He didn't tear his away. Instead, he smiled at me, almost leisurely, and there was a strange twinkle in his eyes.

It threw me so much I couldn't bring myself to smile back.

❧∽◯◯∽❧

Before leaving that day, Beverly stopped me in the back room of the shop before I could grab my handbag.

"Hey, Coral, just a second," she called, emerging from the storefront and locking the door behind her. "Listen, my friend just texted me and told me she saw you at that Italian place at the marina yesterday."

"Yeah..." I trailed off, and I had a feeling I knew where this was going. The *last* thing I wanted to do was relive that memory. It had taken me hours to get over it once we'd gotten home.

"Did you throw a glass at Melody?"

I sighed, tipping my head and squeezing my eyes shut.

"No, I did *not* throw a glass at Melody," I bemoaned finally, shaking my head and letting my shoulders sag. "Technically, *she* threw it, and it caused a scene, and she blamed it on me."

The good thing about Beverly is that she knew all about Melody, and she'd even let me rant to her about Melody more than once. It felt extremely validating to see her eyes widen in shock as I told her the story of what happened.

44

"I can't believe she did that," Beverly said, folding her arms. "That woman is *psycho*. I'll never be able to fathom how your father fell for such a wicked woman. It's like she's an evil stepmother who walked straight out of a fairy tale book."

I snorted, grabbing my handbag from the hook near the door.

"Yeah, except my life is no fairy tale," I replied shortly. "Anyway, I have to go get my sister from school, so I'll see you tomorrow," I said, before heading out the back door. I eyed the beach on my way to the car, but the competition had ended about an hour ago and was mostly packed up now. Only a few people were still milling about.

My thoughts drifted back to Lysander, and I couldn't help wondering if he'd won a prize. Maybe he'd even won the whole competition—he was definitely good enough.

I got into my car and pulled out from behind Snack Shack, heading back up into town and to Kendra's school.

As I pulled into the small parking lot, I noticed the students making their way off campus, and a part of me couldn't help but think back to my school life. Until ten months ago, I'd been a student here. I could still recognize people's faces, though I doubted many of them recognized me. My only friends had been Maya and Matt. Now, one of them was dead and the other an outcast—Matt didn't like high school very much. Or people, for that matter. He was a true lone wolf.

A pang of sadness echoed through me as I remembered Maya. She'd been so lively, so wonderful. The complete opposite of Matt, who was more reserved, but they'd complemented each other perfectly for that reason. I remember how

45

devastated everyone had been when she died. They'd laid flowers by her locker for weeks and lit candles in her honor. I'd had to avoid that hallway because every time I'd passed it, I'd felt like I couldn't breathe.

The sound of the door opening startled me, and I let out a steady breath when Kendra climbed into the passenger seat. She slammed the door shut—she was in a mood.

Awesome, because that was the last thing I needed right now.

"How was school?" I asked, trying to diffuse the air a bit. She huffed, and I instantly regretted it. I remember being in high school and hating it when my dad asked how my day was. It was tedious, and it hardly ever changed. *Good, bad, average...* what did it matter? It was just school.

I don't know why I'd asked her that, knowing how much it used to annoy me. I guess I was feeling disconnected from Kendra right now, and I didn't know how to reach her without setting her off.

I pulled out of the parking lot and was turning onto the main road when she spoke suddenly, "I'm sorry about yesterday. We shouldn't have been fighting in front of Dad."

I raised an eyebrow at her.

"It's okay," I said slowly, and waited for her to continue.

"I just..." she trailed off, and then let out a sigh. "I don't like what you're doing."

I glanced at her briefly with a questioning gaze.

"It's not fair on you, Coral. You should be the one in school, not me. Why are you sacrificing your future for me?"

I shook my head.

46

"I promised myself I'd look after you, and Melody had Dad completely convinced that she needed you. She never would have let up on it until one of us gave in. This is the best way, Kendra. You won't get to study marine biology if you don't finish high school first."

"But what will you do?" she asked pointedly. "Coral, you could be anything you want to be! You could be a champion surfer, renowned worldwide. But instead, you're going to end up stuck here, managing Dad's resort. Or working at Snack Shack your whole life! Is that what you want?"

I didn't reply. I didn't want to admit it, but she had a point—it *wasn't* what I wanted at all. But I couldn't let Melody ruin my sister's life.

Kendra placed her hand over mine.

"You can't live Dad's dream for him—he wouldn't want that."

We continued to drive in silence for a few minutes, but then Kendra spoke again.

"You're wearing Mom's necklace," she noted. I nodded, reaching up to feel where it lay against my neck.

Dad had given us the necklace when we were seven years old, and he felt we were old enough to share it. He told us Mom had left it for us to wear and remember her by. It was a smooth clam shell that shone iridescent under the light. Kendra and I used to take turns wearing it each week, but a few months ago, she'd told me to keep it for a while.

"Did you want it?" I asked her, but she shook her head.

"It looks better on you. It always has," she replied with a soft smile.

I pulled into our driveway, and the gates opened for us when I used the clicker in our car. I continued on up the gravel slope, through the leafy, tropical foliage and dark spruce trees that sheltered our home from view and gave us some privacy. But as I neared the garage, something caught my eye. Through the palm trees on the front steps, a person was sitting, and at first I couldn't make out who it was. Even Kendra frowned while trying to get a better look, but the person's face was angled away from us.

I parked right outside of the garage and turned off the engine. When I stepped out and the door slammed shut, he looked up. My hands began to sweat when I saw him.

"What the..." I murmured, staring at *Lysander*. What was *he* doing here?

"Wow, he's cute," Kendra whispered excitedly in my ear, and I fought the urge to scowl at her.

Lysander's green eyes lightened, and he stood from where he'd been sitting. His black hair was frazzled by the wind— and still seemed damp, even though the surf competition had ended hours ago. He'd changed into a dark sleeved shirt and shorts.

I felt like I couldn't move, and it wasn't until Kendra nudged me that I began walking toward him. Kendra followed behind, nervous energy thrumming from her.

"Uh, hi again," I said, remembering our conversation from earlier, that strange *smile* he'd given me. I couldn't seem to shake the desire and wariness that washed over me at the memory. "How did you find me?" I continued, and the hint of a smile formed on his lips.

"It appears it's not hard to track down Christopher Klassan's daughter," he replied. His eyes locked with mine. "I hope you'll excuse my intrusion. But I did say I'd let you know if I found your board."

My heart leaped a little.

"You *found* it?" I breathed. He gestured to something behind him, and my gaze fell upon my board, which was leaning against the wall, still intact. I hadn't even noticed it with his presence. My eyes must have been wide with surprise, because he offered me a lazy smile and added, "When I was surfing earlier, I saw it in the water. I went back for it and your name was carved into it. So I asked around town and eventually someone pointed me in the right direction."

My heart was racing in my chest, and my mind filled with panicked thoughts. Who had he told? Who knew my surfboard was out on the water? Oh God, it was just a matter of time before this made its way back to Melody's ears—or worse yet, my dad's.

Somehow, I managed to keep my composure as I said, "Thank you. I appreciate you coming all this way to return it."

I was about to direct him to leave—not because I *wanted* him to, but because I had to get this surfboard back inside before anyone else saw it. Not to mention, Melody needed us for her stupid surprise party this evening. But just as I was about to do that, the front door opened, and Melody herself stepped out onto the porch.

I tensed, bracing myself for her reaction.

She eyed the three of us, Lysander in particular, and she seemed to study him for a moment. Notably, Lysander's gaze had darkened in her presence. Melody's lips curved into an amused smile.

"Well, well," she mused, planting her hands on her hips. "Isn't this a surprise?"

CHAPTER FOUR

Coral

We all sat in the living room waiting on the refreshments Melody had sent for. The sea was audible outside, sloshing against the cliffside below the house. Our cornflower-blue painted balcony doors had been left open to let in the summer breeze. Pink bougainvillea flowers grew in clusters along the balcony railing, and a sweet, pungent, honey-like scent drifted from them.

Lysander sat opposite Kendra and I, while Melody hummed and gushed to our dad, who was home from work and had been coaxed into joining us by Melody. He looked tired, but his blue eyes were kind and attentive, and he smiled through his thick, rugged beard.

I stole glances at Lysander, who lounged on the sofa. It was strange, the way he leaned as if he didn't have a care in the world. He only looked my way once, but when he did, I noticed that strange twinkle in his eyes again and quickly looked away as my stomach turned in knots.

"It's so nice to see the girls making new friends," Melody said sweetly to Lysander, as she perched next to our dad. She turned to him, "Right, Chris?"

"Of course," he agreed enthusiastically, beaming at Lysander as he leaned into Melody on the plush sofa. "I don't think Coral has made a new friend in a long time."

I shrank back in my seat, feeling exposed in front of Lysander. He still said nothing, but I noticed his lips curve up ever so slightly.

The refreshments finally arrived, carried on a platter by one of our butlers. I took a glass of ice-cold sparkling grape juice to distract myself as Dad continued talking. The tray of drinks was handed around, and Lysander took a glass. I watched as he sipped the juice and made a strange face as he tasted it. I couldn't tell if he liked it or not from the way his lips puckered.

Dad fixed his gaze on Lysander.

"What brings you here again, Lysander? I think Melody mentioned you were returning Coral's surfboard?"

"That's right," Lysander replied coolly, his gaze flicking between Melody and my dad, who turned to me. My cheeks heated at the mention of it.

"I didn't know Coral was surfing again," he said, eying me with surprise. I wished I could shrink back even more.

"I'm not—not really..."

Melody frowned at me.

"But you were working today, Coral. When did you have a chance to surf?"

Oh boy...

I let out a slow, uneasy breath. Even Kendra watched me with uncertainty, cocking an eyebrow at me. The ice in my drink clinked, the only sound in the room.

"I went out on Saturday night," I admitted. I left out Matt—he didn't need to be dragged into this.

Both Melody and my dad's expressions hardened.

"In the storm?" my dad asked, sounding shocked. He was trying to mask it, but he was failing, and I noticed Lysander shift uncomfortably. I've never wanted to disappear so badly in my life. This was so much worse than the scene Melody had caused yesterday.

"Yeah, I'm sorry. It was stupid," I said, hanging my head.

"My goodness, that's so *dangerous*, Coral," Melody said slowly, emphasizing fake worry as she poked her own drink with her straw. "You could have *died...* "

I glanced up and caught a glimmer in her eyes. She could barely contain a smirk as she turned to Dad wistfully. "And it doesn't show very good responsibility either. Perhaps we need to be stricter on our girls, Chris."

I blanched at her words. *Our girls?*

Melody then added, "If they're going to break curfew, they need to be punished."

"Both of us?" Kendra interjected sharply. "Why *me?* I didn't do anything!"

"It was for Maya" I cut in quickly, and they ceased bickering. "It was her anniversary..."

Dad's gaze softened a little at the mention of Maya, but he still spoke sternly.

"I know Maya's death has been hard on you, Coral, but I didn't think you'd be reckless enough to risk your *own* life. Especially after what she did for you."

I swallowed hard, avoiding his gaze as his words cut into me. He wasn't being cruel, but the truth still hurt... and he was right. What had happened to Maya *never* should have happened, and I was a fool to endanger myself when I'd been given this second chance.

53

I turned my gaze toward the vibrant green potted plants in the corner of the room, blinking hard to avoid the tears stinging at my eyes. Dad sighed and then cleared his throat. "We'll talk about this later," he said, his gaze floating back to Lysander. "We have a guest right now."

Lysander was now watching us with cautious eyes, having straightened in his seat. He reminded me of an animal, aware of a danger in its midst but not quite motivated to run yet.

Dad noticed this and sipped his drink quickly, letting out a sigh of contentment as he swirled the ice cubes. "Oh, my dear, this is lovely," he said to Melody. "We should serve this at our wedding."

"You're getting married?" Lysander chimed in curiously. Melody and Dad beamed back at him.

"Oh yes—the wedding isn't far off at all," Melody breezed, tracing my dad's cheek. I didn't try to hide my frown, and Lysander shifted in his seat.

"Well, I extend my congratulations to the two of you," he said, but his tone was strangely flat. "When is it?"

"It's—"

Melody cut off Dad with a light chuckle and patted his shoulder.

"Honey, I have to tell you something," she said quickly. Dad frowned at her for a moment, and then his expression fell.

"Oh God," he breathed, "you're calling it off, aren't you?"

My heart fluttered in hope for a second, but Melody burst out laughing. It sounded like chimes on the wind.

"*No* darling, of course not!" she cried between her laughter. She was practically buzzing with excitement. "I've moved *up* our wedding day!"

My jaw dropped, and I felt like the world had gone still around us. Lysander's eyes widened at the announcement. Melody continued to beam at our dad, like her announcement wasn't shell-shocking.

"You have?" my father chuckled, relief flooding his eyes, and smiled brightly at her as if he should have guessed as much.

"It was *meant* to be a surprise," she chastised, glancing at me like her untimely announcement was my fault. "I had a whole dinner party planned this evening just to tell you!"

"Well why *did* you tell me?" Dad laughed, entwining her hand in his. Her gaze flicked to Lysander for a moment, and I didn't quite understand her motives, but clearly, she'd wanted him to know she planned to marry as soon as possible. Perhaps it was just her ego driving her.

"I just couldn't wait any longer," she crooned finally, leaning closer to him. "I want to marry you so much—I've already organized all the catering and venue for our new wedding date."

"How did you manage that?" Dad breathed in awe. "The caterers here are booked out with events months in advance."

The scene was so nauseating I had to sip my sparkling juice as a distraction.

"Oh, I have my ways," she replied seductively, then giggled. "In any case, we will be getting married just one month from now."

I spat out my drink, causing Lysander and Kendra to jump in their seats. Everyone's gaze turned to me as I coughed and rasped before finally slamming the glass down on the driftwood coffee table.

"What?" I coughed, eyes locked onto Melody. *"A month?"*

The original date had been set at least nine months ahead.

"I know it's sudden, Coral," she said, her voice soothing like she was comforting a toddler, "but I already feel so part of the family. Why wait?"

Because I haven't figured out how to stop the wedding yet.

The thought flashed through my mind before I could even process it—I hadn't even realized I'd felt that way deep down. Despite all my *wanting* to be happy for my dad and Melody... I simply couldn't be.

"Why the *rush?*" I asked pointedly, cheeks heating as I dabbed the juice I'd spilled with a nearby tissue. I didn't dare glance at Lysander. "It seems like you're in such a hurry."

Melody just shook her head, smiling.

"I don't expect you to understand, Coral," Melody crooned softly, as she stroked Dad's face. "But maybe one day, when you fall in love, you will. And when that happens, you'll have me to talk to about it—I bet you miss having a motherly figure so dearly, especially in your teenage years."

The words were like splinters piecing my heart. I blinked as my eyes stung a little, and I could feel her smirk without even having to look.

"In any case," Melody breezed, as if I were fine. "I am hoping you girls can help me with the last of the wedding preparations. I feel like it would be a good way for us to bond."

I looked up again, my expression now hardened.

56

"That's a wonderful idea," my dad agreed, smiling back at her. Then, a little more softly, he added, "I'm so excited to *finally* call you my wife."

She made dove eyes at him and that was about all I could take as I realized it was too late; Dad was in love with her. He deserved to be happy, but with this treacherous woman, I simply couldn't give him my blessing. The last thing I ever wanted to endure was this horrible wedding.

I stood abruptly, and Lysander's gaze caught mine. I could have sworn I saw pity there, which made me feel worse. He opened his mouth to speak, but before he could say anything, Melody also sprung to her feet, flashing him a forced smile before she turned to me.

"Coral, you're making a scene," she hummed, her eyes narrowing sharply.

Oh, she would know all about *that.*

I turned on my heel and marched out of the living room.

"Where are you going?" Dad called out to me. "You're grounded for Saturday, you know!" He continued to call after me as I stormed out of the house and down the steps. I'd nearly made it to my car when I heard another voice calling me, and I froze.

I looked over my shoulder, and saw Lysander jogging down the front porch steps to catch up to me.

"Coral!" he insisted, and came to a stop behind me. I let out a small sigh, turning to face him properly, and gave him an apologetic look.

"I'm *so* sorry you had to witness all of that," I said, wrapping my arms around my torso as my cheeks heated. He shook his head.

57

"I'm guessing you don't like your stepmother," he commented, and I let out a dry laugh.

"She's wretched," I replied through gritted teeth. "I just thought that maybe Dad would see it before... well... never mind. It's too late now. There's nothing I can do." I buried my face in my hands for just a moment, then added, "Thanks for returning my surfboard. I need to go."

Knowing that I was probably leaving the *worst* impression on him and that I'd probably never see him again, I walked to my car without looking back and climbed in the driver's seat. I didn't know where I was going—just that I needed to get away.

I drove until I found myself at the beach near my house again. I didn't intend to end up here, but I knew it was where I needed to be as soon as I arrived.

The sound of the rolling waves soothed me as I made my way down from the parking lot to the beach. The sun would be setting soon, and almost everyone had gone home for the day.

I sat right there, hugging my knees and burying my head in my arms. The waves tickled my toes in the sand. I let the tears flow for what seemed like hours—though I knew it couldn't have been that long. The breeze felt warm, almost like a caress.

Being near the water reminded me of Lysander again. I remembered his unkempt black hair, each soft curl. I remembered the vivid color of his sea-green eyes. I remembered his voice and how charming it had sounded...

I cursed mentally and shoved Lysander from my mind. How stupid of me to think of him at a time like this! My thoughts drifted back to my dad and I was instantly miserable again.

I stayed balled up by the waves until I heard a voice say my name. It was only faint, like a whisper in the wind, but it was enough to make me look up.

There, standing on the waves, was a figure lit by the setting sun. My heart thumped in shock and fear momentarily as I stared at it, but then I realized...

Those features.

The woman was dressed in a white dress but transparent like the rest of her body. She seemed to shimmer and glow, and it was hard to see her in the sunlight. I couldn't help but feel that without the sun's direct rays flittering through her body, I wouldn't have seen her at all.

But it was her face that unnerved me most. I recognized her from the photograph stuck to my mirror.

"Mom?" I whispered. How was this happening—how was I seeing my mother's spirit?

I had *never* had any kind of paranormal encounter in my life. No number of stories I'd grown up hearing about—mythological creatures such as mermaids and faeries—had proven to be real. And yet, here before me, my mother now stood.

She closed her eyes slowly, then opened them again. An urgency was in her eyes.

"Danger," she whispered.

I leaped to my feet, trembling. I didn't know what to do... but there was my mother, and I'd *never* had the chance to know her, to hug her...

I began racing through the waves toward her. Alarmed, she shook her head and gestured for me to go back.

"Danger," she repeated firmly, and I froze in the shallow water. At the sight of her pointed gaze, I backtracked a few steps, ankles still in the waves. She began to fade, and my heart raced.

"Wait!" I called, reaching out for her, but she was almost gone. I heard her voice again.

"A message. Find me."

Then, she had vanished. I blinked at the spot, but now there was only the pale blue sky. It was like she'd never been there.

Had I imagined it?

I shook my head slowly, staring down at the lapping water. Seaweed brushed my feet, reminding me that I was in the ocean's territory. It wasn't that I was afraid of the ocean, it was just that I knew I was trespassing the domain of other creatures.

My mom's words echoed in my head again. *Danger.*

Somehow, I was compelled to go back to the sodden sand, the cold air now encircling my wet ankles.

I collapsed and processed what I'd just seen.

I didn't know what she had meant, nor how I would "find her." This afternoon had been entirely overwhelming—with Lysander, and then Melody's announcement, and now this. I wanted to curl up and sleep to avoid reality.

But instead, my phone buzzed in my pocket. I pulled it out and checked the message I'd received. It was from Kendra—she'd texted me the address for Dad's surprise party, which was apparently still going ahead, and was asking me to come.

The words on the screen made my blood boil.

It was a freaking *sushi restaurant!*

Of course. Why did I expect anything less from Melody?

My nostrils flared, and I shot to my feet, nearly shaking. Quickly, I brushed the sand from my knees and hands before sprinting back up the slope. *Surely* Dad would realize this was going too far. Maybe there was still a chance to persuade him out of this marriage after all.

And if not, well, nothing could.

CHAPTER FIVE

Coral

As the sun was setting, casting pale orange and pink streaks across the sky, I pulled up at the address Kendra had given me. A narrow strip of small shops lined the road, and it didn't take long for me to spot the sushi shop.

I jumped out of the car, the cool evening air hitting me, and stormed down the street. Fairy lights were strung in the thick tree canopies above the sidewalk, and they passed in a blur—as did half a dozen outdoor tables and chairs. I finally reached the sushi shop and entered. It only took me a second to spot Kendra, wearing a pretty pink dress, seated at a small table across the room. Melody and Dad were there too—Melody wearing a plunging mauve dress, and Dad in a deep red dress shirt.

The table was close enough to a sushi train that they could reach for as many plates as they desired. The train was filled with all varieties—but none of which I knew the names of, having never tried them.

There was a roaring in my ears as I marched through the restaurant toward them. They noticed me just as I reached their table, and I glared at the three of them, knowing this conversation would make or break things.

"A sushi restaurant?" I seethed, struggling to keep my tone in check. Both Dad and Melody turned to me with frowns—but Melody's was obviously fake.

"I heard you'd never been to one before," she replied innocently, tucking a strand of her voluminous hair behind her ear.

"Because of Mom," I replied, narrowing my eyes. "Which I'm *sure* Dad explained to you. It's tradition—"

"Coral," Dad interjected quickly, noticing Melody's faltering expression. "Honey, let it go just this one time."

"No, Dad!" I cried, heart racing. "We *promised!"*

I couldn't believe my ears. Dad was acting like our tradition was nonexistent to appease Melody. It was one of the very few things we had left to honor our mother. I felt sick to my stomach—and it wasn't just the smell of fish wafting from the sushi train. Melody had Dad wrapped around her perfectly manicured finger. There was clearly no stopping her antics.

"Coral, honestly," Melody said, throwing down her serviette and standing, her chair screeching against the tiles. A few people glanced our way. "I am doing *everything* I can think of to include you girls, to bond with the both of you, and it seems like you just *won't* give me a chance! I thought this would be a nice surprise and a nice evening together! But you just *had* to come and ruin it, didn't you?"

I narrowed my eyes at her, noting her stony expression. I would *fight* her, right here, right now if it came to it. My hands were nearly shaking, and a roaring had filled my ears.

"Please darling, don't—" Dad begged, but Melody cut him off.

"No, Chris, I'm tired of this," she insisted, folding her arms. "Coral, I am going to marry your father whether you like it or not. Now, we can do this the easy way or the hard way, but I *hope* you'll choose not to continue hurting your father every time you see the two of us together. Can't you see that I make him *happy?*"

Kendra nodded, with a pleading gaze.

"She's right, Coral, don't you want Dad to be happy?"

I felt as if the room was closing in on me, and I couldn't breathe. *They were ganging up on me!*

I'd never felt so alone and isolated from my family before. My twin had always been there for me and always understood me like nobody else could. My father had always looked out for us and done everything he could to keep us safe and healthy. How could they *not* see Melody for the monster she truly was—her manipulations, her controlling manner, her fake smiles and patronizing speeches?

My fingers dug into the chair in front of me as I gripped it tightly and blinked back hot tears. I was alone in this. They thought I was some ungrateful, stubborn teenager who wanted her mom back and felt threatened by Melody. Of *course* I wanted Dad to be happy—just not with *her!*

I turned and ran from the table before they saw my face crumple and the tears fall. I couldn't even dine with them as a family anymore—not now that Melody had her claws so deep in my sister and my dad.

I drove to Matt's house, which was roughly two minutes away. Once I was there, I knocked on the front door but was greeted by his mom.

"Oh, hello, Coral," she said, clearly surprised to see me. "Matt's out back in the shed."

"Thanks," I replied. I couldn't find it in me to smile, and I felt a pang of guilt at how rude I must have seemed. I headed around the side where I was greeted by a tall wooden fence that encircled the house. The gate was slightly ajar, so I pushed through it and followed the dirt path to Matt's shed—a rusty structure that would have easily blown over in a typhoon. The wall panels were shabby, clearly having been replaced often over the years but never fitted properly. Despite all its flaws, it was his workshop, where he made all of his surfboards—and it was his pride and joy.

I knocked and entered.

Lying on a narrow table was a long, freshly-carved surfboard. Matt had already done a first coat of paint, and he appeared to be mixing colors for the next layer. The heavy smell of paint hung in the air.

"Hey," I said solemnly, and he looked up to meet my gaze. "Sorry to intrude."

"No, it's fine," he replied, jumping to his feet and crossing to me. He wore a light cotton t-shirt and shorts. When he noted my red puffy eyes, a frown instantly crossed his face. "What happened?"

Tears welled in my eyes again, and he guided me to an old sofa where we sat, and I spilled everything to him about Melody and the wedding. He listened from start to finish, nodding and doing his best to hide his own anger.

When I'd finished, he wrapped his arms around me. I noticed how muscular he was—though I'd never seen him as more than a friend.

65

"Oh, Coral, I'm so sorry," he said, holding me as I dried my eyes. "I can't imagine what it's like to have the people you love turn on you like that. And for Melody, no less—she hasn't even been in your life that long."

I was grateful for Matt's words. To his credit, he'd never turned on me or blamed me for Maya's death, even though he'd lost the person he loved. If Matt could still call me his friend after something as terrible as that, why couldn't my family listen to me over Melody?

"Can I... stay here for a bit?" I sniffled. "Just a couple of hours."

"Of course," he replied, and got to his feet. "I'm about to do the second layer for this board. You can help me, if you like. Or just watch, even."

I opted for watching—I was afraid to mess up his artwork. I moved to perch on a chair closer to the table, and Matt paused to tie his locks back before mixing the paint more quickly. His paintbrush clicked rapidly against the bowl he held as the last of his colors mixed together. He was a brilliant artist—some of his completed surfboard designs were mounted in the shed. There were sunsets and abstract designs, palm trees and waves. He'd sold a few to tourists, but the ones he was most proud of he kept for himself.

I remembered lazy summer afternoons spent in here with Maya and Matt, laughing and kicking up sawdust. I remember a surfboard Maya and I had painted together. It had looked terrible next to Matt's artistic skills, but Maya had loved it so much she'd kept it as her own surfboard.

It was at her mother's house now, probably stored in a dark corner somewhere so that it didn't remind her of the daughter she'd lost.

Once he'd finished mixing, he began to paint long strokes up and down the surfboard. I couldn't make out what he was painting yet, but it was warm, bright, and vibrant—perhaps a sunset. I leaned forward as I watched, and I couldn't help but envy him. I could *never* paint like he did—he was truly talented.

After a while, my gaze drifted to all the surfboards hanging in the shed, and my shoulders slumped. I *hated* that I didn't surf anymore... I missed it with all my heart. Surfing with Matt last Saturday, although wildly dangerous and terrifying, had filled me with a small moment of joy.

Joy I didn't deserve to feel... because it didn't feel right to surf anymore. Why should I get to surf when Maya couldn't? Why should I get to surf when she had drowned saving me?

It was wrong.

I let the thoughts go, let them drift away, and let my mind wander once more. There was still so much weighing on it... Lysander... my mother... *her ghost.*

I'd nearly forgotten what I'd seen at the beach, but not quite. I just didn't know who to tell... who would even believe me?

I looked at Matt again, who was deep in concentration, and frowned. Matt believed me about Melody. In fact, he and Beverly were the only ones who *did*. Maybe Matt would believe me about this too...

67

The thoughts became too much, too demanding in my head. I couldn't sit on it any longer, couldn't stay isolated in my drowning curiosity.

"Matt," I said suddenly, and he hummed in response. "Have you ever seen a ghost?"

He paused and met my gaze.

"No. Why?"

I bit my lip, unsure how to even begin explaining what I'd seen to him.

"I know this sounds crazy... but I could have sworn I saw my mother's ghost earlier today."

He leaned back from his handiwork and frowned at me, shaking his head.

"How is that even possible?"

I shrugged, wide eyed.

"I was hoping you could tell me!" I exclaimed with an awkward laugh, before hugging my knees to my chest in the chair. "She said to 'find her'... but I don't even know what that means or how to start looking."

"Wait, she *spoke* to you?" he pressed, narrowing his gaze.

"Yeah," I breathed. "It was only for a few seconds that she appeared to me. I didn't get a chance to ask her anything."

He paused for a moment, as if considering something. Then, he asked, "What time is it?"

I checked my watch. "It's nearly eight thirty."

He pursed his lips for a moment, then met my gaze.

"What if we talked to Maya's grandmother?" he asked, and I frowned.

"Why would we do that?"

Matt stood and began to clean his paintbrush in a nearby bucket of water.

"Maya used to tell me that her family was descended from a line of witches. She never believed the stories, but she grew up hearing them from her grandmother."

I'd *never* heard this, and I couldn't help but frown. She'd been my best friend. Why hadn't I known this?

"So... you think her grandmother can, like, talk to ghosts or something?" I waved my hand absently as I spoke, trying not to show my bitterness, and Matt shrugged.

"Well, maybe? Who knows unless we ask her?"

It was my turn to purse my lips, and I thought it through.

"I don't think that's a good idea," I said, remembering how Maya's mom—who avoided me in the streets—had screamed at me the last time I'd seen her. Her family didn't want anything to do with me.

"Trust me, Maya's grandmother is different," Matt promised. I hesitated again, but I didn't have any other ideas for how I could talk to my mother again. If there was *any* chance that this could work...

"I guess we don't have anything to lose by asking," I said finally, and Matt smiled at me.

"Let's go then," he said, jumping to his feet. My eyes nearly boggled out of my head.

"Now?" I asked. "Isn't she, like, eighty? What if she's asleep?"

"Come on, it will be fine," he insisted, offering me his hand. I let out a single huff before taking it and getting to my feet. Together, we left the shed and headed back to the front of

69

his house. Getting in my car, I took us on a new route—to Maya's grandmother's house.

I'd never met Maya's grandmother, but I knew Matt had, due to them dating. When we arrived at the quaint seaside cottage, Matt led me up the sea-weathered front steps to knock on the screen door. It was about a minute before the hardwood door behind it opened, and a sharp-looking older woman appeared in the doorframe behind the screen door.

"Who—" Her gaze went from me to Matt, and recognition bloomed there. "Matt," she crooned, and her gaze softened. "What a pleasant surprise!"

She was a short, frail woman who shared Maya's dark complexion. Her white hair was worn short, and her vibrant blue dress wore loose on her figure. She opened the creaky screen door to let us both in, and Matt hugged her.

"Ms. Mugo, this is Coral," he introduced. "Pardon our intrusion, but Coral has something important to ask you. I hope it's not too forward. Would you hear us out?"

Maya's grandmother regarded me with keen eyes, studying me a little closer. I noticed how they crinkled in the corners from age and how those lines continued down her cheekbones. It wasn't long before her eyes lit up with recognition—warm and brown.

"Oh, you're Maya's friend," she said softly. "Well, yes—come inside. I'll make some tea. Do you drink tea? I don't know if I have any juice."

"Just water is fine," I reassured her, as we walked into her strange little home. It was so different to the light, airy space of my home. Hers was all dark wood and weathered floorboards, aged from years by the sea. A pleasant gardenia scent hung in the air. Each room was filled with antiques and trinkets, and every wall was covered in wooden carvings and tapestries.

I passed a photograph of Maya on the mantle, illuminated by golden light, and my throat tightened. She was about fourteen in this picture. Her black skin was glossy, and her blown-out afro was just as I remembered it—she used to wear it parted slightly on the left, and the hues would always catch in the sunlight. Her deep brown eyes shone with happiness in the picture.

I felt my eyes grow wet and wiped them with my sleeve quickly before moving on.

We followed Ms. Mugo into the kitchen and sat at her round oakwood dining table. She brought us two glasses of water before joining us there.

"So what can I do for the two of you?"

I glanced at Matt, almost reluctantly, before swallowing hard and speaking.

"I think I saw my mother's ghost earlier today," I began, waiting for her to look at me like I was crazy. But Ms. Mugo's expression didn't change, so I continued. "She died when I was only a few months old. But her ghost spoke to me briefly. I... I think she has a message for me? A warning... but I don't know how to talk to her."

Ms. Mugo nodded slowly, and I felt some of the awkwardness in the air dissipate. I continued, "Matt told me about your

71

family's heritage... and I wondered if maybe you could help me."

She nodded slowly at me.

"I speak to spirits all the time," Ms. Mugo confessed, leaning back in her chair and tucking a stray white hair behind her ear. "I could certainly try to contact your mother for you."

Excitement and fear coursed through my veins all at once. Maybe Ms. Mugo's abilities should have seemed stranger, but I'd already seen my mother's ghost, so it didn't seem so far-fetched...

"Thank you! I'll pay you whatever you want—"

She let out a grunt, cutting me off with the wave of her hand.

"I don't want anything from you," she said firmly, and the look in her eyes sent a wave of regret through me. "You were a good friend to my Maya. That's the only reason you're here."

I paused, swallowing hard. Maybe I shouldn't have come here... but something told me running would be worse. I couldn't *not* say something.

"About... what happened to her—"

"She made her choice," Ms. Mugo said simply. "She chose to save you because she loved you. I'm sure you would have reached for her too, had the roles been reversed. Now, I don't have to *like* it... but Maya was raised to make her own choices, and I'm choosing to remember that fact."

Her gaze remained cool, and her words made my chest tighten. All I could bring myself to do was nod. It was more kindness than Maya's mother had given me. I could still feel her wrath, see her screaming at me across the graveyard when I'd shown up at Maya's funeral...

"Have you spoken to Maya?" Matt asked suddenly, and a strange chill came over me at his words. They hung in the air as Ms. Mugo's expression grew somber.

"Unfortunately... I haven't been able to reach Maya," she replied, her voice small.

I frowned.

"Why is that?" I asked, barely daring to breathe. I wondered if we should stop asking questions about Maya, but Ms. Mugo didn't protest.

"When I cannot reach a spirit, it means they have either moved on... or they are not a spirit," she explained slowly. Her voice cracked as she added, "So I believe Maya has moved on."

Somehow, that filled me with an almost overwhelming sense of sadness and relief all at once. The knowledge that she was in a better place comforted me, but knowing I truly could never speak to her again...

"Do you have anything of your mother's?" Ms. Mugo asked finally. I blinked for a moment, then jolted, my hand flying to the necklace around my neck.

"Yes, here," I said, removing it and handing it to her. Ms. Mugo inspected the necklace in the light for a moment before clasping it in her hands and closing her eyes. She relaxed in her chair and was silent for a moment.

Matt and I waited, watching her.

"Was your mother's name Lorraine?" Ms. Mugo asked finally, eyes still closed.

"Yes, that's her," I said, my voice barely a whisper. It felt as if the room was going colder around us somehow.

Ms. Mugo slowly opened her eyes—they seemed distant somehow.

"She's here," she said. "She has a message for you."

I leaned forward, not trusting myself to speak, as Ms. Mugo grappled to listen intuitively to my mom's spirit. I could only feel the cold and hear an occasional noncoherent whisper.

Then suddenly, Ms. Mugo's eyes became more focused on me—locked, somehow.

"Coral," she said, her voice strangely terse. My gut turned.

Ms. Mugo no longer seemed like herself. It was as if someone was speaking through her. Her usual low voice had a strange, high pitch to it.

"Coral, listen to me," she said. It was unhinging because her expression had twisted to accompany the new presence. "You must keep Melody away from your father and your sister."

As scary as it was to hear those words tumble from Ms. Mugo's mouth, I felt a sense of support for the first time in *months*. Like someone was confirming my suspicions—siding with me, *finally...*

"Why?" I pressed, listening intently.

"Melody is not who you think she is. Your sister and your dad—and *you*—are all in grave danger."

I didn't know how my mother could know this, but maybe it was something about being a spirit. Maybe she saw things those living could not.

"Coral, the necklace—"

74

The trance broke, and Ms. Mugo slumped a little, shaking her head. I stared with wide eyes.

"What happened?" I asked, my voice rising an octave.

"The connection is weak," Ms. Mugo explained. "There was more she wanted to share. Let me see if I can get her back."

She refocused, settling back into her calm position with her eyes closed. I exchanged an anxious glance with Matt, who reached out to squeeze my hand reassuringly before pulling it away once more.

Turning back to Ms. Mugo, her eyes slowly opened again with that distant look.

"Siren," was all she said. I frowned at her.

"Siren?" I repeated, not understanding. "Like... a tsunami siren?"

The connection broke again and she gasped, panting. She seemed pushed to her limit, so I didn't ask her to reconnect again. But Ms. Mugo hadn't even finished composing herself before her serious gaze met mine.

"She meant like those of myths," Ms. Mugo explained, able to speak of her own will again, and realization settled upon me as I finally grasped the impossibility of what my mom was saying. "Your mother's saying that Melody is a siren."

CHAPTER SIX

Coral

"What's a siren?" Matt asked hesitantly, looking between us with an uncertain gaze.

Ms. Mugo rose swiftly from her chair and moved as quickly as she could to the next room. I didn't know where she was going, but I was too busy processing my own thoughts to ask or follow her.

I'd heard of mythological stories growing up. Of sirens and mermaids and faeries. But I'd never imagined they could be true.

Was it true? Or was this just... a display? Had my mother really been here at all? How could she know Melody was a siren?

All I knew about sirens was that they could lure men to their deaths with their voices—their singing power.

I thought about how Melody acted. It was true that my dad seemed enthralled by her in every way and that he sometimes acted in ways I couldn't seem to explain.

I then thought of Kendra and how *she'd* been defending Melody. Was it possible Melody could affect females too?

But if that was the case... why was I clear-headed?

Ms. Mugo returned with a huge book. It had a worn cover, and she blew dust from the top before opening it and sprawling it on the dining table. There, on the aged pages, which smelled as old as they looked, was an illustration of a siren—

near naked, except she was cloaked in a sheer satin shawl blowing in the wind. A description sat next to it.

"A siren can enchant any mortal being with just the use of their voice, forcing them to believe, feel, and do as the siren pleases," Ms. Mugo explained, reading the text before meeting my gaze. "If it is true that Melody is a siren, your father is most certainly under her control, given the amount of time they have been together now."

"But not Kendra and I," I added, frowning. "Although... Kendra *has* been acting weird for a few months now."

Ms. Mugo's eyes fell upon the necklace in her stubby hands—my mom's necklace.

I then remembered my mom had tried to say something about the necklace but had been cut off.

"I'm picking up strange vibrations from this," Ms. Mugo said, holding the necklace up to the light again so that the iridescent shell glimmered. "It's very subtle, but when I hold it in my hands, there's an undeniable power within it."

"Kendra and I used to share the necklace," I explained quickly. "But a few months ago, she told me to keep it. Now that I think about it..."

The timeline between when Kendra started defending Melody and when she stopped wearing the necklace... it *aligned.* If there was a power in the necklace keeping Melody's magic from affecting me, then it would make sense why Kendra was affected.

"That could very well be it," Ms. Mugo confirmed, handing it back to me. "Though it's a shame there is only one necklace. Whoever isn't wearing it would be at risk of Melody's power."

I knew that as soon as I got home, I needed to give the necklace to Kendra. I needed her to regain some sense. And then, perhaps, we would need to switch daily rather than weekly to avoid the longer effects of Melody's control.

But even despite understanding what Melody was and how it had been affecting us... I still had questions. What did she want with our dad? With *us?* And how was I going to get rid of her when Dad was so blinded by the spell she had him under? I would never be able to convince *him* to wear the necklace...

I clung tightly to it and grimaced at my unfolding dilemma. This was worse than I thought—and I was powerless compared to Melody.

"Is there anything I could use against her?" I asked weakly.

Ms. Mugo hummed and flipped through the pages in search of an answer. Finally, she paused and let the page fall from her hands to rest against the other pages. I saw depictions of mermaids on the paper.

"A mer-heart," she answered. "Mer-hearts are said to hold *great* magical power. They are so powerful and so sought after that mermaids are hunted for their hearts."

Mermaids?

I didn't want to believe all of this was real. But seeing my mother's ghost had been strange enough. If Melody was truly a siren, then I supposed it would make sense that mermaids would exist too. I just... had trouble wrapping my head around it.

"So... what? Do I fling a mer-heart at her, or is there some kind of spell, or...?"

Ms. Mugo regarded me with a cool gaze.

"It's complicated magic," she replied. "You can do a lot with a mer-heart, but I believe your best chance is to curse Melody using the magic of a mer-heart. Curses are very difficult to undo, and you would bind her to do no more harm to you and your family."

Of course, that was easier said than done. Where was I going to find a *mer-heart?* And what kind of curse could possibly bind Melody? My head was starting to hurt as a million thoughts raced through my mind.

I only had four weeks to figure this out. Four weeks before the wedding. If my dad was this enthralled with Melody now, I couldn't imagine how much harder it would be to separate them once they were married. Melody would probably keep him locked away somewhere, knowing her.

I glanced at Matt again. He was taking this surprisingly well. Perhaps he had also been told stories by Maya—or perhaps his own family had raised him on them. Either way, he'd been open to bringing me here to reach my mother's spirit, so I guessed he had a somewhat open mind.

Ms. Mugo closed the book and gave me an apologetic look.

"I'm afraid that's the extent of my knowledge. I don't know how else I can help you."

I shook my head.

"You've been more than helpful," I replied. "Thank you for everything you've done."

I rose from my chair, Matt following my lead, and Ms. Mugo walked us to the front door.

"Good luck," she said as we left, and I regarded her with a grateful smile, though deep down, anxiety clawed through my insides, leaving me feeling a wreck.

After I dropped Matt home, I drove back to my house.

It had taken a while for me to convince Matt I'd be fine on my own. Even if Matt *could* have helped me, it would be dangerous to bring him further into this mess. So I'd assured him I had a plan and urged him to stay put—then promised to text him an update when I could.

"You know you can always stay here if you need to," he told me before I left, hovering on his front doorsteps. "You don't even need to ask."

I was grateful for a friend like Matt, but I had to face Melody head on. My entire family was in danger with her around.

When I finally pulled into the garage at our house, it was close to 10:30 p.m., and I expected everyone would be home from the sushi place by now. I crept up the front steps and unlocked the front door, trying to be as quiet as possible as I slipped into the dark and headed for the stairs.

Someone cleared their throat, and I froze.

A light flicked on in the living room, and I could see Melody sitting in an armchair, facing me. *Waiting for me.*

"Coral," she beckoned with her long fingernails. *Siren*, my mind warned me, and I swallowed hard. She hadn't done anything to me yet. Nothing *severe*, anyway. But I couldn't help but wonder what she was capable of.

After a moment, I begrudgingly approached her. She gestured to the sofa opposite her. "Sit down, please."

I gingerly sat on the white sofa and stared at her, taking in her every perfect feature, the lull of her voice, her glittering eyes.

"Where have you been?" she asked quietly, folding her arms.

"I was with Matt," I replied carefully. "I just... needed to get away from everything."

She inhaled slowly, and leaned back in her seat.

"Is he a boyfriend?" she asked lightly, and my blood simmered. *That was none of her business.*

"Oh, so you want to talk boys?" I drawled darkly, before I could stop myself. My mind was screaming at me to shut up, but her presence alone was grating.

Her gaze turned stormy.

"I suggest you stop with the attitude now," she warned, her nails digging into the armchair. "You're already in a lot of trouble from your father and I. This conversation is to discuss what will and will *not* be tolerated from now on—and sneaking around with boys late at night is one of them."

"You're not the boss of me," I growled. She would *not* control me. She may have everyone else under her spell, but she wouldn't get to me.

She studied me with her glittering green eyes, and I felt as if I were being held under a microscope—every imperfection gleamingly visible.

Could she hear my thoughts? Did she know that I knew her secret?

81

"Look, Coral," she said, her voice soft as a lullaby as she sat upright once more, her posture perfect. "I understand how hard this must be, having me walk into your life and seemingly replace your mother. But I wish you knew how sad you make your father when you refuse to get along with me."

If only *he* understood how sad he was making *me* by keeping Melody around. I folded my arms and glared at her.

"You're not marrying him for love," I spat, and her frown deepened. "You want power—you want to control us and control everything we have to offer you. This isn't about love at all, and if it were, I would feel differently about you."

She sprung forward so fast I flinched, and bared her perfect white teeth at me.

"You know *nothing* about how I feel," she seethed, her eyes like slits. "I have wanted your dad since the moment I first laid eyes on him. You've *no* idea what I've done just to be with him."

I dared to breathe, and her lips pulled into a thin line.

"The bottom line is this: there will be no more sneaking out, no more talking back, no more *disobeying* me. And I promise you, Coral, should you continue to displease me, I will punish you in ways you've *never* imagined possible."

Those last words were dark and guttural and sent a shiver down my spine.

"Now get out of my sight," she breathed, shooing me from the room and averting her gaze. I leaped from my chair quickly and hurried from the room, relieved to be free. Swallowing hard, I clutched the necklace around my neck, hand trembling slightly, and I knew what I had to do.

I had to give the necklace to Kendra.

Even though I knew it would endanger me, I couldn't afford to let Kendra sink deeper into Melody's spell. And I knew the truth, so maybe it would be easier for me to avoid Melody's effects. But this couldn't go on any longer—and I could *not* allow that wedding to happen.

In the days that passed, I tried and failed miserably to get Kendra to take the necklace. She simply refused to wear it, and I knew Melody must have had something to do with it.

We were both so busy that I barely had the mental space to think of a way to convince her. I worked my shift each day, dropped Kendra off to and from school, and was then immediately swept up in a daily checklist of wedding-planning chores from Melody. Between fetching items, helping to create wedding favors, and assisting in taste testing, Kendra and I never had a moment to ourselves until it was time for bed.

Only my lunch breaks gave me a reprieve, and I would wander down to the beach in hopes of seeing my mother again—or even Lysander, for that matter. But neither of them ever showed.

Melody seemed pleased by our week-long efforts—especially since Kendra appeared more than happy to help. That ground my gears more than anything, and I knew that time was running out. I had to think of *something* that Kendra couldn't pass up to bribe her into wearing the necklace.

The following Thursday, I joined the family for dinner downstairs. The private chef had cooked moussaka—an oven bake with layers of eggplant, minced lamb, pureed tomato, potato, garlic, and spices, topped with béchamel sauce and cheese. As we were digging in, Melody cleared her throat.

83

"We are having a dinner party tomorrow night," she explained to Kendra and I. "To celebrate our early wedding. We're inviting some of our most important contacts from around the island and close friends—so we expect you girls to be on your best behavior."

Melody's eyes focused on me in particular. I looked back down at my plate to avoid her and spooned the gooey, minced food around. There were still twenty-six days left until the wedding, but I couldn't help but feel as if they were mere hours.

"I'll have suitable dresses delivered to your rooms," she added.

Then, my dad chipped in, "And there will be alcohol, which you are not permitted to drink."

A short pause, and I looked up as Melody's gaze flicked carefully to his, but then, "Well, Chris, maybe allow them just a glass? The apple cider is delightful—a favorite recipe of mine, and I want to share it with the girls."

I didn't miss the sweet croon of Melody's voice—a faint hum sounded from it. I watched my dad's expression as he paused, but then appeared to reconsider.

"Hmm... Lorraine never liked apple cider," he said slowly. A shadow of anger crossed Melody's face briefly at the mention of our mother's name, but my dad continued on, "Alright," he agreed thoughtfully. "*Just* a glass."

Pure revulsion shuddered through me. I'd seen this happening in front of me all along, yet I'd been ignorant to see it for what it truly was because I couldn't fathom that it was even possible. But Melody had charmed my dad right before my eyes just now—probably for the thousandth time.

Kendra was eating her food, not paying attention at all. I quickly returned to my own plate, not wanting to come across as suspicious. I didn't want to know how Melody would react if she knew that I knew her secret.

After dinner, I finally had a moment away from Melody and Dad, so I followed Kendra up to her room.

"Hey, Ken?" I said cautiously, as she climbed onto her bed and pulled out a book from under her pillow. From the cover, I could tell it was a textbook—something to do with marine life—and I refrained from wrinkling my nose. I'd never been fond of books.

Instead, I unclasped the necklace, feeling suddenly vulnerable.

"It's your turn to have the necklace," I said firmly, holding it out to her as she crossed her legs. She looked at it for a moment, then shook her head and instead opened her book to start reading.

"I told you I don't want it."

"You have to," I pressed, trying to sound calm. She looked back at it, eyes cold and vacant.

"Coral, stop trying to make me wear it! Melody is our mom now," she said simply. "Our mom died a long time ago. It's time for me to move on from her, Coral—you should do the same."

I gritted my teeth in frustration.

"Kendra," I insisted, desperation clawing at me. "I'd really like you to wear it—"

At that moment, the perfect bribe came to me.

"In fact, how about this?" I babbled quickly. "I *promise* to be nicer to Melody if you wear it. I mean it—no talking back, no nasty comments, *nothing.*"

She met my gaze with a raised eyebrow, and my heart fluttered hopefully. I walked over to her and offered her the necklace again.

"Please," I whispered.

Kendra pursed her lips.

"If you're nice to Melody for a day, I'll put it on," she decided. "But you *cannot* be nasty or problematic in *any way.* I'll be watching to make sure."

It wasn't ideal—and the thought of being kind and obedient to Melody made me sick—but if that's what it took, I'd do it.

"Fine," I relented, and Kendra finally took the necklace. A wave of relief flooded through me. I just had to make sure she put it on in twenty-four hours' time.

"Thank you," I breathed, and hugged her tightly. She squirmed.

"What's gotten into you?" she grumbled, but hugged me back. I couldn't hide my smile as I left her room; after *days,* I'd finally gotten it into her hands, at the very least.

Now, I just had to figure out how to stop Melody before she could use her controlling powers on me.

CHAPTER SEVEN

Coral

Being obedient and nice to Melody was harder than I thought
it would be—partly because every demand that came out of
her mouth irked me, and partly because there were *so many* of
them.

But every time I was called on to run an errand or help
with preparations for the dinner that night, I plastered a smile
on my face and obliged politely. It was noticeable that something was up with me, but Melody seemed pleased all the
same.

Perhaps she thought her power was finally working on me.
Maybe it *was,* to a degree.

To make it worse, I felt completely naked and powerless
without Mom's necklace, now that I knew what it was. Standing on the rafts of a ladder and tying decorative sashes over
our two-story windows should have been scarier than not
wearing a necklace, but it wasn't.

One of our housemaids, Jenny, was on the floor below,
guiding me.

"A little to the left," she instructed, inspecting the sash
carefully. "That's good. Okay, you can come down now."

I shot down the ladder as fast as I could, feeling dizzy from
the height.

"Are you okay?" Jenny asked, and I nodded.

"I'm fine," I breathed, simply relieved to be off the ladder. She smiled at me from behind her short black bob cut and long lashes, the contrast stark against her pale skin.

"That's good, because I could use some help in the kitchen. Could you walk with me?"

I was about to oblige when Melody's familiar heels clacked in our direction.

"Actually, Jenny, I need Coral's help. I'm sure you can find someone else," she said shortly. Jenny's eyes glazed over a little before she nodded and excused herself.

A chill settled on my shoulders as I turned to face Melody.

"How can I help?" I asked brightly—maybe too brightly, because she frowned at me.

"What has gotten into you today, Coral?" she asked, folding her arms. I shrugged, pretending to play dumb.

"I'm not sure. I just woke up feeling like I wanted to help you," I replied lightly. "I mean, you're always doing so much for us with the resort and helping Dad. It's the least I could do."

Her expression almost sparkled as she watched me, and a deep sense of pride came over me knowing I had her fooled. Maybe she thought she'd never get to hear such words come from my mouth or see the day I willingly did anything for her.

"Well, that's just refreshing to hear," she breathed as a sly smile crossed over her features. "I am having some jewelry delivered for tonight with your dresses, so I need you to bring me that necklace you wear so often."

I faltered, my blood running cold. It took all my effort to keep my expression pleasant.

"Necklace?" I repeated weakly. She narrowed her gaze.

"Yes, the clam one. But wrap it up in something—a hand-kerchief maybe. It's very important that you do that."

Strange. Why would she need it wrapped up? Perhaps she couldn't touch it...

"That's my mother's necklace," I said, feigning resistance in a way that I hoped would come across as something deeply rooted—something her magic couldn't quite take from me yet.

She pursed her lips.

"I realize that—that's why I need it. I want to keep it safe for tonight," she said, a gentle lull to her voice.

A wave of dizziness came over me and panic seized my chest.

"We will have so many guests in the house—you wouldn't want to risk it being stolen while you girls are wearing the other jewels I've prepared for you, right?"

I struggled against the melodic spell, feeling my limbs turn weak.

"I lost it..." I managed to say, before the spell could dig any deeper under my skin. Instantly, the magic eased off. I was silently thankful I hadn't revealed Kendra had it. "Yester-day... I was with Matt again, and I lost it. I don't know where it went."

There was a pause as Melody analyzed my face, eyes narrowed still. Then finally, she let her shoulders sag.

"Well, that's a shame," she said lightly. "I guess I won't be needing it after all. In that case, why don't you head back up-stairs and start getting ready for tonight? I'll send your sister there shortly too."

I nodded, offering her a kind smile that made me sick to my stomach before turning and hurrying up the stairs.

I was trembling from how close I'd come to losing the one weapon I had against her right now. But at least I knew one thing: she couldn't touch the necklace. So as long as one of us was wearing it at all times, she wouldn't be able to rip it from us. It was probably why she hadn't tried that already.

As I reached the landing, I made a mental note to myself—I *had* to get Kendra to wear that necklace tonight and *not* the jewelry Melody had sent for. I couldn't risk Melody getting a chance to swipe it or... or worse, leave Kendra vulnerable to Melody's power.

It wasn't until much later in the evening, when I'd put on the seafoam chiffon gown Melody had sent up to my room, that I heard from Kendra. She entered, wearing a similar gown but in a shade of sunset pink.

I noticed she was fixing an opal earring in her ear.

"Hey, do you have any hair pins I can borrow?" she asked.

"Oh, Kendra!" I said brightly, stepping away from my mirror. "I meant to tell you—Melody is still really busy getting ready, but she asked me to give you a message,"

Kendra raised an eyebrow.

"What message?" she asked.

"Melody decided she likes Mom's clam necklace better than the jewelry she sent you, so she wants you to wear that instead."

I'd come up with the lie hours ago and had been practicing it in my head over and over so as to perfect it for this moment. Now, I stood, silently praying she'd fall for it.

"Are you sure?" Kendra asked, sounding skeptical.

I reached over to my vanity and grabbed a bunch of hair pins, offering them to her.

"I'm certain," I replied confidently. "Why don't you sit and I'll do your hair and then you can go put it on?"

She seemed to loosen up at the suggestion and sat down at my desk. I followed her, grabbing a brush, and began to comb through her short, wavy golden hair. I wasn't very good at doing my own hair, but I'd done Kendra's hair a number of times. Being without a mother, we'd had to rely on each other for such things.

Downstairs, the sound of idle chatter drifted up as guests began to arrive. I began to gather the strands of Kendra's hair and braid it into a half-up, half-down hairdo. I carefully positioned each pin to hold the braid in place. It looked like a crown on her head.

"Thanks for doing my hair," Kendra murmured, and I smiled warmly.

"Why wouldn't I?" I replied. "We always do things like this for one another."

That thought seemed to stay with Kendra for a minute—like she'd forgotten or something. I cursed Melody silently for whatever she'd done to her.

We chatted and laughed like we used to as I did her hair, and all the tension that had surrounded Kendra over the past two days was gone by the time I was done. She was beaming as she turned to admire every angle in the mirror.

"It's perfect!" she exclaimed, and I grinned.

"I'll be ready in a minute too. Shall I meet you down there?" I asked.

"Sounds good," Kendra agreed. "I'll... go put on Mom's necklace."

I bit back a huge sigh of relief as Kendra went back to her room. I wanted to slump against the wall. Who knew such a simple task would be such an ordeal to make happen?

Instead of residing into a heap on the floor, I took one last look at myself before walking out onto the landing and descending the stairs.

The house was packed. All of our best lighting was on—the glittering chandeliers, the elegant lights hanging down the walls, the fairy lights outside. A sweet, orchestrated tune played through the house. Melody had hired servers to work, and they walked around with trays of wine and delicious delicacies—I spotted antipasto platters brimming with salami, olives, apricots, and prosciutto; tzatziki and crackers; and dozens of different cheese selections.

I waded through the people, past tall businessmen and their wives, and inhaled the sickly scents of their overbearing jasmine and melon perfume. I continued on until I'd reached the lounge room. The balcony doors were open, letting a pleasant breeze drift through the house.

I was eager for Kendra to come downstairs so that I could assess her state of mind. Perhaps if she was open to listening with the necklace on, I could explain what Melody was. But meanwhile, I had to be careful not to be overheard by the wretched woman herself.

I spent a moment looking for her in the crowd to make sure I knew where she was, and eventually spotted her across the room, chatting to a couple. She wore a blood red gown, and her hair was twisted up into an equally elegant style. She turned her gaze my way and caught sight of me standing across the room. I pursed my lips, trying to fight the urge to run and hide now that she'd seen me.

I watched her excuse herself and walk toward me. I braced myself to act pleasant again.

"Coral," she gushed, putting on a show. "My beautiful daughter-to-be, come join us with the celebrations!"

"Sure," I replied with a smile, and began to follow her.

"Where's your sister?" Melody asked.

"I think she's still getting ready upstairs," I replied, glancing around the room.

Melody pursed her lips, as if annoyed that Kendra was taking her time.

"She's going to miss the speech," Melody muttered, as we walked. "I've been meaning to ask you, Coral—have you spoken to Lysander lately?"

I frowned at her, wondering why she would care about him, of all people.

"No... why?"

Her expression betrayed nothing as she studied me.

"Good," she said finally, turning her attention back to the crowd. "Best to stay away from that one, my dear—he'll only drag you down into depths you'll never escape from."

I faltered in my steps, processing her words. What did *that* mean?

I shook my head quickly—it was probably just another mind game of hers—then jogged a little to keep up with her. We eventually met up with my dad, who was speaking to some of his business friends. At the sight of Melody, he held out an arm for her to lean into his embrace.

"That's quite shocking news, Christopher," the lady opposite us said. "Handing over island ownership so quickly..."

What?

My eyes boggled out of my head, and my dad noticed.

"Oh, I forgot—I haven't told the girls yet," he chuckled to his friends, reaching to grasp my hand reassuringly. Turning to me, he added, "Melody will be taking over the resort once we're married. I'm going to retire."

His hand was warm, but I felt like I'd turned entirely to ice.

"Retire?" I spluttered. "But you *love* running the resort... and Melody..."

I couldn't think of the right words, and even if I had, I couldn't say any of them in front of my dad. They both waited for me to finish, but I shook my head, pulling free of his grasp.

"You can't," I said firmly. Melody sighed.

"Now, Coral, remember how you and I were talking about how good it would be for your dad to spend a few years sailing again?" She glanced at my dad and added, "He's missed it so terribly all these years."

No such conversation had happened.

Then, she looked back at me, and such a heavy wave of compulsion came over me. "You remember, don't you?" She narrowed her gaze and I stumbled a bit under the forcefulness of it. The edges of my vision blurred.

"Yes, I remember," I replied suddenly, before I could even think. My eyes widened in shock as I realized what had just happened.

Melody smiled smugly.

My mind was reeling as I tried to piece together why Melody would want ownership of the island resort.

What did a *siren* want with such a thing?

Maybe she was just on a power trip. Maybe she was feeling bored of controlling my dad, who was obviously an easy puppet, and now that I was slipping, she needed a bigger challenge.

"You look rather shaken, Coral—why don't you go fetch yourself a drink? The apple cider is rather nice."

Again, the urge to walk off and find the nearest waiter overwhelmed me, but I fought against her words, digging my heels into the ground to stop myself from moving.

"No," I said, as forcefully as I could. Her eyes grew darker and she let out a deep sigh.

"Oh, Coral," she muttered. "You're really just like your mother. *So stubborn.*"

A feeling of shock echoed through me.

"Did... did you know my mother?" I asked quietly.

She let out a single dry laugh and fixed her honey-blonde hair. "I knew her better than you ever had a chance to."

"How?" I whispered. How had they known each other all those years ago?

It occurred to me, all of a sudden, how my mother had known Melody was a siren. Perhaps... my *mother* had been a siren too?

But that didn't seem right. Unlike Melody, my mother had been kind. Or at least... that's how I'd always viewed her to be. The truth was that I hadn't known her at all. I didn't know what to think or believe.

Melody eyed a waiter passing by and grabbed a glass of sparkling apple cider. I felt uneasy as she handed it to me, eyes twinkling and voice sultry with allure, "Drink up, and I'll tell you everything."

I reached out without thinking, my fingers encircling the cool glass. I wasn't able to resist bringing it to my lips. I could smell the acidic sweetness.

Then suddenly, a strong wind blew through from the open balcony doors, and a crackle of thunder sounded overhead. Glasses toppled over, decorations came undone, and loose napkins flew through the house. Guests gasped and cried out.

I glanced around, startled. What the *heck* had just happened?

It was over as quickly as it had begun, but it had been enough to break Melody's concentration. She was glancing around the room as well, lip curled up in annoyance. I quickly emptied the glass in a nearby potted plant, vibrant and green. By the time Melody looked back, it appeared I'd downed the drink in one long gulp.

Melody's smile grew deadly.

"Such an obedient girl," she crooned at me, tucking a stray hair behind my ear. "Your mother and I used to be friends, dear. It was a long time ago."

She glanced over at my dad, then offered me a more serious frown.

"But she betrayed us—it impacted us all. I've never forgiven her for it."

It appeared that was all she intended to let on. I was left reeling as she took my dad by the arm and said, "Come, darling—the speech is about to begin."

The two of them walked off through the crowd toward the staircase, and slowly, the other guests around me followed. I was left alone, standing in the corner of the room.

My gaze drifted and fell once more on the potted plant I'd emptied my glass into. My blood ran cold at the sight.

The potted plant was limp and brown and unmistakably dead.

CHAPTER EIGHT

Coral

There was the sound of a glass being tapped, and a hush fell over the crowd. I spotted Melody standing on the white stone staircase with my dad so that they were both elevated.

"I'd like to make toast," she said, gesturing for us to gather at her feet. She was like a queen addressing her people. I only took a few steps through the crowd to get a better look at her.

"I hope you're all having a wonderful evening and have all had a chance to try the apple cider. I do encourage you all to taste it— it's simply divine."

My gaze fell back to the potted plant—and then it hit me. The reason she'd wanted our dad's permission, and the reason she'd kept trying to sing me into drinking it:

Something was in that cider—something *deadly.*

All at once, cold horror washed over me as I scanned the crowd, a sense of hysteria building in my throat. *How many people had drunk it by now?*

"As you all know, my darling Chris and I shall be married in the coming weeks, and he will be stepping down as resort manager to hand over responsibility to me."

Melody went on to briefly discuss future prospects for the resort. It seemed that everybody knew now that she would be taking it over. However, I'd stopped listening as my attention was drawn to someone else; Kendra was heading toward me through the crowd.

"Hey," she greeted in a hushed tone. "Sorry I'm late—what did I miss?"

Relief flooded through me. I made a move to drag her outside when I noticed a half empty glass of cider in her left hand. My blood froze over.

"Kendra!" I hissed, eyes wide. "Did you drink the cider?"

"What? Yeah," she replied, eyeing the glass. "Why?"

My mouth fell open and my stomach plummeted. This couldn't be happening. My sister had that stuff *inside* of her.

Melody's voice ripped me out of my thoughts of panic.

"I want to thank each and every one of you for coming here tonight. A toast: to my beloved Chris, to our future!"

She held up her glass, and the entire room cheered. I didn't scream fast enough as the room downed their drinks.

"Stop!" I cried, but it was too late. Melody's eyes narrowed at me, and I watched the crowd in horror. It started with a light cough. Then, the coughs multiplied, and before I knew it, half of the people in the crowd were choking, struggling to breathe.

Poison, my mind rang. The cider was poisoned.

People began to fall to the floor, rasping for air. Chills ran down my arms, rendering me numb.

Melody was on the staircase, practically glowing.

No, wait... she *was* glowing!

Her entire figure had become illuminated, bright and white, and I watched in horror as I traced wisps of light back to the fallen bodies. I didn't understand what was happening, but Melody seemed radiant with power.

Then, Kendra started choking too.

Eyes wide, I sprung into action.

"Kendra!" I shrieked. I looked in Melody's direction, locking eyes with my dad. Thankfully, whatever spell he was under hadn't rendered him completely oblivious—he immediately made for us as Kendra collapsed, and I caught her struggling, weak body in my arms.

"Kendra please," I whispered, tears in my eyes.

Please don't let her die... please...

She lurched to the side and began to retch. I never thought I'd be happy to see vomit on my shoes.

I held her steady as the poison came up.

"Kendra," my father's voice boomed, tense with worry. He knelt beside us. "What's wrong?"

"She's been *poisoned!*" I shrieked at him, my entire body trembling. How was it that he *still* couldn't see what was going on around him? "Can't you see that Melody has done this to her?"

"Melody would never hurt you girls," he replied, furrowing his brow. I wanted to shake him, but Kendra was still vomiting. I could feel her entire frame quivering, her frailness, with every heave.

When she finally did stop, she was pale. Sweat beaded her forehead, and her hands were clammy. Her eyes fell closed. She'd passed out from exhaustion.

I noticed Mom's necklace glinting around her neck.

Thank goodness.

"Christopher," Melody's voice rang out—sickly sweet, like honey. He immediately turned to face her. She smiled sweetly at him.

"Bring the girls to me, won't you?"

He turned and offered his arms, as if to carry Kendra. I wanted to hold tightly and never let her go, but Dad was under Melody's spell. He would force me to give her up eventually, and she was too heavy for me to run with. So I shifted her weight to him before following as we crossed the room.

I noticed the remaining people in the room hadn't reacted at all to the deaths—they were kneeling patiently, eyes glazed over, as if they were waiting for orders.

They're already under her spell, I realized.

"Why have you done this?" I asked Melody directly. I was tired of hiding my knowledge, tired of the games, and tired of walking on eggshells around my dad. "What do you want with our family?"

Melody regarded me with a cool gaze.

"You didn't drink the cider," she tutted, looking disappointed. "And it appears you *didn't* lose your mother's necklace either," she added, eyeing Kendra's chest. Her gaze flew back to me. "How long have you known what I am, Coral?"

My eyes bore into hers.

"Long enough," I replied shortly.

"Well, I'm impressed," she said smoothly, walking down a few steps of the staircase. "I didn't expect to be discovered—but then again, you've always been a rather stubborn girl."

She regarded her fingernails briefly, as if checking for imperfections, before trailing a hand down my dad's cheek.

"Chris, my darling, remove Kendra's necklace."

"No!" I cried, going to lunge forward. But someone grabbed my foot, tripping me, and I smashed into the ground. My chin throbbed with pain and tears formed in my eyes. I

101

struggled, looking back. One of the party goers, still kneeling, had grabbed me.

I tried to kick them off but their grip didn't loosen.

My gaze shot back to Kendra, whom my dad had now laid gently on the ground. But when he went to grab the necklace, a light erupted from it, forcing him back.

I watched with wide eyes as it enveloped Kendra, encasing her in a crystalized coffin of sorts.

Suddenly, she was untouchable. A noise sounded from Melody's throat—like she was trying not to scream.

"Lorraine," she muttered darkly. Turning to my dad, she said, "Darling, find something to break the crystal with."

My dad hurried off, leaving only the two of us glaring at each other.

I struggled to free myself, trying to push off the stone floor and stand, which seemed to amuse Melody. She watched the spectacle with sparkling eyes.

"What are you going to do to her?" I grunted. She smiled darkly.

"I'm going to take her heart," she said simply. "I will cut it from her chest and devour it, right here in front of you. And then I'm going to take *yours.*"

Horror washed through me, and she strode slowly to my side before beginning to encircle me. I felt as if I'd gone ice cold.

"You want our hearts?" I asked numbly.

"Yes. The hearts I just absorbed from these willing sacrifices are wonderfully powerful, but they're nothing compared to hearts like *yours,* dear Coral. With your heart, I will seize control of the land. And once the land is mine, the Undersea is a mere *given.*"

Hearts like ours.

"*Mer-hearts?*" I asked, feeling faint. It *couldn't* be...

I thought back to my mother, to the fact that they had been friends once. Was it possible that my mother hadn't been a siren, but rather...

She bared her perfect white teeth.

"So you *do* know," she confirmed. A new fear washed over me as I pieced it together.

Had Dad known our mother was a mermaid?

He returned at that moment, holding a golf club he'd found in the garage. I could barely breathe as he raised it over Kendra's crystalized body, and brought it slamming down.

The crystal didn't so much as crack, but a resounding clink filled the air.

Melody growled, growing increasingly frustrated as she clenched her fists.

"I thought as much," she said. "The necklace contains Lorraine's heart magic. Neither you nor I will be able to break it, Chris."

She turned back to me with hungry eyes.

"Only another *mermaid* can break it."

Currently, that crystal was the only thing keeping Kendra safe. And besides, I didn't know *how* to break it.

"I have no power," I replied stiffly.

"That may be true," Melody mused, towering over me. "But the tides will turn soon enough."

She looked upon the crowd of people still kneeling and commanded, "Restrain her!"

I didn't have a moment to think through my options. With all the strength I could muster, I kicked free of my captor, sprung up from the ground, and ran. Shouts sounded as I wove through the rising crowd Melody had brainwashed, and sprinted in the opposite direction, toward the open balcony doors. My heart thudded wildly, adrenaline driving me, and the night-cloaked ocean drew closer and closer.

"Don't let her escape!" Melody roared after me, her voice resounding off the walls. "I want her heart! *Bring me her heart!*"

Kendra would be safe so long as she was crystalized. But I wouldn't be safe here without a deeper understanding of who I was and what my power was to Melody.

This was my only chance to escape.

I'll come back for you, Kendra, I vowed mentally. And for my dad too—though that would be a harder spell to break.

I reached the balcony adjoining the living room, and without thinking, I jumped the railing.

I inhaled as deep as I could as I plummeted right over the cliffside, toward the dark, deep waters below. I pointed my toes and my hands mid-air, perfecting them for a dive.

The water hit me hard, and icy cold shock came over me as I was swept under by the current.

Panic seized me again, made worse by my already present adrenaline.

I fought the current, trying to find which way was up. The water swirled around me, tugging me in every direction and disorientating me. I decided I needed to swim—I couldn't just keep spinning in it.

No sooner had I started swimming, something grabbed me by the ankles and tugged me down.

My lungs pounded in my chest, and I kicked with alarm. The grip was strong, pulling me down, down, down into the depths of the ocean.

I screamed, and air bubbles rushed to the surface that was now miles above my head. Black haze formed at the corners of my eyes. I grew weaker in my movements. And just as I was about to pass out, I felt something cold and heavy click into place around my neck.

Then the darkness took me.

PART TWO

CHAPTER NINE

Coral

When I came to, I was drifting in a strange, upright position. My arms were pulled in both directions. My head lulled to my left and saw that my wrists were entangled in seaweed—too tight to pull free from.

The hue of colorful lights glowed from above, dizzying in my still-drowsy state, and illuminated all the space around me. I realized I was surrounded by water. I was *breathing* in it somehow.

"You're awake," a familiar voice said, almost comfortingly. My gaze turned head on, and to my shock, I saw that I was in a kind of throne room. An *underwater* throne room, with glass windows that spanned meters high in the air toward a dazzling domed skylight. Glowing crystals grew from the walls, illuminating the space in all different colors, and schools of fish were visible swimming past from outside.

But what shocked me most was the figure lounging on a mossy bedrock throne adorned with various types of vibrant coral—pink and orange and yellow—all twisting out from it.

Lysander tilted his head at me, watching on with clear curiosity in his sparkling eyes. He was dressed differently to how I'd seen him on land—here, he wore a fitted jacket, in the deepest hue of navy I'd ever seen, with silver lapels. And he wore a crown of silver coral in his luscious hair. I wondered if the fine clothes weighed him down, but he stood at that moment, and they seemed to float easily along with him as he descended a small set of bedrock steps to approach me.

Why was I tied up? Why had he been sitting there, watching me? What did he plan to do with me? Panic began to seize me as he strode toward me.

"Where am I?" I asked, unsure if I could talk until I tried it. I didn't know how I was breathing either. But when I spoke, no water filled my mouth—instead, air seemed to rush out of me, dissolving into tiny air bubbles as I spoke. Surprise must have shown on my face, and it seemed to humor him because he chuckled.

"You're in my throne room," he answered gently, and came to stand in front of me. With the other various guards standing around the room, I suddenly felt very closed in.

"Yes, I see that," I said carefully, trying not to show my panic as hysteria built in my chest. "But *where?*"

"In the kingdom of Veranis," he clarified. "In the Undersea—in case that part wasn't obvious."

It *wasn't* obvious. I bit back a retort, feeling a dull ache creep into my arms now that I was awake. How long had I been hanging here?

"Will you untie me?" I asked hopefully, tugging on the seaweed restraints growing from the floor.

"That depends," he breezed, his sea-green gaze meeting mine. "Are you going to try and escape the palace?"

I didn't know how to answer that. I didn't know *what* was going on or who I could trust, for that matter.

"Perhaps I wouldn't feel the need to escape if I wasn't *tied up,*" I answered finally, a hint of edge to my voice. "Lysander..." I added carefully, gauging his every reaction. "I thought we—well, I thought you..."

I was struggling to find the words. It wasn't that we knew each other—we'd only spoken twice, ever. But I thought we'd been on pleasant terms, at the very least.

"Why have you tied me up?" I sighed finally.

Lysander gently touched my chin, which stung with pain all of a sudden. I yelped, thinking he was hurting me, but then I remembered smashing it back in our foyer when I tried to save Kendra from Melody.

"That looks painful," Lysander murmured, studying the graze. I didn't have a clue how bad it was—just that it hurt to touch.

"Why am I tied up?" I repeated, beginning to lose my patience.

Lysander took a step back and pocketed his hands.

"You seem to have a nasty habit of getting caught up in currents. I'd much rather have you alive, therefore, the only way for me to ensure you *stay* alive is to keep you put."

I frowned, thinking back to the times I'd been caught in currents. Earlier this evening—if it was *still* even evening, that was—and that night a week ago with Matt.

A sudden realization washed over me, which nearly left me reeling.

"It was *you,*" I said, as I put the pieces together. "You helped me surface last week when I nearly drowned."

"Indeed," he revealed, seeming smug. "You're lucky I was there."

"But why?" I asked.

He stepped forward again and traced my cheek. A strange mix of discomfort and anticipation settled in my stomach, and I leaned away. I wasn't used to strangers touching me, let alone attractive ones who had me captured.

"I won't allow you to die," he said plainly. "That simply just won't do—especially after all this time, when I *finally* have you."

A chill crept along my neck as I tried to follow his words. Perhaps I should have taken him following me out to sea that day as a red flag.

Turning his back on me, he strode back to his throne and resumed lounging on it. "You're welcome, by the way—I had my men rescue you from your siren stepmother."

Rescue? They had done a rather poor job. I had escaped within an inch of my life, and they had almost drowned me dragging me down here.

"So you knew she was a siren?" I pressed, eager for answers. Who exactly was Lysander? And how long had he sought after me?

"She is none other than the reigning queen of Coronis. And while our court has maintained peace with the sirens for centuries, her particular clan poses a looming threat to our kingdom," he explained. "I wasn't aware, however, that you were Lorraine Quarte's daughter until I laid eyes upon your father. Then, a lot of things began to make sense."

Only parts of this conversation were making sense, but I did my best to follow it.

"My mother—she was a mermaid," I stated, hoping he would let on more information.

"Indeed," was all he replied with, which made me clench my jaw.

"So what does that make you?" I shot back helplessly. He recoiled slightly, but I was far too tense and uncomfortable at this point to care. "Are you a siren or a mermaid?"

It was impossible to tell, but as I eyed his legs, I decided he couldn't *possibly* be a mermaid. Unless... he was like me, somehow.

"Neither," he answered, smirking as he rested his elbow on the throne's arm. "I am an undine—as are all of us you see here in the Veranis court."

What the *hell* was an undine? I'd never heard of such a thing. I decided I was better off not knowing—I had more pressing problems—and it appeared Lysander wasn't going to hand me the answers I needed about my mother, or anything for that matter, on a silver platter.

"You have to let me go," I insisted, tugging at the restraints again. "Melody—she has my sister. I need to go back and help her."

Lysander frowned thoughtfully.

"If Melody has your sister, she is certainly dead," he replied calmly.

"She's not—she's encased in some kind of crystal," I explained. "Made of my mother's heart magic. That's what Melody called it."

I didn't know if that would mean anything to Lysander or if it would make sense, but his features switched to surprise, and he shifted back into an upright position.

"Well, that's unexpected. I wonder how she was able to preserve her heart magic after all these years."

"In a necklace," I said slowly. "I think... it must have been in her necklace."

"Still," Lysander said, "a heart is a heart. It does not just simply *fit* into a necklace. She would have had to have used a spell... or a curse, even."

He seemed to mull over this momentarily, but then shrugged it off.

"No matter—it's not important. What *is*, is ensuring Melody cannot get her hands on you." He rose again and strode down the steps once more. "That is why, sweet Coral, I cannot let you go back. It is too dangerous."

My heart sank in my chest.

"You can't keep me here," I pressed angrily. He raised an eyebrow.

"I am a prince," he stated. "I can do whatever I want. And as long as Melody seeks your heart, I shall not allow you to leave this palace."

"Why does it matter to you whether I live or die," I asked wearily, "or if Melody takes my heart?"

He tilted my face up to meet his with his index finger.

"Because *I* want your heart," he stated plainly.

A sick feeling swept over me. *Both* of them? Was Lysander going to kill me instead?

I remembered Ms. Mugo saying how mermaids were hunted for their hearts in the Undersea, but it hadn't truly settled on me what that was like until now—as I had *become* the hunted.

Were all creatures of the Undersea this despicable?

"And what would you do with my heart?" I asked, my voice barely a whisper.

113

"Now is not the time to delve into such matters," he replied, studying my facial features. "But you cannot imagine what owning your heart would do for me. Not with that strange, human upbringing you've had."

"You *can't* have my heart," I seethed, despite my full awareness that I was his prisoner and he could take it at his own leisure. My words seemed to strike him more forcefully than I thought they would. He recoiled, as if being slapped by them. A grimace formed on his features, and I instantly regretted it.

I wondered how much it would hurt to have my heart ripped from my own chest.

"That will change," he promised. "Nobody except those most foolish, like Melody, would dare try to take your heart from me. I don't need your permission to keep you as my prisoner for eternity, Coral."

I couldn't believe what I was hearing—I'd *liked* Lysander. He'd been kind to me, brought me my surfboard, and now he wanted to keep me trapped down here while my sister and dad were in grave danger. How could I have ever been attracted to such a heartless soul?

I couldn't let him keep me here. I needed to help Kendra and my dad. But how was I ever going to get back to land? Furthermore, how long would I be able to breathe down here? Didn't they realize humans needed to eat as well? The thoughts began stockpiling, and momentarily, I forgot he was there.

It wasn't until a door opened on my left that I came back to reality, and a man strode in wearing a navy-blue uniform. He had short, wavy red hair—the hues ranging from copper to chestnut under the lights—eyes like honey, and stubble. He crossed straight to Lysander and bowed before him.

"Commander Leif," Lysander greeted. "What news is there?"

"It's worse than we thought, Your Grace," he replied, handing him a piece of parchment. "There's a full report in there—but we should speak privately as well."

"Very well," Lysander replied, folding the note without reading it. "I'll be with you momentarily."

The commander glanced at me on his way out—but his expression was a mask.

Lysander turned back to me and flicked his wrist, as if summoning someone. A lady stepped forth, with long black hair that reached her waist. She wore a long but plain navy gown.

"Rue, please show Coral to her room and tend to her needs," he said, and she curtsied.

"Of course, Your Grace," she said, and Lysander made another movement with his hand. The seaweed restraints disappeared, and I drifted to the ground, surprised to find that it didn't feel sluggish to move in the water. My movement was still restricted, but it didn't take as long for me to walk across the threshold as it should have. I rubbed my arms to ease the ache that had formed in my upper arms and glared at Lysander. He ignored me and stalked off through the door Commander Leif had exited. I watched it click shut.

"Come along," Rue said to me, leading me in the opposite direction of Lysander. I debated refusing her, but what good would it do? The palace was full of guards that would stop me, and I didn't know my way back to the surface from here. So I

115

followed Rue begrudgingly, and hoped I might see an opportunity to escape sooner rather than later.

As soon as we reached my room, the guards locked the doors behind us.

The room was much like the throne room—the same tall windows gave me an endless view of coral gardens and schools of fish, illuminated by the lights of the palace. The room was circular, made of stone and bedrock. The crystals glowing on the ceiling seemed to produce more than light; a heat was radiating from them, battling the icy temperatures of the ocean. Perhaps that was how these deep waters felt pleasant despite the fact that the cold should have killed me by now.

The materials of the double bed were strange too—as I ran the sheets through my hand, I couldn't tell if they were soaked with water. Everything was watery around me, and yet the sheets felt nice. Not dry, and they had a heaviness to them, but they still felt comfortable enough to sleep in.

I grimaced as I inspected the rest of the room. All the doors were sealed, and there was nothing I could use to break the windows. Even if I did have enough strength for that, the pulls of the water prevented any such action—which I learned as soon as I crossed to a nearby desk and picked up a book. The cover was tough, like it was made of some kind of strong withstanding material, but it still drooped in my hands slightly, and I knew it wouldn't break a window.

"Can I get you anything, my lady?" Rue asked me, and I frowned at her. I didn't know what to make of her—we had housemaids at home, but I'd never had a personal hand-maiden. I didn't need someone to dress me and bathe me.

But I did need answers. And though I was weary of these people, Rue seemed harmless.

"The prince..." I trailed off. It felt weird to call him that—to *admit* that's what he was. "What does he want from me?"

"It's as he said—he wants your heart," she replied. I tried not to shudder as another chill went down my spine, and I slowly sat down on the bed.

"Will he carve it from my chest?" I whispered, thinking of how Melody described the way she'd take Kendra's heart. "Will he eat it?"

The handmaiden burst out laughing and clasped a hand to her mouth. "Forgive me," she giggled, trying to stifle herself. "You are thinking of it far too *literally.*"

I stared at her.

"You mean to say... he won't take my physical heart from me?" I asked.

"Not at all. He needs you to *give* him your heart, meta-phorically."

I sucked in a breath. So, what he was *essentially* saying was that he wanted me to fall in love with him?

Well, perhaps he shouldn't have tied me up and declared me as his prisoner, I thought bitterly, and placed a hand to my chest protectively.

I felt my fingertips brush something against my neck and looked down. There, sitting around my neck, was a tight neck-lace of pearls I hadn't been wearing at Melody's party. I'd been so caught up in recent events that I hadn't even noticed them until now.

"What's this?" I asked, running my fingers along each smooth pearl.

"Oh that—it's enchanted to keep you alive down here," Rue explained. "Each pearl protects you against something. One is filling your lungs with air. Another is strengthening your body against the water pressure. One is keeping you from getting dehydrated. And so on."

I recalled a vague memory of something clicking around my neck before I fell unconscious and woke up in Lysander's throne room. I guess this explained it.

"Unfortunately, the journey down here was too fast for your body to acclimate, so you did fall unconscious for two days."

I whipped my gaze up at her.

"Two days?" I gasped. I'd already lost two days to Melody? Rue flushed, looking sympathetic.

"I'm afraid so, my lady."

A numbness spread over me. I'd already been gone for so long. *Anything* could have happened between now and then. Was my family even still alive?

I felt sick all of a sudden, and I carefully sat down on the bed. The room was starting to spin, so I laid back, which sent bubbles up in my wake. I stared at the bedframe which was made of the same coral as Lysander's throne. Reds and yellows and blues all sprouted out into a semi-circle formation, twisted to resemble pillars and branches.

I turned my gaze up to the ceiling, toward the surface, toward *land,* however many miles above my head it might be.

Kendra was still with Melody. I wondered what she had done with Kendra's body, even if it was still encased in crystal. I wondered what my dad was doing, what he was *thinking,* if he had any capacity left to think at all.

I didn't have *time* for love—or for Lysander's desires. I had far more pressing problems.

"Rue, I *need* to get back to the surface," I insisted, sitting up again.

"I'm afraid it's impossible, my lady," she replied gently, as she fussed around my room. "At least, without the prince's help. And I doubt he'll let you go."

I gritted my teeth.

"Why me?" I exclaimed. "Can't he woo some other girl?"

"It's not that simple," Rue replied, as she began folding an extra blanket to lay at the foot of my bed. "The royal family of Veranis has suffered a curse for the past thousand years. The prince is certain that your heart is the key to breaking it."

"A curse?" I asked, raising my eyebrows. "What kind of curse?"

"It's hard to explain... and easier to see with your own eyes," she replied, with a grimace. "But I'm sure, in some time, you'll understand for yourself once you get to know him better."

I didn't *have* time.

"Can't it wait until *after* I've saved my family from Melody?"

"You'll have to speak to the prince about that," Rue said. "I can request a meeting for you, if you like."

"Yes," I said immediately. "As soon as possible—I want to speak to him."

119

"I'll see what I can do," she promised with a kind smile, heading toward the bedroom doors. "For now, you should try and get some rest. I'll bring you some supper later—unless the prince requests you dine with him, of course."

I let out a steady breath as she knocked on the door. The guards opened it a moment later, letting her exit. As soon as she was gone, I heard the lock click back in place.

I was trapped, and I was alone.

My thoughts wandered back to what Melody had said about Lysander at her party.

"Best to stay away from that one, my dear—he'll only drag you down into depths you'll never escape from."

If only I'd known how right she'd been.

I woke from an unplanned nap when I heard a knock at the door. For a moment, I'd forgotten where I was, and panic seized me at the unfamiliar surroundings. But as I sat up on the bed, my dress from Melody's party still crumpled around me, and took in the tall windows and glowing crystals above, I remembered.

Rue entered with a tray of food, and my stomach grumbled. I didn't know how long it had been since I'd eaten, and there was no sense of time this deep in the sea where the ocean was near black outside.

She set the tray on my bedside table, and I examined the contents. There was a bowl of kelp, another of algae, and a third of sea berries. I wrinkled my nose.

"No fish," I noted, looking up. Rue let out a squeak.

"My apologies, my lady, I thought—with you being of Mermaid heritage..." she trailed off, looking flustered as her cheeks reddened. My face fell, and I shook my head.

"No, that's not it, I just wondered why," I added quickly. She raised an eyebrow at me.

"Well, it's not custom, my lady," she explained. "The Merfolk don't eat fish, given their... tails and what not. It would be too close to cannibalism."

Understanding came over me. No *wonder* my mother had been so against eating fish.

I turned my gaze back and poked the green kelp.

"So... we're vegetarians?" I asked, noticing the slimy texture. It seemed to shimmer gold as I prodded it.

"I guess you could say that," Rue replied. I picked up a strand of the kelp. It didn't look at all appetizing, but if I didn't eat something, I would starve down here. And my stomach was already growling. So I popped the gross thing in my mouth and forced myself to swallow it, not even attempting to hide the distaste on my face as I felt its slimy texture on my tongue. It was extra salty—probably from the seawater.

"I do hope the taste grows on you," she said, watching me. "And I wanted to let you know, I've requested an audience with the prince."

"What did he say?" I asked, leaning forward.

"That he'll see you when he can. I don't know when that will be."

I groaned. I couldn't just sit around here!

"Surely there's *something* else I can be doing," I muttered, hoping Rue might offer a helpful suggestion. But all she did was tap the bowl of berries.

"You can keep your strength up—it won't do you any good to waste away in this room. These berries are an excellent substitute for fresh water. I heard humans need it."

They'd really thought of everything to keep me alive down here—to keep me their *prisoner.*

"And when you're finished, I can help you change into a nightgown," Rue added, ignoring my bitter expression.

"I can dress myself," I insisted, but took a handful of berries and popped them in my mouth. Their delicious, watery, sweet taste bled on my tongue, and I found myself instantly addicted. It seemed like the skin of the berries kept any salt water from being absorbed, so only fresh water remained within.

"Then perhaps I can ready one for you," Rue replied, crossing the room to a large, ornate wardrobe, the color of deep teal. She began rummaging in it until she found a shimmering silk sheath.

"This should do nicely," she replied, and left it hanging on a nearby hook for me. "If that's all, I'll take my leave for the evening."

I nodded, still frustrated about my current situation. She left quietly, and the doors locked behind her once more. Once I'd had my fill of berries, I changed into the ivory sheath and marveled at how much nicer it was to wear. I hadn't realized just how heavy my other dress had been, and it was almost as if this one predicted my movements and shifted with me in the water.

122

With nothing left to do and nowhere to go, I drifted back to my bed. My eyelids were beginning to feel heavy, and I realized how weary I was from the long events of the past two days.

What was Melody doing to my father? To Kendra?

Had Matt noticed I was gone? Was he looking for me?

Was anyone even still alive on the island? Or had they all been slaughtered by Melody?

I had to stop her. I remembered Ms. Mugo said that I should curse her—that in doing so, I could bind her. But I needed to wield a mer-heart to do such a thing, and I had no clue how to use my own heart to access that kind of power.

Crawling under the covers—and noting how soft and comfortable they were—I hoped I would see the prince soon and that I wouldn't be stuck here forever. I had to convince him to let me go.

The bright crystal lights made it difficult at first, but exhaustion came over me faster than I thought it would, and within minutes I was asleep.

CHAPTER TEN

Coral

I awoke to a figure sitting on my bed in the dim light.

A scream tore from my throat, and I jolted upright. The figure sprung up from the bed.

"What is it?" it cried, and I recognized the familiar voice. He waved his hand, and the crystal lights brightened suddenly. Lysander eyed me with a startled expression, watching as I panted and tried to get my bearings.

"You—" I spluttered, bringing my knees up to my chest. "You're watching me *sleep!*"

He frowned at me.

"What is wrong with that?"

I gaped at him like a fish, unable to believe the words coming out of his mouth.

"You can't just watch me sleep! *It's creepy!*"

"I am certainly not creepy," he protested, folding his arms, and he actually sounded *offended.* He continued to frown at me, a single lock of his black hair falling over his eyes.

Shaken, I scrambled out of the bed, eager to put some space between us. I backed nearly all the way to the desk near the towering windows. His gaze followed me, and his brow furrowed. A moment later, he sat carefully on the edge of the bed again and raised his hands—as if to indicate that he meant no harm.

"Please calm down," he said, watching me with such rigidness, you'd think I was a rabid animal preparing to attack. "You requested an audience with me. So, here I am," he added, gesturing widely as if his presence itself were a gift.

Was this guy for *real?*

I buried my face in my hands, trying to process that my life had come to this; that I was *trapped* in a palace under the sea while my siren stepmother-to-be was murdering innocent people on the island above, and of all the people I could be stuck with, it was a prince who was entirely full of himself!

Taking a deep breath, I slowly looked back at him. He was waiting patiently, an intrigued gleam in his eyes.

"I thought you would summon me—not *come* to me," I answered. Panic flashed in his eyes.

"If you prefer, we can talk tomorrow—"

"No," I said, taking a step forward before he could stand. "No, we will talk now. About everything. Tell me about my mother. Tell me about your *curse.* Tell me—"

He held up a hand to stop me from going on.

"Easy," he replied, and gave me a gentle smile that made my heart waver. "One thing at a time."

He rose from the bed and took a couple of steps toward me. When I didn't move, his smile grew wider.

"So you know of the curse, then? Well, let's start there."

He offered me his hand. I stared at it for a moment but didn't take it. Eventually, he lowered it, then made a gesture for me to follow him as he headed for the door. I scurried to keep up with him. He was *not* leaving me locked in this room again.

125

"After you," he said, opening the door for me, and I frowned at him. What game was he playing here? But I went on ahead and waited on the landing for him to follow. He pointed to his left, and we turned down a corridor as we fell into step, walking side by side.

The palace was dark at night, with the same heated, dim lighting I'd found in my room. The teal wall panels were detailed in carved gold borders, and it all looked very opulent.

We walked down a narrow hallway filled with portraits. A *gallery* of some kind, I realized. Lysander came to a stop at the very end, facing a beautiful female with the same wavy black locks as his. The way she stared at you through the portrait was... eerie. Her eyes seemed blank, and her face showed no emotion.

"This was my mother," Lysander explained, his gaze fixated on the picture. "The portrait was done not long after she gave birth to me. I was told that before that time, she was full of life and laughter."

I held my breath as I listened to him and reached out to touch the portrait. Whatever it had been painted with, it didn't smudge or peel in the water. The texture was like hard wax.

"My father was a heartless, ruthless ruler before he met her. And the moment he saw her, he became enthralled. He would have stopped the currents of the Great Sea if he'd known it would make her happy."

He turned to face me, a strange sorrow evident in his eyes as he told the story.

"When they married, everything changed. My father gained a moral compass, while she lost hers. All her kindness, compassion, humanity... it left her. Eventually, her emptiness drove her mad, and she took her own life."

I couldn't respond for a moment—couldn't find the right words.

"I don't understand..." I said finally, staring at the portrait. "What influenced her to change so drastically?"

"The curse," Lysander explained, and when I glanced back at him, he was watching me carefully. "Coral, do you know what an undine is?"

I shook my head. He'd told me he was an undine earlier, but I'd been too panicked at the time to dwell on what that meant.

"An undine is a water spirit without any humanity. Though times have changed for our kind, and most are now born with hearts, the royal bloodline is still cursed with our original way of being. The only way for us gain our humanity is to fall in love with another being."

I sucked in a breath as I started to realize what he was telling me.

He wants me to give him my heart, because...

"You don't have a heart, do you?" I said slowly. I imagined what that must be like to have no heart, no humanity, no compassion... it would explain his lack of tact. A heartless being couldn't feel emotions the way normal people did—he couldn't consider kindness, empathy, or even respect.

"I have no heart, nor soul," he admitted. "That is, until I saw you."

"And now?" I asked tentatively, wondering what he meant. He took a slow step forward, so close I could feel the heat radiating from him.

127

"Now," he breathed softly. "I feel things I've never felt before. Confusing emotions that make no sense to me, and I cannot place what they are. Sometimes, it's unbearably overwhelming."

"So... you *do* have a heart?" I asked, confused. "I don't understand fully," I said, taking an equally slow step back from him. "You don't seem... *entirely* heartless."

He regarded me with a longing gaze. There was a strangled silence between us that seemed to go on for some time. Then finally, he broke it.

"As it stands right now, I only feel *glimpses* of what it's like to have human emotions—and only when I'm around you. The one way to make the shift whole and unwavering is to gain a heart for myself."

He watched my reaction, but I said nothing, so he continued, "My father loved my mother long before she returned those feelings. After some time, she gave him her heart, unconditionally, and he gained humanity within. But when one gives their heart, they lose it for themselves. She became heartless... and she suffered for it. My father spent the rest of her life trying to fix her, but he couldn't."

My head was swimming. I needed to sit down—and I must have gone pale, because Lysander guided me toward a seat. For someone with no humanity, he certainly seemed to show *some* concern for me.

"I know this is a lot to take in," he said carefully, kneeling before me. "Hence why I didn't want to overwhelm you earlier when you were already scared and confused."

"Lysander, I can't *fall in love* with you," I said firmly, and he physically recoiled as if my words had struck him. "You can't expect me to! I don't have any control over who I fall for—that's not how it works. And besides..."

I let out a sigh.

"Love is the last thing on my mind with my family in Melody's hands. I love *them,* and my priority is *them.* "

"I understand," he said quickly, reaching for my hand. I snatched it away.

"Do you?" I pressed. "Because you've trapped me down here without any regard for how I might feel or what I might want. If you need me to fall in love with you, let me give you some advice: that's a *bad* way to start things off."

He stood before me, a grimace plastered on his defined features.

"I cannot risk losing you," he said firmly. "You are the *only* one who can break my curse, Coral."

"And why should I care?" I snapped back. "Clearly, your actions are purely selfish. People who care for each other don't only think of themselves, *especially* when their actions affect other people."

I went to stand, but he held up a hand to stop me.

"If you agree to stay and you agree to an... alliance," he said, hesitating on the last word, "then my father will send his troops in your favor to stop Melody."

My eyes widened, and I stared at him.

"Why?" I breathed. Surely they wouldn't put their own men at risk just for me.

"Melody's actions do not just affect you. You could say we share a common goal," he admitted. "Coronis has been threatening Veranis for some time. And we have held strong, but Melody grows stronger every day. If we don't do something soon, we will lose our kingdom to her. And you will lose your family."

He reached for my hand again, and this time, I was too overwhelmed to stop him from taking it. I was caught up in the moment—actually considering his proposal. Despite having only just met him, and despite all that had happened, he was the *only* person other than Matt and Ms. Mugo who knew Melody was a siren. Who *believed* me.

But more importantly, he seemed like the only one with enough power to help me stop her. Under any other circumstance, I'd have been running for the doors, fighting my way to escape. I felt like a fish out of water trapped in this strange situation.

"If Melody succeeds in marrying your father, she will become the rightful ruler of the land and sea, according to ancient law. And if that happens, nobody on land nor in the sea will *ever* be able to stop her."

"But that's not possible," I insisted, thinking of the vast world above. "The land is *huge*—I don't think you realize how much of it there is. And there are already rulers and governors in other parts of the world."

"True," he nodded. "But none of them can use ancient magic. And even just a small piece of land is enough to turn the tides in Melody's favor, allowing her to unleash powerful ancient magic on the world. Because your father founded the island—the closest body of land to our kingdoms—she would gain rulership through marriage."

"Then why haven't your troops already stopped her?" I insisted.

"Ancient law declares that we cannot fight on land. We must wait for Melody to return to the ocean, or..."

His eyes studied me again.

"We must change the bindings of the Undersea. And for that, we need you."

"Because I'm a mermaid?" I asked, but he didn't confirm nor deny it. I shook my head at him. "Lysander, I can't even access my heart magic."

"Not yet," he replied, his eyes twinkling determinedly. "But together, we could stop her. All you have to do is stay here with me, Coral."

I could sense the pleading in his voice as he squeezed my hand a little, and I shivered. How could I make a decision of this gravity when there was so much at stake? Not just my family's safety... but *my* future?

I thought about the curse, about what had happened to his mother. Would the same happen to me? Would I go mad if I stayed here with him, never to see the surface again, or my family, for that matter?

I *hated* his proposal—it scared me. And yet... it was a better plan than mine. Surely, sending an army would be more effective than anything I could do on my own. Was it worth staying here if it meant my family would be free of Melody?

And...

I looked at Lysander's eyes and saw just a hint of kindness in them.

Would it really be so bad to stay with Lysander, considering how he felt about me? Would he care for me? Go above and beyond for me?

131

I wanted to say yes. It was on the tip of my tongue. And yet... something was stopping me. A sliver of hope, a silent prayer that maybe, just *maybe*, there was another way, that maybe I didn't have to put my future in the hands of a stranger, that maybe I could have my future *and* save my family, all by myself.

I was quiet for a long time before I finally spoke.

"I need more time to decide."

Lysander's gaze fell, and he looked like he wanted to protest—but he nodded.

"Very well. But you should know one other thing..." he said, and I raised an eyebrow at him. "The people of Coronis—Melody's people—are already making their way to land for the wedding. Our time is running out—and the fate of our kingdom is in your decision."

CHAPTER ELEVEN

Coral

When I returned to my room, Lysander locked the doors behind me once more. He still didn't trust me not to run.

I couldn't sleep after everything I'd just heard and spent hours pacing the length of the room.

There was no question that I'd put my family's safety first—but was this *really* my best option? I still knew so little about the mermaids... about *me*. What if I could unlock my heart magic? What if I could use it to curse Melody?

As I paced, darker thoughts kept rippling through me.

How selfish could you possibly be?

I collapsed on the edge of the bed, burying my head in my hands.

You have the chance to save your family, and you're going to risk it for yourself?

I gritted my teeth.

You don't deserve a future—not when Maya died for you. You've already had your second chance.

I heaved a ragged breath, feeling tears well in my eyes once more. I couldn't do this—couldn't choose between them and me. How could I even allow myself to consider it when just *considering* it wasted precious time and put them in more peril?

I should say yes. I should forget any hopes of having a future.

And yet...

There was that sliver of hope again; that hope that be-longed to me alone, that hope that filled me with selfish de-sire—a desire to be in control of my own future. A desire to do things *my* way.

The idea of staying here with Lysander was... I didn't know what it was.

He hadn't hurt me, but he was clearly obsessed, borderline possessive, even. It felt all levels of wrong to allow it.

But the deeper part of me knew I shouldn't be allowed to have a choice.

Maya had *died* saving me. I couldn't let anyone else die for me or *because* of me. I had this chance to save them, and if I wasted it on myself...

When Rue knocked a few hours later, dark circles had formed under my eyes, and I was slumped in front of the van-ity on the far-left wall after many more rounds of pacing. Rue spotted me immediately, a deep blue dress slung in her arms.

"Oh, my lady, I didn't realize you were already awake," she said, hurrying over, the fabric of the dress swaying with her. "Did you sleep well?"

I grunted, staring into the mirror at my sleep-deprived face. I'd gotten nowhere with my endless debating, my mind run-ning in circles. I was completely and utterly torn, unable to make a decision.

Rue tentatively looked me over, frowned, then said, "Well, erm, the prince has requested you join him for breakfast. How-ever, I'm going to need to ready you for the presence of the king."

"The king?" I repeated dully, and she nodded as she crossed to my wardrobe to find a matching pair of slippers. "He'll be here shortly, and I'm sure he'll want to meet you."

I remembered how Lysander had described the king before he married, and for some reason, that's what I fixated on.

My father was a heartless, ruthless ruler.

I couldn't get the image out of my head. It didn't seem possible that people could change so drastically.

This time, I let Rue do my hair, and I could tell from the dress she'd brought with her that I wouldn't be able to get into it on my own. It was covered in ruffles that cut across my torso and continued in spirals down my skirts—and the effect reminded me of jellyfish. The fabric was delicate, similar to pleated tissue paper, and started in a deep blue color before shifting to a pale pink at the ruffle edges.

"Rue," I asked, as she buttoned me up. "Do you know how I might be able to unlock my heart magic?"

Rue shook her head.

"I'm sorry, my lady—only the sea witch would know something like that."

I cocked my head at her.

"The sea witch?" I asked, and she suddenly went pale.

"Oh, my—I wasn't meant to say that," she whispered. "Forget it, my lady—it's nothing."

My eyes widened, and I sat up straighter.

"*Tell me* about this sea witch," I insisted, but her lips were firmly pressed as she reached around to do the final buttons. I rolled my eyes. "Fine. I'll ask Lysander," I huffed, and she shook her head.

"That's a bad idea, my lady," she said quietly—and something in her tone sent a warning shiver down my spine as she clasped the final button. "You're ready. I'll show you to the dining hall. But I beg of you, don't bring this up with either the prince or the king. It will do you no good."

The last part she said with such graveness, it unnerved me.

My head was spinning as I followed her to the door. She knocked, and the guards let us out. I didn't say anything as we navigated the corridors and grand staircase down to the dining hall, but I couldn't stop thinking about what she'd said.

When we reached the dining hall, I was surprised to find only Lysander sitting at a rather long dining table, surrounded by towering walls and the same wide windows. The food waiting at the table was much the same as the night before too—but there were additional plates of raw fish, finely sliced and arranged delicately with garnishes in the center of the table.

I wondered if they got sick of eating the same thing all the time.

Rue directed me to my seat, then left me. We were alone—staring at each other from opposite sides of the table.

"Sleep well?" he asked politely. I grimaced.

"I didn't sleep at all," I replied, and he frowned, his eyes flashing with concern.

"Was the bed not comfortable enough? I could find you a different room—"

"I was too overwhelmed to sleep," I added bluntly for his benefit, and understanding crossed his face.

"Of course," he replied quietly, averting his gaze and busying himself by plopping a handful of nearby sea berries into his mouth. Just watching him eat them made me remember their addictive sweetness, and I joined him in eating them.

"Have you heard anything about my sister?" I asked finally. I barely dared to breathe, but I knew better than to get my hopes up.

He shook his head.

"I'm afraid we won't know much more until my father returns from his expedition shortly."

I slumped in my chair, and Lysander noticed this. He changed the topic quickly.

"What do you know of the Undersea?" he asked, gesturing for me to talk. I pursed my lips, wondering if he was trying to distract me. But I supposed I could've used a distraction, and I thought about it as I leaned back in my chair.

"Before coming here, I only knew that sirens and mermaids existed. I didn't know there was an entire kingdom down here. Or about your kind. Or about the sea witch."

I'd let my last words slip deliberately, my heart skipping a beat as I watched him, and I didn't miss the way his eyes flashed with fear.

"The Undersea is made up of three kingdoms, actually," he said swiftly, recovering so smoothly I nearly thought I'd imagined those eyes. "They are Veranis, Atlantis, and Coronis. But since the war began, it's really only been Veranis and Coronis."

"What do you mean?" I pressed, narrowing my gaze. Lysander's eyes darted, and he busied himself with his food.

"Merpeople are a hunted species. Very few remain in Atlantis, and those who do are exceptionally skilled at hiding. Most mermaids have been killed or captured by the sirens."

Fear coursed through me at his words.

"How did they take an entire kingdom?" I breathed.

"The sirens are ruthless beings," he shrugged, still not looking at me. "If it wasn't for my father, we, too, would be dead or enslaved. We had an alliance with Coronis when the war began—when my father was heartless, that is—right before Melody took Coronis from Queen Chora."

"An alliance..." I trailed off. "As in... you were killing the mermaids too?"

His eyes shifted, but he finally met my gaze.

"We're not proud of what we did in the past. But it's exactly that—in the past," Lysander said quickly, popping another berry into his mouth. "Not long after Melody took the throne, my mother passed, and that's when things changed. But should Melody marry your father, the situation will only become more dire. I imagine she'll have no use for him once she gains control of the land."

His expression was firm, and that's when I realized he was trying to talk me into making my decision faster.

It was working.

"She's going to kill him," I realized, and he nodded. "Is this the intel your commander brought you yesterday?"

Lysander snorted.

"I don't need Leif to tell me what I already know about the woman," he replied with a pointed gaze.

Despite his words, I couldn't help thinking back to that conversation I'd had with Melody and how defensive she'd become when I suggested she wasn't marrying for love. Maybe there *was* a hint of attachment there, and I could only pray there was.

There was still one thing that didn't add up.

"Why does she want our mer-hearts so badly?" I asked. "If she only needs to marry our father, then why waste energy on our hearts?"

"She likely needs more power to completely subdue him," Lysander replied. "She may be powerful, but her power is nothing compared to yours."

I grimaced. It didn't seem possible that I could be more powerful than Melody. Not after everything she had done already...

"What if she does take control of the land?" I asked him. "What if she comes after me?"

"I won't let that happen," he replied tightly, the possessiveness seeping from his tone. "Even if we can't stop her on land, we'll think of something else."

Right...

"Speaking of mermaids..." I said, switching topics. "How did you know of my mother?"

I was curious, seeing as he had come from a different kingdom altogether.

"Everyone knew of your mother," he replied carefully, but I could tell he wasn't going to say more. Perhaps he planned to withhold information until I agreed to his proposal.

At that moment, the door to the dining hall opened, and a tall man strode in.

I stood. Even without the crown on his thick black hair, I would have known it was Lysander's father. The likeness was uncanny—save for the many age lines in his face and the clear exhaustion in his eyes.

He noticed me, and I was at a loss for what to do. We didn't have royal customs on the island—was I supposed to curtsy?

Lysander gave me a pointed look, subtly clearing his throat, and I took that as a yes. Immediately, I sank into my best curtsy—which was no doubt clumsy from absolutely *zero* years of practice.

I held my breath, not daring to look up, and heard a noise of approval.

"You may rise, child," he said, and I straightened. He regarded me with a cool look, but he didn't seem displeased.

"So you're her," he said finally, looking me over. "You *are* quite different from the other one, then."

I glanced at Lysander, trying to understand what he meant, but he was avoiding my eyes again. Did they mean Kendra? Because she was my twin?

"How was your journey back, Father?" Lysander asked. The king made a gruff noise, but his words were gentle.

"Long. Tiring. The waters are full of soldiers. It's getting harder to navigate, Son," he said grimly. "But we got the intel we needed: Melody's forces have garrisoned the entire island. It's only a matter of time... we'll need to act soon."

His eyes flicked to me again.

"I trust my son has told you of his proposal?" he asked, and I hesitated. There was no accusation in his tone, but I felt as if I was being judged anyway.

"I... said I needed more time to think..." I trailed off, ignoring the way my chest tightened. With every passing hour, it became more and more evident that I needed to make a decision—to say *yes*—and yet, I still couldn't bring myself to hand over my future so easily.

"I see. Unfortunately, time is a luxury we don't have. I'd hoped you might have understood that with your own family's lives at stake."

"Yes, but—"

"Then I must urge you to accept and to do so quickly," he interrupted. His expression was laced in something I couldn't quite place—almost as if there was regret there, but his eyes were full of unrelenting determination.

I swallowed hard.

"What if there was another way?" I asked. The king and Lysander slowly exchanged a look. "If I could unlock my heart magic, then maybe I could face Melody myself—"

The king let out a single laugh—not unkind, but filled with pure amusement at my seemingly obliviousness.

"If that were possible, we would all be saved. But that would be far too easy."

I grimaced.

"Perhaps there is a way," I insisted, but the looks on both of their faces told me my words would have no sway. I was too naïve, too uneducated, too *hopeful...*

I clenched my jaw. I *hated* it when people didn't listen to me, when I was pushed aside like my opinions didn't matter, like my *life* didn't matter, and I shouldn't get a say in it at all. It was exactly how I'd felt with Melody's control seeping into every aspect of our lives over the past six months, that feeling of gradual helplessness increasing day after day.

"I want to speak to the sea witch," I demanded finally. Lysander's face paled. "If she can help me understand my magic, then perhaps she can help me find another way."

The king's eyes became stormy, and his voice became steely and deadly quiet.

"You will not be permitted to speak to the sea witch. Do *not* ask about her again," he warned. It felt as if the sea itself was swaying against my skin from his command, warning me to shut up. Goosebumps trailed my arms, and I didn't dare breathe.

Lysander instantly cut in, moving to stand between us.

"Father, I'll join you shortly. Allow me to see Coral out," he said, placing two firm hands on my shoulders and steering me toward the door. The king eyed us both warily as Lysander hurried me from the room.

As soon as we were safely out in the hallway, I whirled to face him.

"Why did he—"

"He's right," Lysander said, cutting me off with a grave look, and I didn't miss the way his hands trembled as he lifted them from my shoulders. "Please don't ever bring that up again."

I refrained from heaving a sigh as I desperately tried to think of a new plan. I couldn't go back to my room, couldn't stay locked up there—or down here in this kingdom, for that matter. I needed information, *answers,* and I needed them quickly.

"Is there a library here?" I asked finally, trying not to scowl at the words leaving my mouth. I was truly desperate for it to have come to this.

Lysander's strained expression eased.

"There is," he admitted. "But I'd rather you learn from me and ask directly—"

"We don't have time for that," I added quickly, not leaving room for debate. "If I am going to make an informed decision about your proposal, I need to know more about the kingdoms of the Undersea, about what I'd be getting into. Let me look into things on my own."

Understanding came over Lysander's features, and he nodded.

"I'll show you the way," he said, gesturing for me to follow him, and relief swept over me. He didn't need to know that my research would entail far more than the three kingdoms.

CHAPTER TWELVE

Lysander

As I walked briskly to the strategy room, my mind was screaming at me.

Stupid. Stupid. Stupid.

I'd blown the whole thing. Why did I tell her about the mermaids? About us *slaughtering* their people? Of course that would repel her. I hadn't missed the disgust in her eyes, the fear as I'd mentioned it.

Even now, as I felt her presence growing further and further away, all sense was blurring from my mind. Rationality was fading, and my concern was shrinking.

Soon, it would be a tiny thing pressing faintly at the back of my mind—barely a second thought next to the wild, careless desires that usually consumed me.

"I can't fall in love with you."

Her words echoed in my mind, and it was the only thing that rooted me. The same pain and panic that had struck me last night rippled through me once more. All at once, I was reminded of what I stood to lose if I lost *her*.

And after all this time too...

I'd thought it would be easy. Ever since the day I saw her drowning in those waters. Ever since then, I'd dreamed of her, wished and willed for her to return to the ocean so that I might steal a glance at her. So that I might court her. So that I might bring her here, and she could be with me forever.

I should have known there would be complications. That her emotions would be different. That there would be things I couldn't understand—that she couldn't simply give me her heart the way I'd give her mine if she asked.

I pushed on the teal doors of the strategy room where my father was waiting across from a large stone table. A map was sprawled across the surface, marking the three kingdoms.

Coronis, Veranis, and Atlantis.

Leif was here too, standing to my father's left. They were deep in conversation, poring over the map, discussing what to do next with our soldiers.

"Our scouts have reported that Eugene Pryor is moving men closer to our borders," Leif was saying as he pointed out the locations on the map. "Even though they haven't admitted it, it's clear they're preparing an attack. They'll strike as soon as Melody marries Christopher, when her power comes into effect, and we won't get a chance to strike back."

My father nodded thoughtfully, taking it all in.

"We need to strike first, or we will be overthrown in a matter of days," my father replied, placing his hands on the table as he stared at the map. "Even if we move our men west, to Seer's Peek and the Twilight Overpass, we'll only hold them back, and it will only buy us a day or two at most."

He glanced at me, and my heart sank as I prepared to hear what I'd heard a thousand times before.

"Lysander," he began, his voice carrying a graveness in it. "You *must* close this alliance with the girl. I don't care how you do it—we need her."

"Yes, I know," I replied shortly. "But... it's not as easy as I thought it would be."

145

"Of course it's not," my father replied evenly, narrowing his gaze. "I heard you tied the poor girl up as soon as she got here. No *wonder* she's on edge."

I grimaced. I hadn't wanted her to leave—not after I *finally* had her here.

"Well, I didn't think it would be a problem," I huffed, and my father exchanged a weary glance with Leif. He rounded the table and sank into an open-arm pull-up chair.

"I realize how you feel about this girl, Son," he said carefully. "I felt it, too, when I met your mother. But what you are feeling is simply an *infatuation.* Love will come in time, but right now, all you need to do is woo her into saying *yes.* Get her to accept the damn proposal!"

"I don't want to mess this up," I shot back quickly, taking a step forward. For some reason, I felt the need to defend her. I only ever felt these bursts of emotion when it came to *her.* "Kingdom be damned, I *won't* mess this up."

My father raised an eyebrow at me.

"Oh? And will it be *you* who figures out an alternative way to save our kingdom?"

He stood and began striding toward me.

"Will it be *you*, my son, who spends more time chasing tiger sharks in the deep sea than attending your lessons? Who saves us all? Will you trade your precious, leisurely strolls for strategy meetings? Will you fight on the front lines or run off on one of your little expeditions and abandon your people?"

Maybe I should have felt something, but I didn't. I could tell he was upset, but all I felt was numb.

"She is one life compared to millions," my father said firmly, meeting my gaze. "And all hell be damned, I will have you do what's *right* this one time, Lysander."

He straightened, drawing up to his full height, and he glared at me while I stared back, the emptiness in my heart growing and growing.

"I've let you do as you please all these years—let you wander the kingdoms aimlessly, let you skip out on lessons, let you travel to the surface so you could spend your days pining over this girl. Your kingdom needs you—and in less than a year, you will be expected on that throne. You will not be permitted to rule carelessly."

He strode around the table until he was mere feet from me, then added stiffly, "There will be no kingdom for you to rule, no lands for you to wander, if you don't get the power we need to stop Melody's reign."

Selfish, my mind echoed. *You're selfish.*

I'd never seen anything wrong with that until I met Coral. Even now, her words echoed in my head again:

"People who care for each other don't only think of themselves, especially when their actions affect other people."

But why? Why were other people my responsibility? Why did I have to spend my life with awareness for others? It was *my* life, not theirs.

Only when I considered Coral did I *desire* to go out of my way for her, to make her happy—even though that was proving to be an impossible task. Why should I put others first if I didn't care for it?

I'd never asked to be born into royalty. I'd never desired to rule people, to have responsibility for their wellbeing. I

147

wanted to travel, to explore, to spend my days outdoors. I wanted to ride my seahorses and watch tiger sharks. My place had never been on a throne.

My father knew that, and he didn't care.

So I deemed not to care back. The idea of being responsible for thousands of lives was simply exhausting, and I had far more interesting things to do.

My father returned his attention to the map and began asking Leif about potential ways to attack Melody when we gained the upper hand. He began mapping out the best pathways to take, the best ways to gain undetected access to the land, and the best strategies to take Melody out. I watched them both, but I was only half listening.

The moment they'd started talking, I'd retreated to the inner depths of my mind, once again thinking of Coral.

Thinking of the first time I saw her.

Her marvelous beauty, her fascinating personality...

How was I going to gain the upper hand with her? How was I going to convince her to stay here with me?

I remembered all the years I'd waited, all those months spent watching the surface but never seeing her. All that time I'd spent lying on my bed, daydreaming about her.

She was the one—it was clear as day. I'd never felt this way about anybody else.

But she was like a puzzle—one far too complicated for me to solve. So many emotions to navigate, so many feelings to consider... I didn't even know where to start.

Finally, after hours of planning and strategizing, my father left—with Leif telling him he would send a small group of men to be stationed at the nearest valley between here and Coronis. Then, it was just Leif and I, and he regarded me with a careful gaze, his honey eyes studying me.

"Are you alright?" he asked me finally.

Leif and I had known each other for years. He'd started serving as a soldier at fourteen and had quickly climbed the ranks to commander and my personal guardsman. We'd spent a lot of time together, and we'd grown close. Of all the people I knew, he was one of the few I could say I cared about—be it in my own strange way. Expressing that I cared was a whole other challenge and one that never came easily.

"I'm fine," I replied shortly, folding my arms. "I am just wondering what I can do to convince Coral to ally with us— and for her to give me her heart."

Leif sighed.

"I should have known you weren't actually paying attention to our meeting," he grumbled. Unlike me, he had his humanity. All undines did if they were not born into royalty. "You can't force her to fall in love with you," he replied patiently, gesturing for me to sit at the table. I did, and he came around to sit on my right-hand side. He had broad shoulders from years of training, and his jaw was narrow.

"You have to accept that she may *never* fall for you, that she may never give you her heart. Coral is her own person, and she should be permitted to make her own choices."

"Of course," I frowned. After all, I made my own choices, so it made sense that she would too. I just didn't understand why it wasn't *obvious* that she should fall for me. What wasn't to like? I was a prince—I could show her everything in the

Undersea, give her anything she desired. She would be taken care of down here, an entire palace of staff at her command.

Leif glanced at the door, then lowered his voice.

"If I can speak freely," he said—which he knew he could with me— "the king putting a timeline on this is only going to make things worse. The more you push, and the faster you try to woo her, the less likely it is to work. She needs time to get to know you, to learn how she feels about you. And—" he paused, giving me a pointed look, "I can imagine trapping her down here and restraining her hasn't made her grow any fonder of you."

"So what do I do?" I insisted, springing from my chair and beginning to pace. Frustration flooded me. "Do I wait five hours between seeing her? Do I time my advances?"

Leif's eyebrows knitted together, and he looked as if he wanted to smack his forehead, "No, you fool—she doesn't need time like *that*. She needs you to *spend* time with her, however long it takes for the answer to become clear."

I paused and frowned.

"What if it takes longer than we have?" I asked, my heart dropping. The wedding was looming, and if we waited any longer than that...

"If it does, then it does," Leif replied firmly, getting to his feet and facing me head on. "You and your father might just have to find another way to stop Melody if that becomes the case. You can't force this, Lysander."

If this didn't work, my father—I didn't want to imagine his reaction. This kingdom meant everything to him. It was all he had left.

Leif's expression softened as he watched me, and he added, "You can't force this... but you *can* go out there and talk to her. Get to know her. Show her you care. *Put her needs before your own."*

I bristled. It sounded complicated. I didn't even know how to begin doing such a thing. I rarely bothered to put other people's needs over mine—especially not with a palace full of staff tending to me each day. Only my father got what he wanted out of me, and *that* was because he was the king. If I didn't stay on his good side, he could take everything from me with a simple command.

Still... maybe I could mend things with Coral this way.

Dozens of ideas came to mind all at once: things I loved doing, things she might appreciate as much as I did.

"What if we... took a stroll through the garden?" I suggested, as I mentally jumped from idea to idea. "And then, maybe we could have dinner together in my quarters. And after that, I could wake her again and we could go fish-watching—"

"Don't *wake* her when she's sleeping!" Leif scolded, then froze. "Wait, what do you mean *again?"*

"Last night, I went to her room. She'd requested to see me, so I went as soon as I could. But she *did* seem upset about it at first..."

Leif heaved a sigh, throwing his hands up.

"No, Lysander! You can't just..." he trailed off, his arms slumping, and looked lost for words. He pinched the bridge of his nose, then added, "Look, just start with the garden stroll. I need to attend to some matters, but try not to blow it. In fact, don't do anything you wouldn't want me to do."

I nodded slowly, my thoughts shifting quickly, and frowned at him.

"Actually, speaking of *matters,*" I said finally, thinking back to my father's wrath during breakfast this morning. "That thing we spoke of last night?"

Leif only gave a single nod to indicate that he remembered.

"Could you look into it for me? We might need it after all," I said, a tightness forming in my gut. He nodded again, his eyes solemn.

"Of course. I'll send someone to investigate quietly," Leif replied, and turned toward the door.

"Also—" I added, and he stopped in his tracks. "Can you escort Coral to the gardens for me?" Leif looked over his shoulder with a raised eyebrow.

"It's only been two hours—I don't want to seem like I'm rushing things," I added lightly.

His shoulders slumped, his expression defeated. I grinned at him, not sure why he was giving me that look.

"I shall meet her there for our first official date," I declared, rubbing my hands together. He was still standing there with that look as I strode from the strategy room, a bounce in my step.

CHAPTER THIRTEEN

Coral

The library was a massive space, well-lit by the creeping crystal lights on the ceiling and sprawling with dozens and dozens of shelves and books.

And they're intact, I thought, as I picked a title off a shelf and flipped it open. Like the book in my room, this one had a tough cover, and the pages were thick. The water hadn't turned them soggy—they were completely intact somehow. And the ink did not stain and bleed, leaving every word flawlessly written.

I didn't know what magic to call it, but I was grateful for it.

Lysander had left me here, saying he needed to attend a strategy meeting with his father. I didn't know how long their meeting would take or how much time I had to find all the information I needed. But I wasn't about to waste a second.

I walked the entire length of the library, pulling any title that looked as if it might contain useful information and stacking the books in the crook of my elbow. There were dozens of history books containing records of every war in the Undersea, and I grabbed those. But I couldn't find any books on magic or lore, which frustrated me.

The weight of the books on my arm filled me with dread. As eager as I was to find answers, I wasn't thrilled about the idea of poring through dozens of books. Eventually, I returned to the center of the library and found a stone table to lay the books out on before taking a seat.

"Did you find what you were looking for?" a voice asked, startling me out of my skin. I whirled around to face an older female who wore her graying brown hair in a crown of braids around her head. A turquoise silk sheath floated around a dark blue dress, and she pushed a pair of spectacles up the bridge of her nose as she waited for my response.

"Who are you?" I breathed, steadying my racing heart.

"Apologies—I'm the librarian. My name is Deandra."

I nodded, looking back at the piles of books I'd spread out.

"Well, I guess we'll find out," I replied, pulling one closer and flicking it open.

"May I ask what it is you hope to learn?" Deandra asked, taking a seat next to me on a stone chair. "Perhaps I can point you in the right direction."

I shook my head.

"I don't really know what I'm looking for," I admitted. Information about my mother—except I doubted there would be any book in this library detailing specifics of a random person, and certainly not her, of all people. I guessed the same for Melody too—but perhaps there were accounts of Queen Chora in these books. Maybe it would be enough to piece some of the puzzle together.

"Well, let me know if I can be of any assistance. I'll be around," she said gently, before rising and drifting off. I focused my attention back to the book I'd opened and began reading.

I'd never been much of a reader, and I soon realized how that put me at a disadvantage. The information was detailed, written in small handwriting, and there was so much of it to wade through—it was overwhelming. I didn't know why I thought I could sit through all these tomes without losing focus as my mind continuously wandered before I made it halfway down each page.

I tried to scan through and find details about the more recent events of the Undersea, flicking through to accounts of more recent years. But as I continued turning the pages, I realized the first book I'd picked up didn't have any recent accounts of history—it still dated back hundreds and hundreds of years. I sighed as I slammed it shut. How many books would I have to trudge through to find what I was looking for?

After almost half an hour, I'd skimmed through all the books on my table and had learned nothing of use.

I wanted to stop reading. Maybe it *would* be easier to ask Lysander directly. But he would never give me straight answers—he was hoarding the information from me and would continue to do so until he got what he wanted.

So I stood again, gritting my teeth, and did another round—this time, walking slower, scanning more carefully, and taking care to double-check the highest and lowest shelves. That's when I spotted a faded book on the top shelf, the cover well worn. I couldn't make out the title, so I reached up to pull the book down and flicked it open.

It took me a moment to understand what I was looking at. The writing was in an unfamiliar language, but the illustrations depicted an ethereal woman, her gown made up of trails of fabric that snaked around her body like tentacles. Bright, powerful light glowed in her hands, and glowing words spiraled from it until they faded into the surrounding seawater.

155

"Deandra!" I called, hurrying through the library. I continued calling for her until I found her standing beside a row of shelves, her nose in a book of her own. She looked up as I approached her, and I showed her the illustration.

"I'm sorry to bother you—but can you tell me, is this the sea witch?"

"Why, yes, it is," she replied, fixing her spectacles and looking over the illustration.

"Can you tell me about her?" I begged, falling into an empty armchair nearby. "I *need* to know more about her."

She stared reluctantly at the book, and I offered it to her.

"Or maybe you could translate this book for me?"

Deandra placed her own book back on the shelf, then moved to sit in a deep emerald-green armchair opposite me.

"The sea witch is our lawmaker," she explained finally, meeting my gaze. "She is all-knowing and uses her magic to create bindings—rules of the Undersea that all beings must follow. The bindings keep our courts orderly—and deliver punishments when rules are broken."

I frowned. Why wouldn't they want me to know this? It seemed like general, if not *useful* information.

"We get a new sea witch every thousand years," Deandra added thoughtfully. "Our last one died last year, and when a sea witch dies... all of her bindings become undone. And so, new laws can be made—but only by a sea witch."

I nodded as she spoke.

"Where can I find her?" I asked.

"She resides here, in Veranis," Deandra informed me. "But one does not find her—she will summon you if there is to be business between you and her. Nobody but the royals know precisely where she is as she does not wish to be found."

I clicked my tongue. So she was here, in the kingdom—perhaps closer than I realized. If she could get me out of this, then I *had* to find her. There had to be a way... maybe even one where I didn't have to bargain the information out of Lysander.

Deandra studied my gaze as if reading my thoughts, and her eyes crinkled with warning.

"I would not advise seeking her outside of a summoning," she added. "Bindings are not the only magic the sea witch can perform. She can also place curses among any being she chooses and has done so before. Many have suffered for it."

"What kind of curses?" I asked, and Deandra's eyes grew dull.

"Well, the royal curse is one example," she said. "The curse has plagued the royal family for hundreds of years. And unlike bindings, curses do not break when the sea witch passes. There is only one way to break the royal family's curse."

"Lysander said another being needed to fall in love with him... to give him their heart," I recalled slowly.

Deandra smiled a small smile and said, "Except that has not worked in the past hundred years. All it does is pass the curse back and forth between the two lovers—never fully breaking it or ceasing its inheritance down the family bloodline. There is yet another way to break it, but it has not been discovered. Such is why curses are terrible, tricky things to navigate."

I grimaced. I would still seek out the sea witch if it meant saving my family... but not at the cost of my own well-being. And not while another, better option lay available to me, however unbearable it might seem to accept Lysander's proposal.

So I shoved the sea witch from my mind, deciding she wasn't worth my time.

"Are there any books on mermaids here?" I asked, changing the subject. "On anything to do with them—history, magic, I'll take whatever you have."

Deandra's lips curled up in a smile.

"I thought you'd never ask," she beamed, and stood, gesturing for me to follow.

None of the books told me how to unlock my heart magic. But I did learn a lot about how mermaid magic could be used, and harnessed, in general.

As I pored over the books, I was completely enamored by them—in a way I'd never been while reading anything. I devoured the information like it was a lifeline... and I supposed, in a way, it was.

I learned that hearts were the core of a mermaid's power— hence why they were so powerful and so greatly sought after.

I learned that hearts could be wielded by any sea-being to enhance magic, remedy curses, and even use in tonics and potions. It explained why Melody wanted my heart so bad—and it also explained why Lysander thought my heart would break his curse. But it didn't explain why neither had sought another mermaid's heart. For Melody, they couldn't be that hard to come by, and for Lysander... *well,* I imagined that was just a selfish obsession on his part.

I also learned that mermaids could manipulate the ocean using their magic—but in what way, I didn't know. It seemed to depend on the mermaid's strength and power, for a start. And the specifics seemed to differ too—or at least the ancient text of the book made it sound that way.

The last bit of information I learned was the most useful so far—and the most interesting. Mermaids could summon impenetrable crystal shields, and only another mermaid with pure intentions could thaw it and pass through.

I realized that was why my mother's heart magic had protected Kendra the way it had. And I realized that if Melody ever got her hands on me again, she might use me to try and thaw it. I was probably the only person who could break Kendra free of it, which meant she was safe but also trapped until I could reach her again.

Yet another reason *not* to stay down here with Lysander for the rest of my life.

I didn't hear the library door open and didn't sense a tall broad figure come up behind me until he cleared his throat, his voice unfamiliar. It was lower than Lysander's, and I glanced over my shoulder to see Commander Leif standing there, peering over my shoulder.

"Oh, you're reading about the history of Atlantis?" he asked. I glanced back down at the book, flipping to the front cover to check the title, and he was right.

"You must be a fan of this book to have recognized it from a mere page," I replied, looking back at him.

"Well, it's my job to know these things," he said quickly as he shrugged. "And to read up on them."

"I'm not much of a reader," I admitted, pushing the book toward the pile of scattered tomes I'd gathered.

"Me either," he replied with a small smile. "I much prefer being out on the field with a sword. But I do a lot of paperwork."

I guessed that made sense—he *was* a commander, after all. He added, "I've come to escort you to the gardens. Prince Lysander is waiting there and wishes to take a stroll with you."

"He couldn't come get me himself?" I asked, raising an eyebrow. Lysander was doing a rather poor job of courting me so far.

Exhaustion crossed the commander's face—like my comment had struck a pain point—as he replied, his tone short and brisk, "He needed a few minutes to prepare, so I came."

I glanced back at my messy pile of books. Deandra had told me to leave them when I was done, that she would put them back, but I felt bad leaving her with so much work to do. Commander Leif shifted impatiently though, and I got the sense that I had no choice.

Standing, I followed the red-haired man to the door. He was tall, and his hair was a lovely color. And he radiated kindness, so different to that of Lysander's desperate energy.

As we walked, I tried not to stare at the commander's strong back and broad shoulders evident beneath his navy uniform. Instead, I thought back to the tomes I'd been reading—and all I'd learned of the mermaids and their kingdom.

The descriptions had been so vivid, it had been easy to imagine their bustling, vibrant kingdom built on the ruins of an ancient sunken city—the many ginormous columns and pillars, the temples and buildings they had claimed for their own. The texts had described it as a hidden kingdom only accessible through caves, so the climate was sheltered from the harsh ocean currents. The waters were always pleasant and warm and swimming with light rays.

But that was a long time ago. I imagined it was nothing like that now, what with all that had happened.

I wondered what it had been like to grow up there, to venture through the waterways to the surface with your family on your sixteenth birthday, as had been tradition, and visit the many hidden rock pools along the coast, collecting treasures to bring back and remember forever. I wondered if my mother had done that with her parents many years ago before the war.

"Commander," I said quickly, hurrying my pace to catch up with him as we walked the corridors of the palace. He glanced idly over his shoulder at me. "Lysander said that mermaids were a hunted species and that they've been almost entirely wiped out or captured."

He nodded with confirmation, and his expression was sympathetic.

"Only a few mermaids are said to remain in Atlantis—including the royals," he explained to me.

I stopped in my tracks, and he did too.

"The royals are still alive?" I asked, and he nodded again. "But... how could they let this happen to their kingdom?"

The commander's expression remained composed.

"The royals used their magic to encase the Alta Palace entirely in impenetrable crystal. They've resided there for two decades, evading capture and keeping Atlantis from being entirely razed or overthrown. But they are trapped there, helpless and unable to save their people."

I thought of the kingdom, once beautiful and vibrant. Could it ever be that way again?

Maybe the *mermaid royals* could help me unlock my heart magic. Maybe I could reach them somehow. And maybe I could return the favor someday for their kingdom. But how would I ever convince Lysander to let me roam the Undersea? Especially to a place that sounded so desolate and dangerous?

Suddenly, the commander cracked a crooked smile, and my breath caught in my throat.

"What are you scheming?" he asked, raising an eyebrow as he studied me.

"I'm not scheming," I replied quickly, folding my arms and hoping the heat I felt on my cheeks wasn't evident.

He chuckled, breaking that serious composure.

"I have sisters, and they wear that exact same expression when they're scheming," he explained, grinning. "If you're half as good as them at it, then I bet whatever idea you just had is a good one."

I let out a steady breath.

"What if I told you I wanted to visit the mermaid royals?"

"Then I'd tell you that you're mad," he replied seriously. But then he lowered his voice, stepping closer to me. "But I'd also tell you it's a better plan than what we've currently got."

My heart began to thud in my chest.

"Then perhaps I'll bring it up with Lysander," I breathed.

"Perhaps you should," he replied, his eyes twinkling slightly. "It'll give you both something to talk about."

162

He was standing so close, and every inch of my skin felt warm. But the spell broke instantly as he stepped back.

"We should go. The prince is waiting for you."

I fought the urge to shake my head. Had that conversation been as strange as I thought it was? We continued down the corridor, my idea lingering in my mind. It was just an idea... but perhaps it could become a reality.

CHAPTER FOURTEEN

Coral

When I stepped outside into the courtyard, my gaze was drawn upward toward the sky—where schools of fish passed overhead in rainbow varieties.

It was *beautiful.*

"I like watching them too," a voice said, and I looked forward to see Lysander leaning against a statue—one of a man, but not one I could recognize. Lysander followed my gaze to the towering stone statue and added, "This was my great, great, great grandfather—King Maverick. He was a fine ruler."

"I can imagine," I replied, staring at all the intricate details while folding my arms—the creases of his cape, the grooves on his staff, and the replicated gems in his coral crown. "I assume it's not just anyone who gets a statue around here."

Lysander smiled and gestured to the path, which sloped down and weaved through dozens of vibrant coral gardens. Fish darted from coral to coral, like butterflies might do with flowers. Commander Leif had already gone, leaving us alone.

"I thought you and I could get to know each other properly. Maybe spend some time talking..."

He began walking, so I fell into step beside him. *Best get this over with...*

"And what would you care to speak of?" I asked. Small talk was the last thing I felt like doing with everything at stake. So, if he wanted to talk, he could at least do the honors of coming up with topics.

"Tell me about things you enjoy doing. Do you like dancing?" he asked.

"I hate dancing," I replied, wrinkling my nose. "I've never been any good at it. I much prefer surfing."

"Ah. That's a shame. My mother loved dancing. Or, at least, that's what I heard. She would spend hours dancing in the ballroom, here in the palace. I thought maybe... we could try it sometime."

"Like I said, I much prefer surfing," I replied shortly, keeping my focus on the sunset-colored gardens ahead. For someone who wanted to get to know me, he sure brought up his own family a lot.

A school of fish dived, sailing just above our heads, and Lysander reached his hand up. They circled back to nuzzle him, each one drifting against him before they continued on their journey. I stared at the strange spectacle.

"As for myself, I like animals," he told me, grinning. "I especially love sharks. They are very interesting creatures."

"I can see that," I replied, a little stunned.

Perhaps he would get along with Kendra better than I. She was the one interested in marine life.

It didn't take long for the shock to wear off.

"Well, this has all been very enlightening," I huffed, unable to help myself in the light of things. Maybe he would deem this a loss and let me go back to my room. But he seemed to misread my words, breaking into a glowing smile, and I cringed inwardly.

"Lysander, listen—" I began, but he stopped me.

"Please... I know this must be hard for you," he said quickly. "I know you're worried about your family. I want to save them too... because it matters to you. And I know I brought you here unwillingly, and I've kept you here, but I'm doing my best to make this situation better for you."

I studied him, and his gaze was nothing but genuine.

"In all honesty, Leif suggested I try to talk to you. It all feels very foreign to me, and I'm afraid of messing this up. I fear that I already have."

I raised an eyebrow. So the *commander* was playing matchmaker now, was he?

The way Lysander stared at me with those pleading eyes... maybe I was being too harsh on him. I didn't *truly* know what it was like to be him, to feel things the way he did. If he was truly doing his best, could I really fault him for not being better? Could I expect better from someone who didn't know how to *be* better?

I sighed, feeling my walls come down.

"I appreciate that you're trying," I replied gently. "But in all honesty, I don't want to get to know you. Not like *this*. Not when I'm sick with worry over my family. Not when I know I might never get to see them again. It's tearing me apart from the inside."

My eyes began to sting, and I blinked away tears. His expression fell as he watched me.

"What can I do to help?" he said. "Aside from taking you back to the surface—I *can't* do that, but anything else I can do, I will. I swear it."

I stared at him, trying to read any hint of deceit in his eyes—but if there was one thing I couldn't fault Lysander for, it was his honesty. His lack of tact made him an open book.

"If you truly mean that," I began. "Then there *is* something you could do for me."

And then, with him listening intently, I told him of my idea.

Lysander didn't bother to knock on the commander's office door, instead opening it and striding inside. Leif was seated at a desk centered in the room, poring over pages of books and papers. He didn't seem surprised when he looked up to find the prince had let himself in. He did, however, appear surprised to see me hovering in the doorway.

"Don't tell me he blew it already," Leif huffed, eyeing the two of us.

"Actually, I think we found a topic we agree on," I replied with a smirk on my lips. "Didn't we, Lysander?"

Lysander nodded, a determined look in his eyes as he turned to the commander and said, "We need to organize a trip to Atlantis."

Leif just stared at us both for a moment, his expression unreadable.

Then he looked at me as if to say, *are you serious?*

I grinned back, but that expression didn't turn to delight like I'd expected. Not even a hint of admiration shone in his eyes. In fact, the more we stared at each other, the more horrified he seemed to appear.

I thought he'd *liked* the idea?

"You can't do such a thing—it's far too dangerous," he said finally, standing and rounding the desk to face us head on. "Melody has her soldiers everywhere, on every road between here and Atlantis. You'll never make it past them."

"I understand, but Coral's proposal is too good to refuse. Too good for *Atlantis* to refuse." He turned to me and gestured to Leif. "Go on, tell him."

I felt a sense of pride wash over me and stepped forward to speak, "I want to propose an alliance to the mermaid royals on your behalf—one with the sea *and* land. Surely it's too good for them to refuse, to have two territories backing them when they're on the brink of extinction."

Leif's face paled—and I knew it was because I was right. Because he'd be stupid to turn this down, even with the risks. Because aside from me allying with Lysander outright, there were no better plans, no stronger options.

Plus, Lysander wasn't going to let me go alone. No, he would venture with me to Atlantis just to keep me in his sights. Leif was pale because there was no stopping any of this from happening.

"We're not powerful enough without Coral," Lysander added, backing me. "But an alliance with the mermaids *and* the land would be even more powerful."

"But they don't have a kingdom. Or an army," Leif said quickly, as if he could talk us out of it.

"The royals alone are powerful enough," I replied. "If those tomes I read from are true, they have *incredible* magic.

That power is currently keeping the sirens from getting into their palace. What if that power could be used to contain the kingdom of Coronis once and for all? To keep Melody contained?"

"It's... it's not solid enough..." Leif insisted, tapping his chin as he began to pace. "Melody's men outweigh both of our kingdoms combined. Getting them all into one place would be difficult."

I turned smugly to Lysander.

"Didn't you say the people of Coronis are making their way to land for Melody's wedding?" I asked. Which made sense—because it was the one place they couldn't be attacked.

"There are soldiers at our borders though..." Leif said, appearing to think the idea through now. "But... you're *right*. There's only a handful of them, scattered in groups. We could sneak past them and then our men could take them *if* the mermaids helped us contain Coronis. And then... we *would* stand a better chance of facing Melody on land."

Then he shook his head.

"But the mermaid royals are currently trapped in their own palace—if they leave, it would mean surrendering their kingdom to the sirens. And they would never even *entertain* the idea of an alliance with us. Not after..."

He trailed off, his eyes haunted, and I remembered Lysander telling me they'd once allied with Coronis. They'd *killed* mermaids, perhaps for years...

"Not to mention," he added, skipping past the thought entirely, "that getting in and out would be difficult. There are still sirens patrolling those lands for survivors. You'd have to disguise yourselves as sirens."

He looked me up and down and said, "For you... it might not be so difficult. You're beautiful enough that you could pass as one of them. You'd have to cover up that scrape on your chin though."

My eyes widened—I hadn't been expecting him to call me beautiful, and I averted my gaze.

"But Lysander... he's a public figure. It will be more difficult to disguise him without magic. Perhaps there's a potion we could use..."

Leif was *really* considering this! He continued to muse aloud, "Neither of you have tails, which helps. You'd have to learn siren mannerisms, but I'm sure you could master it..."

Every obstacle that came up, he worked through it. We passed ideas back and forth until finally, he seemed satisfied. He leaned against his desk, facing us, and said, "I don't like it... but I think it could work. However, we'd need to pass it by your father."

He looked to Lysander who nodded and added, "I can convince him. If you can write up a detailed report of how we'd go about it, I'll take it with me and propose the idea this evening."

I cleared my throat, and both of them turned their attention on me once more.

"I just have... one condition," I said, and they both seemed to hold their breath.

Here goes nothing, I thought.

"In return for allowing me to go and to ask the royals about my heart magic, I will accept Lysander's alliance proposal—but *only* on the condition that the royals reveal no other way to save my family."

Lysander's eyes widened.

"Really?" he breathed, and I nodded, my lips pulling into a tight line.

"I'll do whatever it takes to save my family. But I want a chance to save myself first. I want..."

I trailed off, trying not to let the hope overwhelm me.

"I want to use my heart magic, if it's possible to do so, to save my family. Because it means I get to choose my own future."

The two males were silent. Lysander looked wounded, like he'd been punched—like it was only just dawning on him the position he'd put me in. Leif, on the other hand... he was smiling like he'd expected as much.

"I'll get started on the paperwork," he said, nodding to both of us.

I headed for the door, and Lysander followed me out. He didn't speak to me once we were outside, and when I glanced at him, he wouldn't look at me.

I don't think he knew what to say. Perhaps he was ridden with guilt.

Good, I thought. He needed to understand what he'd done. And now that he did... maybe things could be different between us.

"I'm going to my room," I said finally, and he nodded. "Please tell me what the king says as soon as you know."

I headed back the way we'd come, knowing the staircase was down the hall, but then stopped to look over my shoulder and added—because I knew he wouldn't, "And please knock before you enter my room again."

171

CHAPTER FIFTEEN

Coral

Word came that evening that our request to travel to Atlantis had been approved by the king. I couldn't contain the smile on my face, and when Rue arrived with my dinner, I was still grinning from ear to ear.

"Well, I heard the news," Rue huffed, laying the tray of food on my bedside table. "And I don't know how you pulled it off, but consider me impressed."

She offered me a smug look, and I couldn't help but beam at her.

I was getting out of here! I was going to learn about my heritage, my family, my *magic!*

It felt so good to be doing something other than sitting around, debating back and forth in my head for hours and agonizing over what to do about Lysander's proposal. At least I could push that to the back of my mind for a few days.

"You'll need to pack tonight as you'll be leaving first thing tomorrow," Rue said, but she began working her way around the room as she piled clothes and shoes on the end of the bed—she was packing for me.

"Don't I need to disguise myself?" I asked, and Rue's eyes widened.

"Oh, yes, you'll have to dress like a siren. I'll find you something appropriate," she promised. "And you'll need to act like a siren too—they are creatures of savage beauty. They can

172

tear you apart without breaking a single nail, and they fuss if they have a stray hair out of place." She turned up her nose at the thought. "I don't know how they get anything done," she muttered, shaking her head.

"So act like a princess?" I asked, and Rue frowned at me. I then realized my mistake. "Oh, not a literal princess—it's an expression. It, uh, means to be spoiled and fussy."

"Well, yes, that sounds about right," Rue replied thoughtfully. "Most sirens are demanding, cold-hearted, and self-centered. They love using their magic to enslave others into serving their every need. But sirens can also be prideful creatures. They'll go to any lengths to show you what they're really capable of if you anger them... so don't go angering any of them!"

It sounded simple enough. I'd been around Melody so long that I could mimic pretty much all of her mannerisms and habits. She was always tossing her hair, checking her nails, and sitting straight as a board—as if any imperfection would suggest a weakness.

Rue gave me an ointment for my chin before bed, which stung when I applied it but did wonders to heal the wound by the time I woke and checked it in the morning. There was only the faintest sign that I'd injured myself—weak scarring where there had been a raw red injury—and when Rue returned to help me get ready, she assured me that the wound would be fully healed in only a few more hours.

Lysander came to fetch me not long after that—and to my relief, he knocked at the door *and* waited outside. It was a miracle!

Rue had finished packing a large, drawstring bag for me the night before, and she was just finishing the touches on my braid, claiming it would be easier to keep tidy.

"Be careful," she insisted, patting out the creases of my traveling dress—a stunning deep purple ensemble that still allowed me room to move in. I didn't know if she meant of myself or the dress, but I made a note to be careful of both.

When I finally exited my room, satchel slugged over my shoulder, I stopped short in my tracks upon seeing the figure waiting there for me.

Lysander was *blond.*

It took me a moment to realize it was his disguise: He had golden locks and was dressed to the nines in a stunning maroon coat and leather traveling pants. His crisp white shirt was slightly unbuttoned, revealing his muscular chest, and his eyes were a lighter shade of green—not the pretty sea-green I'd grown accustomed to.

"Woah," I noted, looking him over and folding my arms. "Who *did* this to you?"

He frowned.

"Does it not please you?"

"Oh, it pleases me," I reassured him with a smirk—but not for the same reason he probably thought. He looked ridiculous, like a shiny, pompous lord's son.

"Leif found a potion. It's supposed to wear off in two days or so..." he trailed off, sounding uncertain, and I snorted.

"I'll be disappointed when it does," I said, eyeing him wickedly. Messing with him like this was far too fun—he was so gullible.

Lysander led me through the palace until we finally reached a foyer, and two guards opened a set of double doors. Bright ocean hues flooded in—kind of like how sunlight blinds you when you step outside. But it was short-lived as my eyes adjusted to the dimly-lit waters and the cavernous surroundings.

After spending so long inside, feeling like I might never leave, it was still glorious to be standing on the front steps, taking in the surrounding ocean. Far, far above us was a cavern roof, suggesting that the Vera Palace was nestled deep down in the ocean, away from the exposed currents and marine life.

"Unfortunately, the kingdom is too crowded for us to ride through, so we'll need to walk until we reach the stables. Leif will be meeting us there," Lysander informed me, and I nodded.

We descended into the coral gardens I'd been admiring for days from my bedroom window, and down a sloping path. At the foot of the slope were towering walls, and the entrance gate was heavily guarded. The guards spotted us approaching, and they swung the iron gates open.

Then we were walking through, and my eyes beheld the sight before me.

The kingdom sprawled below us—sloping forever and ever down, gradually panning further outward as it filled the entirety of a canyon.

As I looked up at the cavernous ceiling, which spanned hundreds and thousands of miles upward, I saw a blanket of tiny turquoise stars.

"Bioluminescent microorganisms," Lysander explained, watching my transfixed gaze as I stared at it in awe. It was absolutely beautiful, making the entire kingdom seem as if it were showered in a starry night sky.

We continued down the sloping gravel roads, the rocks the size of my hand under my feet, and every single one different from the other: from cream to slate to gray with speckled patterns to smooth, rippling lines.

Before long, we were walking among houses, which were narrow and made of smooth silvery stone, then peppered with bedrock texturing. The tiny homes were nearly stacking on one another as they grappled for space on the sloping cliffsides of the canyon. Algae grew on stone trellises of many homes, attracting schools of vibrant, colorful fish that darted from door to door as they nibbled leisurely.

As we walked, we passed many people—the streets were bustling and crowded. I stuck close to Lysander, not wanting to get separated—even though it would have been so easy to slip away. But I would lose myself in this giant kingdom, and getting back to the surface alone would be a challenge.

We walked and walked until we reached a market square where we passed dozens and dozens of stalls packed with boxes and goods on display. There were food vendors, their stalls piled high with freshly caught fish. Some were displayed on spears next to the stalls. I couldn't smell down here, but I gagged anyway, knowing exactly what the vulgar odor would be like.

A group of kids ran past, playing a game of tag. I watched them swipe a handful of fresh red sea berries from an older vendor's stall when she wasn't looking. Her gaze turned in my direction only seconds after the children had vanished into the crowd, and her aged expression glared at me—like she knew she'd been robbed, and she was just looking for somebody to place the blame on.

I turned my gaze away and kept walking quickly.

We passed the food stalls and found ourselves surrounded by merchants of wares and luxuries. One stall was cloaked in cloths and silks of every kind. Another proudly displayed silverware and jade bowls. A third was selling polished wooden storage boxes, marble statues, and handwoven seaweed baskets. Then a jewelry stand caught my eye, glittering with diamond earrings and shimmery pearl necklaces. I reached up to feel my own pearl necklace, wanting to reassure myself that it was still there.

"Oh my," Lysander breathed all of a sudden, coming to a stop in his tracks, and I followed his gaze. He was eyeing a stall where the most *beautiful* cloaks were being sold. The details were so fine, so intricate, with shimmering threads weaving all sorts of patterns and swirls and shapes into the materials.

"I would imagine a cloak would suit you so perfectly," Lysander said wistfully, staring at a particular one in a shade of deep red coral. He turned back to look over me, as if considering it, then shook his head. "Alas, a siren would never hide their beauty under a cloak. Which is a shame, as these roads get quite cold."

He looked genuinely disappointed, like he would have bought me the entire stall's worth of cloaks had I asked.

I pursed my lips, not sure what to say in response. It was flattering... but ridiculous, all the same. No one had ever

177

fussed over me in such a way—not even my sister, who was an excellent gift giver.

"Come on," I said, urging him to keep moving as the crowd bustled around us, and we kept walking.

The markets were huge and so packed that it took us even longer to navigate through than the first half of the city, but once we were through, the rest of the journey through the city was much faster. The crowds thinned as we ventured further and further to the city gates. My gaze was focused overhead, at the schools of stunning fish that kept gliding past—some small and some big and all in an array of rainbow colors.

"Your kingdom is beautiful," I admitted to Lysander finally. He beamed back at me.

"I'm glad you like it. My mother did too."

I stole a glance at him, but there was nothing in his eyes. No sadness, no happiness, no lingering emotions of any kind. Every time I thought of my mother, I couldn't help but wonder what things might have been like for Kendra and I growing up, how different it would have been to have a mother to read us bedtime stories, to confide in about our problems, to cook us homemade meals...

I couldn't help but feel longing when I thought of her. But with Lysander, there was just nothing. I couldn't imagine living so coldly and detached.

When we finally reached the city gates, two hours had passed, and my legs were aching from walking for so long. The guards said nothing as they oversaw us leaving, and Lysander led me down a narrow bedrock path until he came to a stop near a small cave on the city outskirts.

I spotted Commander Leif near the cave entrance, tending to a group of giant yellow seahorses. My eyes nearly bulged out of my head as I stared at them.

I'd never seen seahorses—and I'd *certainly* never seen any larger than me.

Bright orange eyes bore into mine, and the lines of their skin seemed to go white at the edges. It took me a moment to recover as my heart slowed its beating.

"So... which way is Atlantis?" I asked Lysander, as I eyed the creatures warily. I spared a quick glance at my surroundings, but I couldn't see anything but dark waters ahead and sprawling ginormous seamounts.

"It's that way," Lysander said, pointing aimlessly to his right. "But we aren't traveling the remaining distance on foot there. It's not princely to travel by foot."

I rolled my eyes. *Of course.*

Lysander mounted himself swiftly on the back of the nearest seahorse—like he'd been doing it his entire life—and then glanced at me and waited for me to do the same.

I tentatively approached one of the other seahorses, wondering if it would allow me to just climb onto it. I'd never ridden a horse in my life, and certainly not a seahorse, so I didn't have any idea how to mount it. Lysander watched me but made no effort to help. Perhaps it hadn't occurred to him.

"May I assist you?" Commander Leif asked, coming around to stand beside me. He angled his hands as if offering to boost me.

I nodded and turned back to the seahorse. It was as peaceful as ever, even seeming to nuzzle me gently as I reached up to grab hold of its neck for balance. The commander's strong hands found my waist and hoisted me. With his help, I swung myself onto the seahorse's back, finding a comfortable groove in its bony exoskeleton to sit.

I smiled down at him, "Thank you."

He offered a small smile back, then quickly rounded the seahorses to mount the final one.

I turned to Lysander, but he looked away quickly and murmured something to his seahorse so low I couldn't hear him. He seemed tense, and I frowned, wondering if we'd upset him somehow. But then, all three creatures lunged forward, causing me to grip tightly to mine in sheer panic. Their tails sprung up and down, propelling us through the dark seawater.

Lysander stole a single look back at me, and upon seeing my awestruck face, all the tension in him melted. He beamed at me once more.

I felt a strange tingle run through me and looked away, simmering quietly.

The farther away from the starry, cavern-lit kingdom we traveled, the less I was able to see with my human eyes. Though I could *somewhat* see in the otherwise pitch-black waters, which I think my enchanted pearl necklace had something to do with. Still, I prayed the seahorses didn't lose each other—I would hate to find myself all alone in the dark sea without Lysander or the commander.

We rode on for hours and hours. My arms grew stiff from holding onto my seahorse, so tight so as not to be left behind in the current by its quick, frantic movements.

"There will be soldiers up ahead, in the valley," Commander Leif told us, as we approached a dark, looming shape up ahead in the murky waters. It wasn't until we grew nearer that it revealed itself to be a wide seamount, the ranges tall and rounded at the top. And dead center, there was a narrow dip—the valley—leading through dark waters.

As we traveled closer and closer, I felt the waters grow more treacherous, tugging at my clothes and hair. I was grateful that Rue had thought to put my hair in a braid—it would certainly be a mess by the time we reached Atlantis.

"Be careful up here," the commander warned, and our seahorses slowed their pace.

Slivers of light trickled from glow-crystals growing on the peaks above, but this resulted in the valley being coated mostly in shadows of darkness. Dull, thick seagrass sprawled on both sides of the worn path—and it was long enough that anything could be hiding in it. Rocks twisted from the peaks, creating all sorts of crevices and caves where looming shadows swam.

I held my breath as we traveled deeper and deeper through the valley, my heart thudding in my chest. The waters were especially murky here, making it hard to see even just a few feet ahead. Specks of dust floated in the water around us.

Above our heads, large creatures swam—too cloaked in shadow for me to make out what they were. We were definitely not alone here in this eerie dark passage. But nothing attacked us. Nothing dared to loom close enough to pose a threat.

"Something's not right," the commander murmured finally, barely loud enough for us to hear. "There should be Coronis soldiers here—my men reported as much."

"The scouts?" Lysander asked quietly, and the commander nodded. His hand was inching back toward his spear, which was sheathed on his back. I felt like I couldn't breathe.

The murky waters cleared for a moment as we crossed what appeared to be a deep, narrow chasm below us. The crack traveled a long way ahead of us, through the length of the valley. Looking down, I saw a deep dark space that looked less than inviting.

Lysander murmured again to the seahorses, who began a slow and steady pace around the edge of the chasm, taking the long way around, closer to the rocky mountainside. As I stared deeper into the chasm, I noticed the stronger currents pulling past me—as if the chasm was sucking down everything that came too close.

I wanted to get away from this place. Something about it was making my chest ache. In fact, I'd never felt my chest ache quite like this before. It was a strange, tingling sensation, one that filled me with urgent dread.

We were silent for a few more minutes as we crept around it until Lysander turned his gaze back to me. His expression stiffened at the sight of me.

"Coral," he hissed, and I frowned—blood turning to ice.

"What?" I breathed back, overcome with terror as all the hairs went up on the back of my neck at once. Was something behind me?

"Your *heart!*"

I looked down and saw that my chest was faintly glowing—the same way Mom's necklace had done before it had encased Kendra with crystal.

What the—

I stared at it in horror, but I was wearing only a dress. The glow grew brighter and was shining right through it—I had nothing to cover it up with.

"What's going on?" I asked frantically, feeling my heart pounding in my chest. It only seemed to make the glow worse.

"Your heart magic is stirring," Lysander replied quickly. "It means there's danger around—you're going into defensive mode."

"I don't even know what that means!" I cried, not even trying to keep my voice down now.

"We'll never pass through Coronis like this," the commander hissed from the other side of me. "She's like a beacon—a dead giveaway!"

"We need to turn back," Lysander said firmly, pulling on his seahorse to steer it around. "We'll find a place to camp and regroup."

"We can't turn back!" I insisted. "We can't afford to waste any more time!"

I was about to protest more, but it wouldn't have mattered anyway—at that moment, four creatures sprung up from within the chasm lightning fast. They hissed, baring their razor-sharp teeth, and I screamed.

My seahorse bucked, throwing me from it, and I sailed to the ground as the creatures lunged at us.

Lysander jumped from his seahorse, drawing a spear I hadn't even known he had tucked away under his coat. The first siren came at him with claws for nails and scales running from the length of her neck to her arms and ankles—which was all that was visible beyond the floaty tendrils of dress she wore.

I kicked up from the ground as a second siren—a male—tried to grab me. This wasn't like land though—I was a human in the deep depths of the sea. The water slowed me down. I couldn't move fluidly the way Lysander and the sirens could.

I kicked desperately, trying to swim away from our attackers, but one grabbed my leg and yanked me back. I shrieked, clawing at the water desperately, but it was no use.

"Coral!" Commander Leif shouted, and he jumped from his seahorse, rushing toward me. But the third siren tackled him into the hard bedrock floor. The commander sprung to his feet, and suddenly, they were engaged in a deadly fight, his spear ringing and clashing against the siren's agile dagger.

I needed my heart magic power. I needed it *now*. But I had no idea how to unleash it!

The siren, still grasping me in his iron grip, pulled me fast toward the chasm. I clawed at the ground, but it was bedrock—completely solid with nothing to dig my fingers into. The siren yanked on my waist, ripping me backward as he shot down in the chasm with me.

I screamed as I was pulled into the murky depths.

"Coral!" Lysander bellowed from above, but I was falling so fast—the space around me growing darker and darker as we spiraled down, down, *down...*

I pleaded for my heart magic to awaken on its own somehow, but all it did was continue to glow uselessly in my chest.

My back suddenly slammed into something hard yet mushy, knocking the breath out of me. I gasped, straining to breathe for a moment.

The siren came to float over me and crooned softly into my ear, bubbles tickling my neck.

"Don't breathe."

Water rushed into my mouth and lungs, and panic seized me. I was so focused on choking that I didn't feel the slime spread until it was too late. It was all over my body, sealing me to whatever surface I'd been shoved against. The substance was green, like algae, but stronger.

I rasped desperately with panic, spluttering for air. My chest throbbed with pain.

"A mermaid," the siren growled at me, eyes devouring me hungrily. Then another siren emerged in the dark shadows next to him.

"But where's her tail?" the second one asked, leering at me. "The tails are good for skinning."

A scream of agony and dread caught in my throat, gargled against the water—I simply couldn't get it out as I watched the two sirens. They were only illuminated by my glowing chest.

"Eugene Pryor will want her heart," the first one said slowly. "But such a rare prize... and such things we could do with a treasured mer-heart."

He continued to contemplate, like he couldn't decide what to do with me. Either way, I was facing certain death. Black spots began to swim in my vision.

And then, someone came crashing down on the siren's head, and a spear plunged clean through his skull.

Like a snap in the air, the spell broke. Blood seeped out into the murky, dark waters, staining it. Air returned to my lungs, and water spluttered from my mouth. My scream finally unlatched where it had caught in my throat, echoing shrilly in the chasm.

Lysander swung angrily at the other siren, stabbing clean through its chest as its anguished screech turned to a choked whimper. Both bodies slumped in the water, blood trailing after them as they drifted down slowly to wherever the depths of this chasm led to.

Lysander was immediately at my side, tearing the algae from the rough surface beneath me to help me get free as I reeled in deep breaths, able to breathe again. I didn't realize I was shaking until now.

"Are you alright?" he demanded, eyes boring into mine. He held me by the shoulders and took in every inch of me, scanning for wounds.

"F-fine," I managed, but it came out barely audible. "Can we go back up?"

Without warning, he swept me into his arms so that my nose was flush with his chest—*way* too close for comfort— and kicked off the rock, shooting us back up and out of the chasm.

The seahorses had scrambled a distance away in the conflict but were now waiting for us to return. I didn't see the other sirens—maybe they'd been slaughtered too.

As soon as we were out, Lysander set me down. I spotted Commander Leif running over to us, sheathing his spear.

"That was too close—we must go back immediately. This venture was a mistake," Lysander babbled, his gaze fixated on me. I was shaking so violently that his gaze softened. "You are cold," he added softly, and immediately removed his maroon coat.

I could have laughed at his oblivious stupidity had I not been in such a state.

"She's in shock," Commander Leif countered, striding past him to kneel beside me. He looked over me for wounds, and I didn't miss the diligence of how he scanned every inch of my body.

I hugged my body in an attempt to still the shaking. I'd been through this before when Maya died—when I'd realized what she'd done and what I'd survived—I hadn't been able to stop shaking for hours.

But we didn't have hours. I needed to stop shaking *now*. I willed my body to relax and focused on taking deep breaths.

Lysander was studying me. I didn't know if he understood Leif's explanation. Eventually, he wrapped his coat gently around my shoulders anyway.

"Humans do not shake unless something is wrong," is all he said. "So I must see that you are tended to immediately."

Despite what had just happened and how welcoming the Vera Palace seemed in comparison to continuing this journey, I knew I was closer to answers now than I had been before.

The memory of my family in peril swept through my mind again, and it gave me enough strength to shake my head firmly.

"No," I said. "You need to take me the rest of the way to Atlantis."

He opened his mouth to protest, but I cut him off.

"I'm fine—look," I said, showing him my arm from under his jacket. It was shaking considerably less now. "It's wearing off. I'll be okay. We made it this far—I want to go the rest of the way."

"It's not safe," he replied darkly.

"You *promised* me answers," I reminded him, and he grimaced, looking torn.

And I promised you my heart, should I not find them.

I didn't say the last part.

After a moment, he let out an exasperated groan.

"I can't say no to you," he sighed, shaking his head at me. "Tricky human, you are. I should have known better."

But he summoned the seahorses over regardless and gestured for me to get back on.

"Leif, we'll camp tonight near the grove instead," he ordered, and the commander nodded. He stood by, eyeing me to see if I needed help mounting again. But this time it was easier, now that I knew the grooves of the seahorse and where to haul myself up.

I was grateful that Lysander had listened to me—that *had* to be progress.

We rode off once more, and it took me a moment to realize Lysander's jacket was still wrapped snugly around me—like a comforting, protective cloak.

CHAPTER SIXTEEN

Lysander

There was an intense, twisting feeling in my heart that I'd never felt before, like a dagger was continuously piercing through it.

We had stopped for the night, nestled in a grove situated only a couple of hours from Coronis. Long snaking lines of kelp grew all around us, hiding us from any passing travelers, and long jagged thermal cracks surrounded our campsite. They'd been long since established in the bedrock of the ocean floor and provided heat against the midnight chill of the deep seawater.

We'd tethered our seahorses nearby and then promptly dug into our rations—each of us completely famished from the long day's journey. The food now lay sprawled on the open flap of my satchel—there was salmon and cod, rainbow trout, sea berries, oysters, and clams. I'd had my fill of clams, but Coral and Leif were still devouring the food. It didn't matter if we ate it all—we could get more tomorrow in Coronis.

Coral avoided most of the selection, her nose wrinkling at the raw fish, but dug into the flavorsome sea berries. Leif, on the other hand, heartily ate the remaining food, his eyes nearly rolling back in his head as he savored the taste of each fish he popped into his mouth.

I sat hunched against a rugged rock, my eyes darting between the two of them. They'd been conversing with ease for hours as they ate. It seemed as if they had endless things to talk about, but I hadn't been paying close enough attention to recall specifics. My mind kept going to that dark place, the tormenting, twisting feelings continuing to prod at me.

Why was it so easy for Leif to talk to her, but when it came to me, it felt like pulling at teeth? Was I not good enough? Did I need to impress her more? What would she be impressed by? It seemed like my title, the life I could offer her, and the endless gifts I could buy her were not tempting enough. *Not good enough!*

I ground my teeth, watching the pair silently, and felt that strange feeling tear at me from the inside.

"Do sirens love fish as much as undines do?" Coral asked with a frown, as she watched Leif wriggle an oyster free and slurp it from its shell. Leif had the decency to look sheepish as he swallowed his oyster and wiped his mouth.

"They don't enjoy oysters as much," he admitted. "To be honest, the sirens are rather materialistic—and their eating habits are no different. Caviar and crustaceans are favored among the higher ranks because it's more a status symbol— but mer-hearts have always been a prized food."

Coral shuddered and looked away, and Leif returned her grim expression.

"It's barbaric, how they've hunted your kind. We may eat fish, but we'd never go as far as to kill your kind for food. Or for power, even."

"But mer-hearts are still valued," she pressed, with a pointed look. "They're used in tonics and potions. They can revert curses... even if you didn't kill mermaids, you could still weaponize and use them for their power, couldn't you?"

190

The unsaid statement lingered in her face.

Just like you want to harness and use me against Melody.

Leif shifted uncomfortably.

"Mermaids have incredible power, yes," he said carefully. "But I personally would never want to weaponize a mermaid to harness that power."

He returned a pointed look, and some kind of understanding passed between their faces.

"Speaking of power, though," Leif added quickly, as if eager to change the topic, "we should discuss how we'll get past Coronis with that heart magic of yours."

The glow... I'd never seen it before, but I'd known it could happen. I didn't expect Coral's heart magic to react when it was still dormant. But that could only mean one thing: that it was stirring. And if *that* happened...

I pushed the thought down and shifted closer to the pair of them, joining the conversation.

"You said to expect siren soldiers back in the valley," I said to Leif, who nodded in confirmation. "They were clearly hiding—waiting to ambush us—which means they must have been tipped off that we were coming, somehow. Even with our disguises, they must have known to look for three travelers."

Leif nodded again, agreeing.

"I don't know how they found out, but we definitely took care of them all. Nobody could have run back to spread word in Coronis, which means that if we can get into the city and *blend in*... we should be okay."

We'd been lucky. We couldn't risk anyone else knowing—*especially* not the likes of Eugene Pryor...

Leif glanced at Coral and added, "The problem is getting in before Coral's magic senses a hint of danger and tips them off."

"How exactly does it work?" Coral asked tentatively, and Leif looked to me for an explanation. I only knew so much—and for the first time in my life, I regretted not attending my daily lessons. "I couldn't even *feel* it," Coral added with a frown. "Well, unless you count that strange tingling I got in my chest beforehand. But I thought I was just scared..."

"No, that would have been it," I confirmed. "But because you're not in your mermaid form, you can't do anything with it, as far as I know. That might be why you barely felt it."

Coral nodded, processing my explanation.

"Plus, your heart magic didn't react straight away, which means it only reacts when it senses hostile enemies approaching. Had those sirens only been passing by, or had they stopped to question us, the situation might have played out differently."

The glow had been so bright—perhaps I should have bought her that exquisite cloak back in Veranis. I wondered if it would have done much to hide the illuminance.

Then again, a part of me was glad I hadn't. The way she was now, in that sleeveless traveling gown, I could see her bare shoulders and the curve of her neck. She looked radiant in it, and a part of me wanted to trace my fingers from her ear to her jawline.

"Well, she can't wear your coat into Coronis—it'll be a dead giveaway. No siren would ever cover their chest and shoulders like that," Leif said, his brow furrowed like he was thinking. "Perhaps the best way to avoid a reoccurrence is to convince Coral's heart magic that she's in no danger and can protect herself."

"She has us to protect her," I said, waving a hand between us, and Leif looked as if he wanted to roll his eyes.

"Yes, but she needs to feel that safety for *herself.* I think she should carry a weapon on her."

He examined his own bulky spear, which he'd placed next to him while we rested, and frowned,

"Mine is far too long—it wouldn't suit her at all. And the weight would be difficult to manage—especially if she's never carried a weapon before."

I unsheathed my own spear from where it sat hidden under my jacket. It was slightly narrower, and unlike Leif's heavy weapon, mine was designed to be lightweight and discreet.

"She can have mine," I decided, unbuckling my shoulder straps so that she could sheath it on her own bodice. She took the small spear from me carefully and let out a noise when she felt its heaviness in her hands. Leif was watching with approving eyes.

"What about you?" Coral asked, meeting my gaze. Was she concerned about me? Did she fear for my safety?

The twisted feelings from earlier faded a little.

"I have Leif," I replied, looking at him with a trusting gaze. He nodded firmly, and there was a seriousness in his eyes. Leif's job was to lead the military, but he also acted as my personal guard more often than not.

Plus, Leif and I both had other weapons on us—smaller blades we could use if needed. But Coral needed something substantial if we were going to pull this off.

While Coral busied herself fitting the straps and the spear I'd handed her, Leif said something about scouting the perimeter before bed and got to his feet. He disappeared into the thick kelp and was gone.

I took the opportunity to shift a little closer to Coral, and she glanced at me as I settled beside her. She didn't smile at me, but there was no sign of hatred or distrust in her eyes.

That was a good sign.

The sea flowed gently around us, kelp waving in its rhythm, and I watched the stalks drift back and forth for a while.

"Lysander," she said finally, her voice quieter than usual. "Thank you for saving me earlier today."

I remembered the way she'd been gasping for air, her eyes bulging as those despicable sirens were torturing her, the way I'd slaughtered them, the metallic stench of the blood seeping into the waters... and a hint of satisfaction came over me.

"Why wouldn't I have?" I replied earnestly, and she met my gaze.

"I don't know... I guess I just didn't know what to expect from you. You say you only feel glimpses of humanity around me, and it's evident you don't fully grasp a lot of social cues and emotions as a result of that. So when I was taken... I didn't know if you'd care enough to come after me. To put your own life at risk for me."

A faint understanding came over me. She hadn't trusted me before... and I realized that my actions must have mended a gap between us.

"Like I said, when it comes to you..." I trailed off, trying to find the right words. "It's like my heart makes decisions for me. It's like... even though I don't fully understand what I'm feeling or why certain desires come over me... I know to act on them. I know it's *right.*"

She nodded slowly, taking in my words.

"Would you have done it for Leif?" she asked, and I had to think on that for a moment.

"Yes," I decided finally. "Because he's one of the only people I know I care for—even though it's difficult to acknowledge and feel. I would do it for my father too... because he's my father. But for anyone else..."

I paused, playing out the scenario in my head again, and finally, I shook my head.

"Honestly, for anyone else, I would have let them die. And I wouldn't feel bad about it because I just don't care. I suppose... that's what you'd consider a selfish act, right?"

Coral avoided my gaze.

"I think it depends on the situation," she said finally, and her answer made my heart skip a beat. *Interesting...*

Before I could press further, she stifled a yawn, then blinked a few times. I pushed my curiosity to the back of my mind.

"You should sleep," I said finally. "Leif and I will take turns keeping watch."

She nodded without any protest and found a place to curl up on the ground. There were no soft places to sleep here, but she seemed far too tired to care about that. As she nestled near a large boulder, I had the urge to run my fingers through her hair. Something told me not to act on it, so I didn't move.

Before long, her breathing slowed and steadied, and she didn't even stir when Leif's heavy footsteps signaled his return. He emerged from the surrounding kelp moments later, noting Coral's sleeping figure, then quietly sank back into a sitting position near her.

"We're safe," he told me in a low voice. "I'll do another check in a few hours before we switch shifts."

That was my cue to find my own patch of bedrock to sleep on, but instead, I stayed sitting with him. A current rippled the waters around us—the water lukewarm from the nearby thermal cracks.

Leif eyed Coral wearily, then glanced back at me.

"Before we left," he said finally, his voice barely a murmur, "Deandra reported that Coral was investigating the sea witch in the library."

My blood froze over.

"What did she tell her?" I demanded quietly.

"Coral apparently found a book. But Deandra only told her facts that any of our kind would know. Not about... the *other* thing."

My heart was pounding. I thought I'd gotten rid of all the books—how had I missed one? Unless the sea witch had planted it there herself...

"The thing is," Leif continued quietly, "my men also reported back to me. They uncovered a spell that could undo everything... but it requires a visit to the Sea of Souls."

I let out a low huff.

"Nobody who ventures there ever comes back," I replied lowly, my gut turning, and he nodded in agreement. After a moment of consideration, I shook my head.

196

"Then keep looking. There has to be another way," I said, my gaze landing on Coral once more. Once again, the proximity between Leif and Coral gnawed at me. I hated how close to her he was—wished he would move to the other side of the grove to sleep.

Coral slept peacefully, completely unaware of our conversation. I couldn't lose her again... and yet, it felt like there were endless threats trying to take her from me.

I'd never expected to feel threatened by Leif, and I didn't understand it. Why would Coral want to spend time with Leif when she could have me? And why would I support their friendship if it threatened the potential of Coral bonding with me?

I pondered it and pondered everything Leif had told me, even after I'd laid down to sleep. The thoughts kept me awake for hours as I tried to see things a different way—and failed. That strange, uncertain feeling lingered—and no matter how hard I tried, I couldn't shake it.

CHAPTER SEVENTEEN

Coral

I awoke to being nuzzled and sniffed. Slowly, I opened my eyes and saw a small grey creature bumping along my arm.

I startled, jumping up, and shrieked, every hair on my body rising as my heart pounded.

A shark!

Commander Leif was alert in an instant, springing up from where he lay on the bedrock and grabbing his spear. Lysander emerged from the surrounding kelp mere seconds later, eyes wide with panic. But when they saw the shark, their shoulders relaxed.

Mine didn't, and I sat rigid as the shark bumped its nose against my arm playfully. Patterned markings ran down the length of its back. I didn't dare breathe, and my hands grew clammy. Finally, I couldn't take it, and I scrambled backward, away from the creature.

Lysander began to laugh, the sound resounding throughout his entire frame. The commander had the decency not to, but I could see how his lips were curving upward.

"It's just a baby tiger shark," Lysander reassured me finally, crossing to my side and placing a steady hand on my upper arm. "It won't hurt you."

The shark swam toward me, tail fin wagging back and forth, its mouth slightly parted to show its razor-sharp teeth. I reached upward to grip Lysander's arm.

"Do something!" I pleaded, wide eyed.

To my horror, he reached forward and patted the shark. The shark seemed to like it—nuzzling against Lysander's hand.

"You're scaring Coral," he told it. "Please be more considerate. She's not used to sharks."

The shark looked at me, and I could have sworn its beady eyes seemed apologetic.

Lysander gave it one last stroke before adding, "Off you go. This is our hiding place, and you'll reveal us if you stick around."

The shark scampered off, and I watched it go just to make sure. My heart was still pounding.

"You can talk to sharks," I said finally, my voice dull.

"To all sea creatures," he corrected with a wink. "Perks of being an undine prince."

"Did you not realize this with the seahorses?" the commander added, an eyebrow raised. I frowned, shaking my head, and he let out a single laugh. "The undine royals have always been able to speak to marine life. In fact, undines invented seahorse riding—we taught the other kingdoms how to tame the animals."

Lysander gave me a pointed look and added, "You were never in any danger. Your heart would have started glowing if you were."

"That is also true," the commander added, getting to his feet and sheathing his spear onto his back. I folded my arms. Heart glow or not—I didn't want sharks sniffing me when I was *sleeping!*

A short while later, we set off down the path leading toward Coronis. My back was aching from having slept on the hard ground, and that made riding my seahorse even more uncomfortable. The capital city quickly came into view, and the seahorses kept a brisk pace as they traveled toward it.

A towering ironclad gate waited for us ahead, and we needed to pass through it. There was no way around Coronis—it was surrounded by too many seamounts, each one more jagged and unforgiving than the last. Lysander had told me we'd exhaust our seahorses trying to scale them and lose too many days taking a longer route to Atlantis. With only twenty-one days left until the wedding, it was a risk we couldn't take.

Commander Leif did a once-over on me from his seahorse—checking my attire, the spear sheathed at my side, and gave an approving nod.

"Remember—they have no reason to attack us if we appear calm and confident. We all look the part, and we're only going to be passing through."

The capital city—if you could call it that with its fortress resembling walls—was surrounded by dark, dreary waters. Shadows bathed the kingdom from the surrounding seamounts, and there was a heaviness weighing down around us—a feeling of death and suffering.

"Coral, just a warning," the commander murmured, guiding his seahorse closer to me. "You might not like what you see in Coronis. The mermaids..."

He trailed off, and I understood what he was hinting at. They were hunted. *Enslaved.*

"Got it," I replied stiffly, swallowing hard. *I could do this.*

The gates of the capital were heavily guarded with soldiers. Commander Leif and Lysander both projected confidence as we came to stop in front of them, but I could see the stiffness of their shoulders. We were ordered to dismount our seahorses, and I felt even more vulnerable as my feet hit the ground—the speed of my seahorse lost should they attack.

A tall muscular soldier stepped forward to greet us and raised an eyebrow as he surveyed us.

"Been traveling, have you?" he asked finally. Lysander stepped forward, his voice honey smooth as he flashed a dazzling smile.

"My enchanting wife insisted that we venture to Veranis to find the most *exotic* of wedding gifts for Queen Melody," he drawled lazily. I didn't let any surprise show on my face, aiming for an expression of disinterest instead. "We'll be venturing to the surface in the coming days to witness the union."

The soldier looked to Commander Leif.

"And you?" he asked.

"His brother," the commander added, and regarded the soldier with a cool expression. The soldier then looked at me, and I held my breath. He stepped forward once, and I noticed Lysander twitch slightly.

I met the soldier's eyes, feigning confidence and channeling the energy I'd seen Melody strut with for months on end.

How dare you question me, I thought, narrowing my gaze. *How dare you assume I cannot rip you to shreds should you displease me.*

Eventually, the soldier stepped aside and waved us through. I had to stifle a gasp at the sight of the city as we breezed past him, guiding our seahorses in tow. It was *much* more beautiful behind the fortress-resembling walls—rows and rows of stunning golden homes lined with ruby gables glittered before us, and blood-red coral gardens bloomed alongside polished quartzite paths and roads.

Only once we'd well and truly entered the city did we let out a collective sigh of relief.

"Wife?" I drawled finally, and Lysander turned to face me with a serious look.

"The females have more power than males here," he informed me, his voice low. "Marriage is considered a way to lay claim on a male—it only made sense that you, as a siren, would have us do your bidding."

Right...

"And Melody... is a *queen* here?" I added, looking around. It was so dazzling to look at, I could have needed sunglasses. Each home was sprawling and huge, spanning multiple stories, and the corners of each home were lined in glowing crystal— similar to the ones in the Vera Palace. Except these ones were a golden shade.

"The Pryor clan were the most powerful warriors in Coronis for decades—and they were highly respected," Commander Leif explained lowly, as we walked through the spacious streets. "When Melody challenged Queen Chora for her throne, she won purely because raised here status enough that she was considered more powerful than any other siren. Only the most powerful sirens can control other sirens... and are seen fit to *rule* them."

I grimaced. Melody might be considered a queen here, but I'd never acknowledge her as one.

Leif and Lysander steered me off the main path, down alleyways and narrower streets, to keep us from crossing more soldiers than necessary. The soldiers here were dressed in blood-red uniforms, and each one was stunningly handsome. I didn't see a single female soldier, and based on what Lysander told me, I suspected it was a unanimous feminine decision. Why do the dirty work when your males could work for you?

As we trudged deeper down the alleyways, I caught my first sight of a mermaid. I nearly froze in my tracks, stomach twisting at the sight.

The mermaid was shackled and collared by a beautiful siren who was leading it through the streets—as if it were a dog. The mermaid wore scraps that barely covered her chest, and she was covered in dirt and filth. Her hair was matted, her vibrant green tail covered in bloodied cuts and bruises. I wondered if she'd been whipped from those markings...

The siren, in comparison, wore her midnight-black hair piled atop her head, with a revealing glittering-red gown and skirts that shimmered transparently. There was no question who had the power here—especially as the siren tugged harshly on the chain and bared her teeth at her slave.

"Coral," the commander murmured, and with a gentle nudge, prompted me to keep walking before I drew attention to myself. We passed the mermaid, who didn't acknowledge us, and kept walking. Anger simmered in my veins, and I felt sick. I couldn't stop clenching my hands as I forced myself to keep my gaze ahead, to not look back.

How many mermaids were living like this, ruled by sirens? How many more had been slaughtered or used for their hearts?

We rounded a bend, and only then did I get a good look at the Cora Palace in the far distance—which sat centered in the capital city atop a seamount. The gardens around the palace were red coral, entirely covering the seamount and making it look as if the palace sat upon blood. The palace was tall, grand, and jagged—with hundreds of steps leading up to its arched entryway and massive towers topped with deadly-sharp golden spires. It glittered like a red jewel bedazzled in golden embellishments. Humongous whales and sharks circled the mammoth palace—and I got the sense that they were guarding it.

No commoner would ever get close to it—that much I knew. But thankfully, we weren't heading there, and we continued walking.

We reached a marketplace not long afterward, and this one was even larger than the one in Veranis. As we passed the food sector, the commander frowned with distaste at the lack of fresh fish displayed at each stall.

"Is this all they have?" he muttered. I wondered if he was regretting eating so much last night.

Lysander scoped out the varieties on offer, then turned to the commander.

"My father did mention that trade's been down in recent years, as a result of Atlantis being... well, abandoned."

"Surely they have their own farmers," the commander muttered, stalking the rows of market stalls.

"I would assume so—and I would guess that the freshest produce goes straight to the wealthiest sirens," Lysander replied, hands in his pockets as he strode after him. I walked briskly to keep up with them both. "Leaving whatever scraps

204

are left here for the commoners. Besides, Atlantis was closest to the surface, so it was the entire Undersea's biggest source of trade. Anything the sirens harvest now would be farmed and directly delivered by their personal slaves."

The commander grumbled something about the lack of food, then stalked off to another section to sulk. Lysander turned back to me and offered me a small smile.

"Shall we keep moving?" I said, not wanting to linger in this place longer than we had to.

"Of course. However... I did have a thought," Lysander replied quickly, and eyed the spear at my side. "As much as it pleases me to see you with my spear, perhaps a dagger would suit you better. And Coronis is known for its daggers—it's the weapon of choice among their kind."

I had to admit, the spear felt rather heavy at my side. And I wasn't used to feeling it brush against my thigh. A dagger would be easier to conceal and easier to handle.

"Fine," I agreed, and Lysander's eyes shone at my words.

"Excellent. Come along then," he said, and waved Leif back over to explain our plan. He nodded.

"I'll restock our supplies, then come find you," he replied, and we parted ways. Lysander led me in the opposite direction, through the thick crowd.

As we walked, a strange comfortableness fell over us. Despite his flaws, I felt safe with Lysander. I trusted that no harm would come to me with him around. He'd proven as much yesterday—

I cringed, remembering the blood, and shook those thoughts from my mind.

"Coral, may I ask you something?" Lysander mused, as we walked.

"Sure," I replied, weaving with him through the crowd. There were so many sirens here, and each one dressed more eloquently than the last.

"You told me you like to surf... but when we met, back on land, you said you didn't compete anymore. That it was complicated."

I inhaled deeply, knowing where this was headed. Was I even ready for this conversation? But as I met Lysander's gaze, his eyebrow was quirked innocently. And something about that made me give in.

"I don't surf anymore because I got in an accident last year," I admitted. "A wave took me under, and a current held me there. I fell unconscious in the water. My best friend Maya... she was competing with me, and..."

A lump formed in my throat, but I was used to it. I forced it down and kept talking.

"She went under to save me. She shouldn't have, but I guess she thought she could reach me. The current took her instead, and she died. We never recovered her body."

Lysander's eyes grew wide, and he'd stopped in his tracks. I stared at him, wondering if that was pity he was grappling with. Or perhaps... sympathy? It was impossible to tell... and I didn't want to ask.

"So you don't surf anymore... because you're afraid?" he asked finally.

It was silly, but his question filled me with relief. Most people apologized, tried to find the right words... but there were no right words. At least with Lysander, he didn't know to apologize. In a strange sense, he was a breath of fresh air.

"I don't surf anymore because how could I?" I replied carefully. "She's dead, and I'm not. She doesn't get to surf anymore because she *died* saving me during a surfing competition. It seems... wrong."

Lysander was struggling to understand—that much was evident from the way his brow furrowed. I sighed and shook my head.

"Never mind," I said, turning away from him, but he grabbed my wrist to stop me. I glanced back.

"What if she wants you to surf?" he asked.

I couldn't accept that thought. I couldn't even face it, couldn't acknowledge it.

"Why did *you* surf that day?" I asked quickly, changing the subject. His eyes sparkled suddenly, and a lazy smile appeared on Lysander's face as he replied.

"Because I'd never done it."

I frowned and shook my head.

"But... you were so *good* at it..." I trailed off. He had been as good as a professional.

"I know the sea," he explained. "I feel every motion, every current, every tide. It was easy to surf because I could predict every movement."

"I see," I said, nodding at him.

We continued walking again, but he surprised me as he added, "The other reason is that I wanted to feel the freedom of it."

I glanced at him once more and noted his withdrawn eyes.

"I've always wanted... something different than the life I have. My father expects me to rule, but I'd rather see the world. Most days, I dream about what it's like to be normal, to be uncursed, to live leisurely. I *crave* normality, and the surfing... it seemed like a fun, normal thing that you humans do."

I was a little stunned. I'd known Lysander was a complex creature as a result of his curse, but I never expected to find a complex being *beneath* that curse. It was like peeling back the layers of an onion—and suddenly, I was uncovering all kinds of depth to him.

"Plus, if I can be honest... I enjoyed showing off to you," he said finally, and there was a hint of amusement in his eyes.

A smile grew on my lips, and my heart sped up slightly at the sight.

I liked this side of him. I wished he could show these parts of himself all the time.

"Be honest with me always, Lysander," I said, offering him my arm. "It's your best quality."

And it truly was—because for a being who was lost in endless glimpses of humanity, forever chasing those feelings... his honesty made it easier to understand the *real* him.

His eyes softened, and a real, genuine smile appeared then.

"As you wish," he promised, his voice low and his eyes full of that sparkle that made my heart skip a beat. "Now then, let us find you a dagger worthy of your *endless* beauty."

CHAPTER EIGHTEEN

Coral

It didn't take us long to find a stall selling daggers—or for me to spot a dazzling blade that called to me from where it lay displayed, front and center of all the other blades, on the massive stall.

The handle was entirely mother-of-pearl, and the blade was sharp and silver. It sang with promise, the blade gleaming with a razor-sharp edge.

"You like this one?" Lysander asked, coming to stand beside me. His warmth radiated on my shoulder, and I felt comforted by his presence.

Abandoning my manners, I threw him a lazy smile and channeled my best Melody-inspired siren order, "*Darling husband* of mine, I simply adore this one. You must get it for me."

It was all for show, of course—but his eyes flicked with something like desire at my words.

"Anything you wish," he responded, and pulled out a heavy bag of coins. The merchant and him haggled for a bit—she didn't seem to suspect a thing as she handed the blade to Lysander, who then offered it to me.

I held it in the light, examining the glint, the detailed handiwork, and the cool, smoothness of the mother-of-pearl handle.

Much like how Veranis was lit by the bioluminescence, Coronis was lit by the glow-crystals radiating from every nearby building.

"I love it," I breathed normally, once we were out of earshot, and I meant every word.

We walked away from the stall, and Lysander scanned the crowd.

"We've lost Leif," he noted, as if only just realizing. He said he would be restocking our supplies, but surely it wouldn't have taken this long...

"Why don't we go back and check near the food sector?" I suggested, and Lysander agreed. As we waded through the crowd, I unbuckled Lysander's shoulder straps and spear, handing both back to him. Then, I tucked my dagger into my boot where it would be safe. It wasn't as comfortable as I'd assumed it to be, after seeing people hide weapons in their shoes in movies. But I decided I'd deal with the pressing wedge against my heel.

We weaved back through the crowd, and I could have sworn I noticed more soldiers appearing in each street we passed. Their shiny silver uniforms glinted in the rare rays of sunlight that beamed through the shadowy waters.

Lysander noticed it too. He subtly stepped closer to me, weaving his hand into mine. I let him, sensing that something was wrong, and prayed my heart wouldn't start glowing. I didn't feel a tingle... *yet.*

"Where's the commander?" I hissed, and Lysander shook his head ever so slightly as we made eye contact.

"We need to run," he murmured. "When I say so—got it?"

The hairs rose on the back of my neck, and I nodded back ever so slightly, my eyes flicking to the soldiers who strode through the streets. They were scanning the crowd, but it didn't seem like they'd spotted us yet. It would only be a matter of moments though.

"Did we do something wrong?" I asked quietly. How had they figured us out?

"I don't know," Lysander replied, guiding me toward a narrow side street. I glanced to my right nervously, and a soldier locked eyes with me. Then his gaze skittered to Lysander, and his eyes narrowed.

I squeezed his hand in warning, and Lysander growled, *"Now!"*

We took off running down the alley, Lysander shoving hard against the crowd to part the way for us. He drew his spear immediately, and I found myself wishing I hadn't stuck my dagger in my boot. Grabbing it now would only slow us down.

The soldiers shouted behind us, and I noticed how melodic their voices were. A strange lull came over me, tugging at every part of me, making me want to turn back. My chest began to ache in that familiar tingling way.

I faltered.

"Coral," Lysander hissed insistently, through gritted teeth—and I realized he was fighting it too.

I forced myself to keep running, but it felt like I was wading through sludge with every step I took.

We were done for. They would make us give up our weapons in an instant. I'd felt the power of Melody alone, and it

211

had been overwhelming. This was a few dozen soldiers *at least.*

Lysander was faring better than me. He took a sharp right, nearly ripping my arm out of its socket as he dragged me along with him. We raced down another street, and he took a sharp left. The more distance we put between the soldiers, the more my head cleared—and the easier running became. My calves burned, but it felt good to be running. It was nothing I couldn't endure with my sporty background.

Then suddenly, another hand grabbed my free arm and tugged me left. Lysander felt my hand tug on his, and he whirled. A hand covered my mouth.

Eyes wide, I made to shove backward with my elbow, but relief flooded Lysander's eyes when he realized who had grabbed me, which made me stop. I turned and found myself chest-to-chest with Commander Leif, whose own eyes were fierce and determined.

"I overheard soldiers in the market talking," he explained lowly to us, as we stepped further into his shadowed hiding place, pressed against the buildings around us. The commander was still holding me steady, the three of us crammed in the tiny space. "They have one of our men—they used a siren spell on him. That's how we were discovered before."

"They've made him into a spy," Lysander realized, his voice seething. "Who is it? Do you know?"

Commander Leif shook his head, finally letting me go, but he added, "All I know is that the male slaughtered our unit that was stationed nearby. Nobody could report back to let us know, and that's why we never encountered them on our way here."

"So they know to look for us," Lysander nodded. "They know how we've glamoured ourselves. We'll never get out of here—there are too many of them."

"Well... there is one way," the commander suggested, and a shadow crossed Lysander's face.

"No," he growled darkly, and the commander's gaze became pointed.

"We don't have another choice. The alternative is that we all die here. Or worse—you lose Coral to the sirens, who will undoubtedly deliver her to Melody so that she can carve out her heart."

I swallowed hard, wondering what they were talking about.

Lysander gritted his teeth, looking pained.

"I *can't*—"

"You must," the commander said shortly. *Firmly.*

Another moment passed. It seemed to drag on for too long, and we heard voices approaching. Heavy footsteps. My heartbeat began to quicken, and I felt the magic stirring before the glow began again. Lysander's eyes widened with panic, and the commander's expression was pleading as he waited for Lysander to reconsider. Lysander scrunched his eyes shut.

"Fine," he hissed finally, and pulled a large conch shell from his jacket. He brought it to his lips like a horn and blew. I heard nothing, but Commander Leif winced.

Lysander shoved it back into his jacket just as the soldiers rounded the corner and spotted us hiding in the shadows.

"Halt," the closest one ordered—his voice sweet and strong, and a dizziness came over me. I felt sluggish and detached from my body. "Drop your weapons," he said to Commander Leif and Lysander, and I heard their blades clatter to the ground a moment later.

My heart was fully glowing now, and their eyes locked onto it with predatory intent. My stomach turned.

"You will come with us," they said, and my legs moved on their own. I couldn't even look back to Lysander and the commander to see if they followed. The sirens led me back out through the maze of alleyways and backstreets until we emerged in one of the main streets. There were sirens everywhere now, but they cleared at the sight of the soldiers marching us through—and they watched with hungry eyes.

I truly didn't know what would become of us... what would become of *me*.

We made it almost halfway down the long, wide street when a shadow loomed over us and darkened the entire city—possibly more than it already was. The soldiers looked up, and I felt the compulsion weaken ever so slightly.

I looked up then—and saw a giant manta ray gliding over the city. My eyes widened at the sight of it—its pale underbelly, its long, wide mouth, and its massive fins.

It darted low and hurtled straight for us.

The soldiers lunged out of the way just as it crushed the sector to our left side. Screams echoed, and a thundering sounded from the impact. The entire ground shook, and someone grabbed me by the waist to pull me aside. It was Commander Leif, who shoved me behind him. He and Lysander stood together, watching the manta ray with wariness.

It sailed upward again, then aimed toward us. But instead of flattening us, it aimed to our right side, taking out half a dozen soldiers as it landed on the ground. It flattened itself, as if it were a mat laid out just for us, and Lysander raced onto its back.

"Coral." He offered me a hand to pull me up, and I gaped with confusion. Commander Leif shoved me, urging me to climb its back, so I did. It was strong but fleshy as I stumbled toward Lysander. He pulled me into a sitting position, and the commander came to sit behind us.

"Let's go," Lysander ordered, and the manta ray lifted with the massive sweep of its fins. I desperately yearned to hold onto something, but there was nothing. However, Lysander appeared to balance himself with ease, and I remembered him saying that he could feel every push and pull of the current. He noticed my panic and offered his arm for balance.

I accepted without second thought as we tore through the waters and sailed away from Coronis.

CHAPTER NINETEEN

Coral

We traveled in silence for an hour through silent, rippling waters.

My heart had taken so long to stop thundering, the glow disappearing slowly as the minutes ticked by. Lysander was very still as I clutched his arm.

Commander Leif was the first to break the silence by clearing his throat, and said, "I got more supplies earlier. It's not much... but it's enough to get us through another night should we need it."

A few more minutes went by silently and then I spoke, "Why didn't we travel this way from the start?"

I felt Lysander's muscles tense beneath my fingertips.

"Manta rays don't usually travel this way—it would have attracted too much attention," he replied quickly. I couldn't help but think that there was another reason from the way he avoided my gaze and the way he'd reacted back in the alleyway.

"Also..." the commander added carefully, and Lysander threw back a glare at him. The commander decided to ignore it as he said, "Lysander called upon a great power to summon the manta ray. He'll owe a debt now—one that needs to be paid back later."

"The conch shell?" I asked. "That was a summoning tool?"

Lysander nodded, shifting in his seat. He still wouldn't look at me.

"I suppose one benefit is that our journey will be faster now," Commander Leif said, and when I looked back again, his eyes were trained on Lysander's back. "Instead of taking two more days, we will reach Atlantis in a matter of hours."

"But we will also be followed," Lysander replied stiffly, as he stared ahead.

"Undoubtedly," the commander agreed. "Which is why we must make haste and seek refuge quickly within the Alta Palace."

"*If* they let us in," Lysander replied, and Commander Leif's expression softened.

"They would be fools not to," he said, and his eyes fell upon me briefly.

The alliance... the plan... It had seemed so brilliant and simple days ago. But now that we were so close to Atlantis, I was wondering if it had been too risky, too bold. What if Lysander was right? What if they *didn't* let us in? Lysander and Leif had been forced to leave their weapons back in Coronis too. I was the only one still armed—and I had *no* idea how to use my dagger.

I tried not to think about that as we continued to travel in silence once more. We stayed like that for a couple more hours before the commander suggested trading places with Lysander, and they did. I was far too scared to move, so I went from gripping Lysander's arm to gripping Commander Leif's, and Lysander took the opportunity to relax behind us while Leif took control of the manta ray.

217

"Wow, that's a tight grip you have there," the commander joked, glancing at where my fingers were clutching his upper arm.

"Sorry. It's just that... every move of the water makes me feel like I'm going to fall off," I replied, avoiding his gaze.

"It's fine," he replied, his tone breezy, and when I finally mustered the courage to meet his gaze, he smiled at me. "Oh, while I remember..."

He stuck his free hand into his coat pocket and pulled out a small cotton bag, offering it to me. I frowned as I took it.

"What is this?" I asked, awkwardly shifting to pry open the strings. Inside were dried fruits—apricots, peaches, prunes, and berries. My eyes widened, and my mouth began to water.

Real food.

I didn't know how the fruit was staying dry underwater, but something was keeping it that way.

"Where did you get this?" I gasped, immediately digging in. He grinned.

"I spotted it in the markets, and I thought of you. I'm glad you like it."

"This is *amazing,"* I gushed, my mouth full of flavor as I relished the taste. It was better than anything I'd eaten down here in days. "Thank you," I added earnestly, and he beamed. Then I offered him the bag. "Would you like to try one?"

His nose wrinkled.

"No thanks—I much prefer fish," he said quickly, and I stifled a laugh.

"Suit yourself," I mused, secretly glad I didn't have to share. I was going to *devour* this entire bag myself.

By the time we reached Atlantis, it was nightfall. The closer we'd gotten to Atlantis, the lighter the waters had gotten—but now they were almost black again.

The manta ray dropped us off in a field of seagrass. My limbs were stiff from holding on to Lysander and the commander so tightly—though I'd spent so long chatting with the commander, I didn't think I could call him anything but *Leif* now. Everything else seemed too formal.

Ahead was a large wall of caves and coral, spanning thousands of feet in height, and Lysander had told me we would be passing through it to reach Atlantis.

"Over here," Lysander insisted, pointing to a dark, uninviting cave. We had nothing to light the way, so we ventured in darkness through the narrow space. I supposed one good thing about the darkness was that it confirmed our safety—if we'd been in danger, my heart would have started to glow.

We walked in silence, single file, deeper and further down into the depths of the cave for what seemed like an eternity. But then, finally, I noticed a bright yellow glow. I immediately recognized the coral—I'd seen it in one of Kendra's textbooks. It was called sun coral. It grew all over the roof and walls of the cave, illuminating a soft glow in all shades of orange and yellow. They looked like tiny suns because of their dozens of tiny tentacles. They reminded me of the poorly-drawn suns Kendra and I used to do in the corners of our art projects as children.

Kendra had loved them for this exact reason.

"They don't actually need *any* sunlight," she'd told me once, as she was doing homework at the kitchen table and I was texting Matt. "And yet, they have this amazing glow, and they're so beautiful!"

My chest felt heavy as I thought of Kendra, and I wondered if she was still safe.

Eventually, the cave expanded into an opening, and we stepped out onto sandy ground. This was the first time I'd seen sand, and not bedrock, since being down here. Then I looked up, and my mouth went dry.

The kingdom was made of ruins—literally *built* on the ruins of ancient Greek temples and sunken structures. Half of it had collapsed into crevices of the ocean floor, and the rest was entwined in the caves surrounding the kingdom—like the space of the kingdom *itself* was another crevice, and we were in it. It was massive and like a stone jungle of columns and algae. I looked up to see millions of fish swimming through the crystal-clear waters above us.

I realized we were closer to the surface than we'd ever been from how clearly I could see, even though it was nighttime.

The road ahead was lined with shells and starfish, and it zigzagged through numerous structures—all of which were quite clearly abandoned from the lack of movement and sound around us.

"Stay close," Lysander murmured to me. "There are likely soldiers roaming here. We'll stick to the shadows."

Leif and I followed him as he led us toward the nearest building, and we stayed close to the stone walls as we crept through the city. I hadn't yet spotted the palace, so we must have been quite far from it.

Everywhere we went, there was lush algae, seagrass, purple acropora coral gardens, and iridescent lighting from the cavern waterways that shone through the deserted waters. It seemed as if the city were frozen in time with how still it seemed. Even the waters barely rippled, and the seagrass barely swayed.

We navigated from one building to the next, and Lysander led us across an open space toward a temple—

Something shoved hard against me. My side throbbed as I fell to the ground and was instantly pinned by a siren soldier. He plunged a dagger straight into my shoulder, and white-hot pain flashed. I screamed, and the pain grew worse as salty water stung at the wound.

Leif tackled the soldier off of me, but both Lysander and Leif were weaponless. I forced myself upright, gritting my teeth as pain shot through me, and reached for the boot that had my dagger in it.

The soldier threw Leif off of him, and before Lysander could grab him, he lunged at me again. He swiped at my face with his claws, and I ducked. He missed, but he ripped my necklace, and two of the pearls came loose.

A crushing pain began in my chest—like my lungs were filling with water. I couldn't breathe. I couldn't even *scream.* Toppling over in pain, a severe chill settled on my skin. It was agony and hell all at once. Every movement made it worse, but I was the only one armed.

The dagger, I thought, and even though I was choking and my chest was crushing me, I kicked my boot free and wrapped my fingers around the handle. I pulled it free just as the siren came at me a third time. He was fast, but I was already moving, and I thrust the dagger into his chest.

He froze, his eyes bulging for a moment, and black spots appeared in my vision. I heard faint cries around me, but my focus was on the siren as I pushed the dagger further into his heart. I watched his eyes glaze over, as the pain from my chest and shoulder became excruciating. My limbs grew weak and then the blackness took me.

Air rushed back into my lungs as my eyes fluttered open.

I rasped, coughing and spluttering as giant bubbles of water heaved from my lungs, spilling out of my mouth. It felt as if a huge weight had been lifted from my chest. The water was pleasantly warm around me, and two figures hovered above me with anxious gazes.

"Coral?"

There was still pain throbbing in my shoulder, and I winced as I tried to sit up again. Leif gently held my other shoulder, easing me back down.

"Stay where you are. You're losing a lot of blood," he instructed. Lysander brushed the hair out of my eyes, and my heart fluttered at his touch.

"We need to hurry. Any nearby sirens will smell the blood a mile away," Lysander urged, but he was remarkably calm in his mannerisms.

"Is he dead?" I croaked, and Lysander took a moment to register what I was asking.

"The siren? Yes, you killed him," he reassured me, holding up my dagger to prove it. It was covered in blood. Leif threw him a scolding gaze, but Lysander didn't seem to grasp it.

Killed him.

I killed a siren. With a dagger. With *my* dagger.

I didn't know whether to feel proud or ashamed of myself. It had been in self-defense... but I'd still taken a life.

"I'm taking the dagger out, and I'll wrap the wound. But it won't hold for long," Leif said, holding a bunch of thick seaweed in his hands. "She needs proper medical attention."

"I'll pull the dagger," Lysander said, reaching for the handle that was sticking out of my right shoulder. I winced as his grip nudged the blade where it wedged in my flesh, sending hot pain through me again.

"How did you—the necklace...?" I asked, still trying to get my bearings.

"It's enchanted. We just needed to attach the pearls again, and it fixed itself," Leif explained quickly. "Okay, on my count."

I squeezed my eyes shut, but nothing prepared me for the pain of them ripping the dagger out of me. I screamed again, and tears formed in my eyes as Lysander held me upright while Leif wrapped the seaweed bandage around me. He tied it quickly, then got to his feet.

"We need to hurry. Can you walk?" he asked me.

My head was spinning, and I felt sick to my stomach. I thought I might faint as I tried to stand, and Lysander offered me his hand. I grasped it so tightly that my knuckles turned white, but he didn't protest as he drew me up to my feet.

I swayed a little, but he held me steady with his arm.

"You're doing great," Leif told me, and we went to keep moving. But a shadow of movement to our left stopped us, and Lysander went rigid in my grasp.

"She's human," a quiet voice sounded from the shadows. There, peering out from behind the ruins of a building, was a young wide-eyed female. She had a fierce scar down the right side of her face, and long mouse-brown hair that fell in curls. She emerged from her hiding place, and my eyes widened at the sight of her vibrant green and blue tail and the many thick strings of pearls that hid her chest from view.

A mermaid.

I wanted to gape at her, but I was still swooning. She simply regarded me with confusion.

"Why do I sense a mer-heart if she's human?" she asked, directing the question at Lysander.

"I'm Lorraine Quarte's daughter," I answered slowly, not sure how else to explain. It seemed complicated to go into any more detail—and I couldn't think very straight as it was.

The female's face paled, and all at once, the tides changed around us—stirring with an almost wary energy.

"You mustn't be here," she whispered quickly, and swam over to us so fast she was next to us in mere seconds, and I nearly recoiled from shock. "Why did you bring her here?" she demanded to Lysander and Leif, her tone seething with anger now. "You'll doom us all!"

"She comes with a proposition," Lysander replied smoothly, folding his arms. "For the king himself."

The female snorted.

"You'll never reach the palace. Not with all the soldiers," the female muttered. "And *that's* if the sea witch lets her get that far. You're lucky the sea witch hasn't yet drowned her for being here."

What did she mean? Why was my presence here such a bad thing?

She whirled to me and narrowed her gaze, "You will leave. *Now.* Before you curse us all—"

"We are going nowhere," Leif interrupted firmly. "We request refuge in the Alta Palace. There are more soldiers right behind us. And Coral needs medical attention. You cannot risk us leaving now."

The female's face turned stony, and she glared at them both.

"There is only one way into the Alta Palace, and siren soldiers are swarming every inch of the exterior palace."

"Then you will present yourself as a distraction so that we may pass," Lysander ordered haughtily, and this time, I did gape. "It is of highest importance that we meet with the king."

"No!" I insisted, and he recoiled as I glared at him. "Don't order her to sacrifice herself just so that we may pass! Surely, there's another way."

"There is," Leif interrupted. "We could use the fish." He looked up at the thousands of schools swimming above us. "Even if just for a minute, if we can distract the soldiers, it would buy us enough time to get inside."

Lysander scowled at Leif.

"So it's fine to use fish, but not to use a mermaid?" Lysander drawled back. I continued to glare at Lysander, but he had a point. Where did we draw the line?

Still, from the look in Lysander's eyes... it was clear that even *he* was willing to sacrifice a few fish for my safety. His lips were pulled into a tight line, but his eyes were defeated.

I turned to the mermaid, whose expression had progressed to glowering, and said, "Don't mind him—he's heartless."

I turned back to Lysander, who now glowered at me, and added, "We don't have much time, right? So can you get the fish to help us?"

Lysander's gaze softened as he took in my state, and nodded. But the soft gaze—which seemed reserved just for me—disappeared in an instant as he turned back to the mermaid.

"If you," he pointed begrudgingly at her, "can get us close enough to the palace, then I can facilitate a distraction for us."

The mermaid was still seething, but she nodded too. It seemed that we were all in agreement—though none of us were happy about it. When the mermaid waved for us to follow her, we did.

She began swimming in the opposite direction, darting between ruins and almost immediately vanishing from sight. She was twice as fast as us, and we had to race to keep up with her. It proved challenging in my current injured state, and the water made me sluggish in my human form.

Lysander noticed this, then without warning, reached for me and swung me onto his back. My shoulder throbbed with pain, but it was faster this way, so I didn't complain.

The mermaid was not making it easy to follow her. I wondered if she was *purposely* trying to lose us. But then, I noticed her pause near a cluster of seaweed and peer around before looking back at us and gesturing for us to hurry up.

It continued like that as she made mad dash after mad dash between hiding spots. I began to feel unnerved, like there *was* danger around that I didn't know about. But still, my heart remained normal, no glow in sight.

Finally, a shipwreck came into view in the murky distance. The mermaid was making a beeline for it. And behind the wreck was a towering palace—the Alta Palace. It glowed in the water and appeared like a glittering green diamond, magically barricaded from all unwanted outsiders. It was beautiful and haunting all at once.

"We should have brought the seahorses," Lysander grumbled finally, and I thought of where we'd left them all the way back in Coronis. I wondered what had become of them—whether they'd be rounded up or whether they'd escape on their own.

Lysander seemed puffed and agitated as he swam through the open ocean, and even Leif was starting to turn red. I felt my chest tighten as I thought of Lysander bearing my weight. He'd probably never done anything like this for anyone in his entire life. His warm body was comforting, and his strong hands were holding me in place.

When we reached the wreck, we followed the mermaid into an open hole in the side of the ship. Timber had rotted away, leaving crevices for light to stream in everywhere. A melodic, gentle creak sounded repeatedly as the water ebbed and flowed through the wreckage. We moved through the narrow space as she led us down deeper into the abandoned cabin and revealed another hole on the other side, leading straight to the front doors of the palace.

It was guarded by at least seven siren soldiers, with plenty more patrolling. We would only get one shot at this.

"Do you know how to get inside?" the mermaid asked me as Lysander finally let me down, and I shook my head. "The palace is encased in crystal, but you can pass through it if you present pure intentions. You and I can pass through easily, but your escorts would need to hold our hands to pass with us."

"I see..." I trailed off. "But then... how come the sirens don't use mermaids to pass through?"

"Because the sirens don't have pure intentions," the mermaid explained. "And the magic will pick up on that. If either of your escorts have any hidden intentions whatsoever, then none of us are getting through. So you'd better be certain before we do this."

I turned to Leif and Lysander and raised an eyebrow. I trusted them both, but...

"You know I wouldn't even be here if it weren't for you two and your ridiculous plan," Leif smirked, placing a hand on his heart.

Lysander's gaze fell upon me, and he added, "I don't even have a heart to swear to—but everything I do is for you, Coral."

I rolled my eyes but nodded and turned back to the mermaid, "We're good."

"Then call your fish, and let's do this," she said. Lysander nodded and put two fingers to his mouth. He blew a low whistle, and I noticed the sirens immediately tense at the sound. But before they could act, a low rumble sounded from above.

I didn't dare peer out of the ship, afraid to reveal our hiding spot, but in seconds, the fish came crashing down around the palace in a swarm. Only then did I dare look. It was chaos, with millions of flailing fins and slimy bodies attacking the sirens.

"Now!" the mermaid insisted, and we ran for the palace. My shoulder throbbed in agony, and my head spun, but I pushed through the pain. I saw her grab Leif's hand, as he was closer, and I grabbed Lysander's as the fish parted an archway around the front door. It glittered, frozen in front of us, and my mind was convinced we were going to smack straight into it.

But my gut told me otherwise, and I closed my eyes, envisioning us passing through.

We kept running, and we didn't hit anything. I felt our feet slap onto polished marble, the roaring of the fish vanished, and I heard the soft, melodic sound of a harp. My eyes opened, and the four of us were face to face with two soldiers wielding bows and arrows—these ones dressed in gold breastplate armor—as well as a finely dressed male and female donning crowns.

My eyes widened because I didn't need to guess at who they were. I sank into a curtsy that made black spots dance in my vision. I didn't know how to address either of them, so I simply stayed that way. I didn't dare look up, because what I'd seen...

The female had long brown hair—sleek as my mother's.

229

The male had the same triangular face I recognized in my sister and I and the same upturned brown eyes as my mother.

It *couldn't* be...

"Nerissa, dear, who have you brought us?" the female asked finally. Out of the corner of my eye, I watched the mermaid rise from her bent-tail curtsy and gesture to the three of us.

"The Crown Prince of Veranis, Prince Lysander. His companion, Commander Leif."

She looked at me and swallowed, like she didn't know how to continue. Lysander stood then and gently pulled me out of my curtsy to present me. My head spun.

"This is your granddaughter," he announced proudly. "The long-lost Princess of Atlantis—and *heir to the throne*—Princess Coral."

That was the last thing I remembered before I collapsed.

PART THREE

CHAPTER TWENTY

Coral

It was three days later, and I paced the elegant quarters I'd been shown to, absolutely *fuming*.

Nerissa, who had been assigned to me as my handmaiden, was zigzagging around me at twice the speed I could manage, preparing a gown fitting of royalty, but that was the last thing I cared about right now. Despite our long travels, all I wanted were *answers*—not to freshen up so I might be deemed pre-sentable at *court*.

My mother had not only been a mermaid, but she had been *royalty*.

I'd been born thirty-six seconds before Kendra. It used to come up in arguments before I realized Kendra couldn't care less and wouldn't back down from a fight just because I was a few seconds older than her.

Now, that made me the heir to the kingdom of Atlantis—a deserted kingdom, overrun by sirens, where the only remaining royals hid themselves in a crystal palace.

What was worse is that mere moments after Lysander had dropped that bombshell on me, I'd passed out from my injuries and spent the past three days in bed recovering. Nerissa had been changing my bandages and applying a fast-healing ointment to my wound—and much like the cream Rue had given me for my chin, it had done wonders to improve my shoulder. Now, it was only a dull ache, the wound almost entirely closed.

I'd gotten out of bed as soon as I'd felt well enough—and I'd been pacing ever since as I fumed over the events that had happened. It was obvious Lysander had known about my heritage, and that could only mean that Leif had too. How could they hide something this *important* from me?

Nerissa pulled me out of my thoughts, zooming to my side so suddenly it startled me.

"Perhaps a bath," she suggested, wrinkling her nose at my attire. I was still wearing the bloodied purple gown I'd arrived in.

I frowned at her.

"How am I to bathe *underwater?*" I asked, and she smirked.

"I don't believe we have the same understanding of the word," she replied, and gestured for me to follow her. Out of mere curiosity, I did.

As we climbed a staircase leading out of my room, I noticed gold accents on the mother-of-pearl walls—which glimmered brightly under the light of jellyfish that bobbed along the ceilings of the palace. The upper floor was made of the same pearl as the staircase, and potted seagrass tastefully decorated the space. A set of golden doors lay up ahead.

Nerissa gingerly pulled at my purple traveling gown like it might bite her. It had become muddied and ripped at the skirts from venturing through the sea kingdoms, and Nerissa shook her head as she inspected it.

"We must remove this immediately."

"And trade it for what, exactly?" I asked, eyeing the simple dozens of pearls that draped her chest and hid her breasts.

"I'm sure we could find something more suitable," she told me, with a mischievous smile.

I was still thinking about what might pass as a bath in this place as I peeled the muddied dress off of me. At this point, I was used to random strangers seeing me naked, especially when it was their job to dress me. Nerissa practically threw the dress over her shoulder, like it was garbage, and let it float aimlessly as she dragged me toward the doors.

As soon as I stepped through, I understood. A set of rounded steps led up to a gorgeously-lit cavern, shining with glowing crystals—until they finally met with where the ocean surface rippled above us.

The cave had a giant air pocket.

I glanced at Nerissa who gestured for me to go up the stairs, so I kicked off my traveling boots and ascended.

As I poked my head out into the air pocket, gloriously warm air settled on every inch of my skin—heated by the crystals that illuminated the space in rainbow spectrums. It was more like being in a sauna than a bath—but I guess Undersea creatures didn't use water to cleanse themselves.

I climbed all the steps and found that the water still swirled at my feet as I stood in a smooth, shallow tub—the water rolling effortlessly into it from where the stairs ended. I sat in the shallows, feeling the blissful warmth, and let out a sigh.

I hadn't felt the air for a long time. It felt rejuvenating, like I'd been withering slowly underwater.

Slowly, I let my head fall back into the water and rested there. As I stared up at the cave, I let my eyes follow the trail of rainbow light sprouting from each crystal. The water was gloriously warm against the heated air, and I let my eyes fall closed.

It had only seemed like minutes, but I suddenly startled awake and jolted back up with a splash. Scrambling to the edge, I plunked my head back into the ocean and peered down the stairs, but Nerissa was gone. The door was shut, giving me complete privacy.

I decided I was done relaxing, and I descended back down into the ocean water once more, toward the doors of the bedroom. Still naked, I pressed my ear to the door first to listen for noise. When I heard nothing, I carefully pushed the doors open and peered out into the bedroom.

I felt something brush against my arm and looked down. Hanging on the handle was a new dress—made of the same material as Lysander's fine clothes and the bedding, it seemed, because it felt a lot lighter. My boots were gone, replaced with a pair of flats that had been left against the door, and my dagger was resting atop of them.

Had Nerissa left this for me?

I picked it up and examined it. The sleeves were transparent and puffed like balloons, embodied with translucent pearls that shimmered. A flowy light pink material made up the remainder of the dress—the skirts floated gently in the water, and it cinched in the middle with a bronze belt.

I quickly changed into it, not wanting to be caught in the nude, and marveled at how much nicer it was to wear. I hadn't realized just how heavy the other dress had been.

I descended back down the steps into the quarters I'd been given and scanned the room, but Nerissa was still gone. There was only the empty clamshell bed I'd been sleeping in, piled with soft kelp to serve as a mattress, pearlescent tables and chairs, a wardrobe, a bookcase, and a mirror. A soft kelp-stitched rug spanned the entire room, but other than that, it was empty. The gold detailing on the walls made up for it, making the room seem much grander than it actually was.

As I neared my bed, I realized a tray of food had been left for me—a bowl of plankton covered in a glass dish, more kelp and algae, and more sea berries. But my bag of dried fruit had been transferred to a bowl too—or, at least, what was left of them. They were the most colorful food on the platter, a vibrant array of oranges and reds.

I reached for the dried fruit and was debating whether to eat the handful I grabbed when a knock at the door sounded. I figured it was Nerissa returning, but when it opened and I spun around, I saw Leif in the doorway.

Immediately, anger flooded my veins again.

"You," I seethed, and marched toward him. He quickly closed the door behind him and held up his hands in protest.

"Wait—Coral—"

"How could you keep this from me!" I cried. If I'd been handed a tiara, I would have ripped it from my head and flung it at him. But instead, I settled for flinging my dried fruit at him. It was satisfying and disappointing all at once, and he looked equally hurt that I'd thrown his gift at him.

"I'm sorry—I had no idea," he said quickly, his honey-brown eyes pleading.

I raised an eyebrow assumingly.

"Oh, but you knew who my mother was?" I pressed.

"Well, yes, everyone knew who Lorraine Quarte was—"

"So you just *happened* to not put two and two together?" I drawled, narrowing my gaze. He narrowed his own gaze and shot back.

"It seemed that neither did you."

I faltered, spluttering for words. I hadn't realized that my mother was *royalty*. How could I have *possibly* put anything together?

Then again... maybe that was the extent that Leif had known too. After all, I still didn't know the full extent of my mother's history. And why was she referred to as Lorraine Quarte and not *Princess Lorraine?*

I took a deep breath, then relaxed my shoulders.

"You're right. I'm sorry," I said, and he relaxed too.

"I believe Lysander knew—but perhaps he didn't realize what a shock it would be for you. You still have every right to be mad at him though."

I rolled my eyes. *Typical Lysander...*

Had I only mattered to him because I was *royalty?* Was that why he was so certain that I was the one who could break his curse? It seemed like a perfect match—a prince and a princess...

Leif reached out and gently touched my good shoulder comfortingly.

"Are you okay?" he asked me finally, and I nodded.

239

"I'm fine. I just... I want answers. I'm tired of all these surprise discoveries. When will someone sit down with me and give it to me straight?"

I strode to collapse in a nearby armchair, and Leif followed me across the room.

"I didn't know the story of your mother all that well. I just know that many years ago, a sailor fell from his boat. Your mother rescued him and took him to shore, but because she could not venture further onto the land, she felt such longing for him that it drove her to leave her old world behind, just to be with him. Everyone knew of her because to do something like that... it was the ultimate betrayal of mer-kind."

I stared at Leif as I processed what he said. My mom had saved my dad from drowning? My dad had never told Kendra and I how he and our mother met—just that she was one of the first inhabitants of the island and had been there for him in his first years of building the resort.

"Melody said she was once friends with my mother," I added, trying to think of how that could possibly fit together. "Do you think that has something to do with why she targeted our family?"

"I don't know," Leif admitted, and he sounded truly apologetic. "But listen... maybe you should discuss some things in private with your grandfather before we approach him with this alliance of ours. Especially if there are more things you do not yet know that might affect the alliance."

"And how could I possibly request a private audience with the king?" I asked glumly. Leif raised an eyebrow.

"You need only ask—you're royalty. You need not ask anyone else's permission but his."

Realization came over me, and I sat forward in my chair. He was *right.* I knew very little of courts and customs, royalty and rules—but I knew this much. Why hadn't it occurred to me sooner that I could have simply demanded answers anytime before now?

"Would you like me to escort you to his quarters? I've learned much of the layout of the palace while you were resting," Leif offered.

"Yes—but not yet. There's still something I need to do," I decided, and it couldn't wait any longer.

CHAPTER TWENTY-ONE

Lysander

My quarters were outstanding, but I missed my room back home.

Back home, I had my own study attached to my quarters, filled with books and tomes I enjoyed. I had a view of the coral gardens where fish would visit at all times of the day. And I had a massive bed softer than powdered sand.

Here, the quarters were half as large, lacking in comfort, and overly lavish. Everything was far too *shiny,* and the waters seemed too bright.

I'd been doing my best to stay occupied, even though everything in me wanted to visit Coral. She was still recovering, and Nerissa refused to let me see her. I'd tried once or twice, but she'd slammed the door in my face. She was quickly becoming someone I heavily disliked.

My father would be wanting an update on our journey by now, and I could send messages through fish to him. But that would require me to leave the palace somehow—or get a fish inside. I was debating making some inquiries into it when a knock at the door sounded and then the heavy marble doors swung open.

Coral stood there—sweet Coral, in a transparent pink dress that complemented her perfectly and a fierce look in her eyes. Her shoulder was no longer bleeding, wrapped tightly in a bandage.

I strode to her in a matter of seconds, the overwhelming urge to embrace her coming over me. Somehow, I refrained and came to stand in front of her.

She smelled of air—how was that possible? All this time underwater had infused the scent of salt into her hair, so the new scent was strangely out of place.

"Your hair is back to normal," she noted, and I frowned. It had returned to normal days ago—but I suppose this was the first time she'd seen me since then.

"Yes, it is," I replied finally.

She grimaced, then added, "We need to talk."

She folded her arms, and I tried not to shrink back. This couldn't be good—she didn't seem pleased to see me, even though *she'd* been the one to seek me out.

"What is it that you wish to discuss?" I asked carefully.

"You knew about me being royalty," she pressed, and my gut turned. Suddenly, I felt as if I'd done something wrong, but I didn't understand why. Leif *had* tried to tell me this earlier, but... well, I'd ignored him because I'd been so sure I *hadn't* been wrong.

"I did," I admitted finally.

"Why didn't you tell me?" Coral demanded, and her tone made me flinch. "We came all this way for an alliance that probably means *nothing* to these people—because why would they need my alliance when *I'm* their heir?"

It wasn't that I hadn't thought of this. It's just that I hadn't thought we'd get this far. In truth, I'd agreed to this journey because it was what Coral had wanted. And I'd *hoped* that by spending time together, she would come to accept my proposal. That we would turn back, satisfied.

243

Instead, we'd made it all the way here, and she was right. This alliance *would* fall on deaf ears.

"I'm sorry," was all I could offer, and her gaze softened a little. Despite her hostility, I was glad to see her alive and well. There was a hint of color in her cheeks, and a part of me wondered if it could be darker. If *I* could be the one to make her blush furiously through various words and touches...

What was I thinking? I mentally shook my head as my gut flipped, and a strange sensation came over me.

"In any case," she sighed, and she averted her gaze from me. She was fidgeting with her hands, and I watched curiously. "I need to know... was this all because I'm royalty? Is that the only reason you care about me at all?"

My eyes widened, and I reached for her hand immediately.

"Of *course* not!" I replied, and squeezed her hand firmly. "Coral, I didn't even *know* you were Lorraine Quarte's daughter until I met your father the day I returned your surfboard. I've wanted you *long* since before then."

I'd told her this before, but she seemed to have forgotten. Her eyes widened as the memory struck her, and I could have sworn I saw relief there.

"Right. I forgot..." she trailed off, and her cheeks flushed again. That feeling rippled through me again, and I swallowed hard. I wanted to trace her reddened cheek... then *keep* tracing down every inch of her body.

Pull yourself together.

"Coral," I said, and my voice was guttural. Her eyes widened at the sound, and I swallowed again, trying to mask it. "I care about you—I really *do*, even if I don't always show it.

244

And I need you to know that I'm glad you're well. I wanted to come see you, but Nerissa..."

She shook her head.

"I told her not to let anyone in," Coral admitted. "I wasn't ready to talk to you. I was... so *angry* with you for what you did... but I realize now that you didn't mean to hurt me."

She was too good for me. And who was I to keep her here, in this place she longed to be free of? She wanted to be with her family, she wanted to return to land.

I didn't know how I'd ever let her go, but I also didn't know how I'd live with myself if I forced her to stay.

We'd come all this way for an alliance that would fall through, and she'd promised me she'd stay if it did. Now, we were at the end of the line, and I didn't know what to do.

"Perhaps there is another way to convince King Malvin—"

"No," Coral interrupted quickly. "I'm going to speak to the king in a few minutes. I need answers from him and then I'll bring up the alliance myself."

I froze.

"What will you say?" I asked her, and she hesitated, her eyes darting away.

"I'll propose our idea... and if he refuses..."

I held my breath, and she met my gaze.

"I made you a promise—"

My heart began thudding in my chest, and I couldn't tell if it was from anticipation or panic.

"You don't have to do this," I said quickly, taking a step toward her. She shook her head, pressing her hands to my chest, and her touch alone set me on fire. I wanted to wrap her in my embrace. I wanted to feel her lips against mine. I wanted to explore every inch of her body—

"My family is what matters here," she said, her voice shaky. "We're running out of time, and if I can't save them, then this is the next best thing. And besides... it's not such a bad thing."

She cocked her head at me shyly, her lips parting ever so slightly, and my heart went crazy. It took all my willpower not to lean in and kiss her. Instead, my hands found hers, still placed against my chest, and I let my fingers drift along her arms. She shivered, and I suppressed a noise in the back of my throat.

"Coral," I whispered, my voice rough, and I gently touched the bandages on her shoulder, tracing their soft texture. She didn't flinch, didn't move away. If anything, she leaned into it, and I let my fingers drift, light as a feather, to her collarbone. "When you were stabbed, I thought I would lose you right there and then. And when you stabbed that siren, I was in awe of you. You're everything I *crave*... and yet..."

I couldn't finish the sentence. I couldn't tell her that I'd let her go, and I hated myself for it. I couldn't bear the thought of her leaving me.

She let out another shaky breath—but this time, it wasn't one of despair. It made my heart flutter, made my insides melt, and I had to step back from her because I *knew* if I didn't, I wouldn't know when to stop. My mind was racing, my heart *thudding,* my hands sweating...

"If you knew what kind of thoughts are running through my head right now..." I breathed, and her eyes darkened. She seemed frozen by my words, and instantly, my chest tightened. *I shouldn't have said that...*

"I can't keep the king waiting," she replied finally, her voice a whisper. There was a strange, throaty undertone to it, but if she felt the same as me, she didn't reveal it.

"Let me come with you," I said, and this time, I wasn't going to budge. "I won't say anything about the alliance—the decision is yours to make. But let me be there with you, at the very least."

She considered my words, then after a long moment, she nodded.

"Fine," she agreed, and she turned toward the door.

This was it. The moment we both got answers—and despite having longed for this for so long, a small part of me wasn't ready for it at all.

CHAPTER TWENTY-TWO

Coral

As I exited Lysander's room, my heart raced and my mind whirled. I tried not to let my thoughts show on my face—because the way he'd looked at me, the way he'd *spoken* to me... it had done things to my body.

I could barely breathe just replaying it in my mind. These things I was *feeling* for him... I'd never imagined I'd ever feel this way about him. That I'd feel so *strongly* about him at all.

Leif was waiting for me down the hall, and we walked quickly to meet him.

A part of me was afraid. A part of me didn't know what it would be like to be with Lysander. The idea of being with him, of *staying* down here with him, left me both enthralled and terrified all at once.

Even more terrifying was how badly I wanted him. How damn *attractive* he was with his defined cheekbones and broad shoulders...

I managed to pull myself together before we reached Leif. He'd been leaning against a marble column waiting for me, but once he spotted Lysander and I, he straightened. He escorted us straight to the king's wing, where guards greeted me. I requested an audience, and they went inside to deliver it.

After a minute of waiting, they opened the door and waved me inside.

"Shall I wait here?" Leif asked, but I shook my head.

"No need," I told him, glancing at Lysander. "I think we'll be fine."

Leif wished us both luck, then turned to head back to his room.

Lysander and I entered the wing. It was somehow even more opulent in here than it had been in my quarters—the ceiling glittered with a rainbow array of jewels, marbled columns lined every doorway, and potted seagrass was twice as regularly scattered throughout the dozens and dozens of rooms spanning off from the main entrance. The king swam through an open door to greet me, his vibrant green tail shining under the lights. His salt-and-pepper hair was thin, but his eyes were kind.

"My dear granddaughter," he spoke softly, his gaze flicking from me to Lysander. "And the prince," he added more tersely, before waving us further inside. He guided me through another set of doors, toward a sitting area, and gestured for us to make ourselves comfortable on the plush gold couches. I settled in an armchair, and Lysander sprawled on a nearby sofa. I was glad for our distance because I could already feel the tension between us, and I wasn't quite sure I could take it if he'd been sitting right next to me.

The king sat opposite us, centered on another sofa—his tail straight and rigid, and his entire body poised.

"Forgive us for intruding," I began, uncertain of how to begin. I thought about what I wanted to know, but I didn't even know where to begin.

"You look just like Lorraine," he said, after I didn't speak for some time. His words were kind enough, but I noticed a gruff undertone. "You should have been raised here, with us,

249

dear child. But given the events that have unfolded... I'm glad you were safe elsewhere."

"I... never knew my mother," I confessed finally. "I was hoping... you could tell me about her."

He shifted slightly—the only sign of discomfort he showed—and bowed his head.

"What do you wish to know?" he asked.

"How did she come to live on land? To meet my dad?" I asked, inching forward in my chair. "I know that she saved my dad from drowning, and I know that she gave up her life down here to go to land. But... how?"

The king nodded thoughtfully and met my gaze once more.

"What your mother did..." the king began, and his eyes were heavy with sorrow. "Humans like yourself cannot comprehend the immense power of those who reside in the Undersea. Your mother gave up her home, her power, and her *family* to do what she did—and look where it got her: exactly where the binding curse said she'd end up—as nothing more than foam in the sea."

He shook his head, avoiding my gaze, and my heart stilled at his words.

Sea-foam?

"I *told* her what would happen—but she didn't listen to me."

"My... my dad told us she fell ill," I swallowed. I suppose that was easier than telling two toddlers she turned to seafoam. But had *Dad* known what had truly become of her?

"No, child," the king said softly. "She betrayed her court and asked the sea witch to give her legs in place of a tail. She sacrificed her life in the Undersea to be with your father. No other being has committed such an open act of betrayal against their own kind—to give up her power and her *responsibility* for a mere human. She could never return—could never even *touch* the sea without turning to foam."

I was silent for a moment as I processed what he said. Then I asked, "But why did she go near the ocean if she knew that would happen?"

Why did she leave *us?* Leave *me?*

"She did it to save you all from Melody," the king said, leaning back into the sofa and relaxing. "She gave her life in exchange for a blessing—one that would enchant the waters of your island to protect her family. Even now, the enchantment stands. Every river and pond, every *body* of water... is sacred. She gave her life to ensure you would always be protected by her."

I felt choked up, and tears welled in my eyes as I realized the extent of what she'd done. The tears simply mixed with the seawater. Lysander watched on with a sympathetic expression.

"But Melody still came... she's taken over *everything..."*

"Unfortunately, the enchantment can only do so much," the king explained carefully. "Lorraine would have known this. Every curse has a loophole, and every blessing has its limits. When our late sea witch passed, all the bindings of the Undersea were undone. Our kind were able to venture on land again—so it was only a matter of time until Melody's own magic wore the island's defenses down."

The king paused, then said, "Perhaps Lorraine hoped it would be enough time for you to learn the truth... and protect yourselves from Melody."

"How did they know each other? Melody and my mother?" The king sighed.

"Things were different back then," he began. "When Lorraine was a child, she had a habit of going off to explore, despite our attempts to keep her close to home. But she was rebellious, and she was always sneaking through the waterways to the rockpools on the surface. That's how she met Melody—the two of them loved going where neither of them belonged."

"Lorraine was still smarter than most merpeople her age—and she somehow charmed Melody by sucking up to her. So Melody decided Lorraine would be her friend, and that instantly protected her from other sirens—especially at court, seeing as Melody was Lex Pryor's daughter. Very few beings of the Undersea are stupid enough to cross that family."

The expression on his face turned distasteful as he scrunched up his nose.

"Though her mother and I didn't like it, we let their friendship continue. I wasn't ever entirely certain if Lorraine considered Melody a true friend or if she was strategically using her for protection. Regardless, it didn't stop the two of them from exploring the ocean together as they grew up."

A pause, then he added, "I think Lorraine always craved *more.* When she had exhausted the surroundings of the Undersea, she longed for new discoveries. Perhaps that's why the land fascinated her so much."

"And when my father fell into the sea, she had the perfect excuse to venture there," I filled in, nodding with understanding. "I wonder why Melody chose their friendship over my mother's heart back then, if mer-hearts were so powerful and desired?"

My grandfather shook his head, "Back then, merpeople were not hunted. Queen Chora did not have a suitable reason to declare war on us... that is, *until* your mother betrayed us and went to land. She was the only one who had been to land in centuries, and Queen Chora used it to justify war against our kind. Lorraine is the reason our kingdom has been wiped out."

I stared back at him in shock and horror.

"What?" I breathed. "But... surely she didn't mean to—"

"It matters not what she meant to do," the king cut in quickly. "She was a lady of court, a future ruler, and she offended Queen Chora by going where no other being could ever set foot, abandoning her duties to her kingdom. The queen thought the punishment fitting, to remind Lorraine that her actions had consequences. It put Coronis in a position of power, and not long after that, the Pryor clan took reign of the kingdom—with a vengeful Melody leading it."

I thought over his words. Lorraine had followed her heart, going to land to see more of the world. Chasing a man I believed she'd loved deeply. Protecting her family, even when she'd jeopardized her own kingdom. And some vengeful siren queen had started a war over it, wiping out the merpeople, so that Melody could step in and make matters even worse?

"So how did it work when my mother traded her tail for legs? How much power did she lose?" I asked finally.

I knew she'd given up her old life. I knew she couldn't touch the sea again. But she'd still infused the waters of our island, according to Lysander. And her heart magic was in her necklace... so had she truly lost all her power?

253

"Lorraine searched for weeks on end to find a spell to transform her. It was around that time that she fell out with Melody, who, from what I heard, had wanted to drown the sailor who fell from his ship—your *father*—and keep his soul. When Lorraine saved him, and *then* was able to go to shore to be with him, it only angered the sirens more.

"But when she did find the spell, she left so quickly we didn't get a chance to say goodbye. After that, we were only able to watch each other from our own domains. If she got too close to the sea..."

He didn't need to finish.

"So the spell gave her humanity—but with a sensitivity to the ocean," I said, thinking it over.

"Yes," he confirmed. "The ocean recognized the heart magic sealed within her—recognized that she was not where she belonged. She could not perform magic like she used to. And as with all bindings, the binding keeping us from the land would try to restore peace in any way possible. The only way to return her to the sea—the one place she could harness her magic fully—was to ensure she could not leave it again. And so, when she finally did touch the ocean, she turned to foam and was nothing more."

So it had truly been the only way to protect us.

"It was no secret that the sirens were furious with her—as was all of the Undersea. But word spread on the tides. Even as a human, I have no doubt she could hear whispers on the wind. Melody wasn't going to stop until she found a way onto the island. It could have taken days, months, or years, but eventually it would have happened. I guess Lorraine knew Melody would target that man of hers... and *you* girls."

So rather than wait and risk not being able to protect us, she had done so as soon as she knew. When we were barely old enough to remember. Was that why it had taken almost a year for Melody's songs to start working their true power on us? Because the island had weakened her somehow?

This wasn't just about power for Melody. This was pure revenge. She had *wanted* our dad's soul from the moment she laid eyes on him, and Lorraine had thwarted her time and time again until the day she died.

Now, Melody was so close to succeeding, so close to undoing everything our mother had done to stop her. Instead of immediately killing and coaxing every person she met, she'd bid her time on the island. Perhaps she knew my mother's spirit was watching on, helpless, as Melody dragged out a slow revenge on us, tearing our family apart.

Anger bubbled inside of me.

"I need to stop her," I said darkly. "She has Kendra... and she'll kill my dad. I'm their only hope—I'm the only one who understands about the beings of the Undersea and the only one who isn't under Melody's control. But I need my heart magic to stop Melody—I need to know what the spell was that my mother used."

My grandfather shook his head.

"Lorraine took the spell with her to shore. That's why it was impossible for Melody to follow until the bindings of our old sea witch broke."

My heart sank, and I couldn't help the annoyance I felt.

So the *whole time,* the answer to my problem had been back on the surface? Where could the spell be? Tucked in a box of my mother's old things? Buried in some secret location on the island? How would I *ever* find it?

Lysander had shifted at the mention of the sea witch, and I glanced at him. I'd almost forgotten he was here—he'd been so silent. When he said he wouldn't interfere... he'd meant every word, it seemed.

"Is there anything you could tell me about the spell? Anything that might help me act sooner?" I begged, turning back to the king who shook his head.

"The only thing I can say that might help is this," he offered. "No creatures of the Undersea except for merpeople are capable of true, unconditional love and kindness. That is what makes mer-hearts so powerful... and what makes Melody so vicious. If you seek to use your own power, you will find it in that one strength."

That was hardly helpful. Nobody ever won wars with love and kindness. I nearly scoffed out loud imagining how that might go down in a standoff with Melody.

I sucked in a breath, readying myself for the next topic I needed to discuss with him.

"In truth, we didn't just come here to seek answers about my mother," I admitted. "In fact, before coming here, I didn't know that I was the heir to Atlantis. But we came here to propose an alliance—one between the land and the sea."

The king frowned at me, and Lysander leaned forward in his chair.

"How would that possibly work?" the king asked.

"Well, my father is the founder and owner of Odyssey Bay—the island which Melody seeks to gain control over. And it is my understanding that doing so will grant her access to ancient power that could disrupt life on land *and* in the re-maining Undersea kingdoms.

"If we work together to stop Melody, then I will be the heir to the land—making me the heir to the land *and* sea. An additional alliance between Veranis would mean we have backing from three territories, granting us enough power and resources that we could take back the kingdom of Atlantis. We could overthrow Coronis, rescue our people—"

"I must stop you," the king interrupted, his gaze hard. "We do not wish to go to war. Our kingdom has always been one of peace, and if we counter-attack Coronis, we are no better than them."

I gaped at him.

"Counter-attack? You've been *wiped out!* This isn't about morality—this is about *survival."*

He shook his head.

"It is in our best interests to stay here, in the palace, where we have stood our ground for two decades and can stand our ground for centuries more if need be. Nothing will penetrate our forces that isn't welcomed."

I narrowed my gaze at him.

"It's all fair and well for you to sit in the safety of this palace and do nothing, but I've *seen* what the sirens have done to our people. They have them in chains! They *whip* them and slaughter them!"

"I'm aware of this," the king replied shortly. "But up until now, we have not even had an *heir* to rebuild the kingdom for. We are too short on men. And we have no desire to go to war and risk the few lives we've preserved here."

I glared at him, but he remained stony-faced.

"So I am to face Melody alone?" I pressed, and he shook his head.

"We cannot offer you a kingdom, but you are welcome to stay here with us. You will be safe within these palace walls."

Lysander snorted—the first sound he'd made since walking in here—and I didn't fault him for it. I couldn't abandon my family and hide here for the rest of my life!

"In any case, your proposal is bold and reckless," the king stated, leaning back in his chair. "You are thinking *exactly* like your mother—and look at where that got her. We will not risk our people, and we will *not* side with the one remaining kingdom that *contributed* to our downfall."

He was referring to Veranis's original alliance with Coronis, and Lysander's gaze narrowed.

"Veranis is extending our hand to help you rebuild," Lysander cut in, in an attempt to persuade him, and I didn't protest.

"You are extending your hand because you are under just as much threat from Melody as we were two decades ago," the king scoffed. "Our refusal means your kingdom would crumble, just as ours has."

"And would that serve you?" I challenged, raising an eyebrow. "Would it serve anyone who is left down here enduring Melody's reign of terror?"

The king sighed and leaned back once more.

"Listen to me, Coral, as this is my final word," he began, his voice rough now, "This alliance is a weak promise. We don't need an alliance with Veranis because they have nothing to offer us that *you* cannot already offer alone."

I paused, and I knew I'd come to the end of the line. There was only one card left to play—the most damning card of all.

"That's not true," I said, and swallowed hard to stop my voice from shaking. "I have promised Prince Lysander my heart—and with it, I am bound to *his* kingdom first and foremost."

The king's face paled, and Lysander went very still.

"So no," I continued, throwing my shoulders back. "You have *not* secured an alliance between the land and sea through me. You will only be granted that if you agree to *my* terms, which are as follows: you will assist us in stopping Melody, you will teach me how to harness my magic, and you will ally with Veranis. Otherwise, you will lose *everything.*"

I watched as the king's eyes turned stormy. Meanwhile, Lysander was watching me with clear awe in his eyes.

"What have you *done,* child?" the king growled. I folded my arms, knowing I'd forced his hand—but I'd be *damned* if I let Melody wreck more havoc than she already had. She'd already torn my family apart. I wasn't about to let her destroy the Undersea, or the land above, for that matter.

And if I was truly the heir to Atlantis, its people deserved a better ruler than my grandfather. One brave enough to leave the confines of this ridiculous palace and *fight* for their freedom.

I watched the king, waiting for his response, and after a long moment, his shoulders slumped with defeat. The corners of my mouth turned upward, and I knew we had a deal.

CHAPTER TWENTY-THREE

Coral

Lysander and I walked in silence back to my quarters. My mind was still reeling from what had happened, and the rush of making demands had worn off.

I kept trying to convince myself that I'd made the right choice. That I was an idiot to keep running from this perfectly good alliance—one that would save my family. One that might have *already* saved them had I not been so selfish as to venture across the sea kingdoms in hopes of finding another way.

I should have done this days ago. It was clearly the right thing to do.

And yet...

I still couldn't shake the feeling that I'd backed myself into a box. It was a feeling I absolutely *loathed.*

A tiny part of me wished there had been another way, if only to prove that I could have saved myself and my own future. That I could have avoided the fate of staying here with Lysander.

But... something had changed between us. I could sense it.

When we reached the doors to my room, I turned the knob and pushed the doors open.

"Can I come in?" Lysander asked from behind me, his voice hoarse, and I paused. After a brief moment, I swallowed hard, then nodded and let him follow me inside.

Nerissa had been by while I was gone. She'd cleaned up the dried fruit I'd thrown at Leif and laid out an embarrassingly skimpy nightgown that I had no intention of wearing.

I crossed a few paces across the room, not ready to look Lysander in the eye.

It was done.

The alliance was sealed. My heart would be his.

I felt like I'd given up my entire life in one moment. Now, it was just a matter of time until the tides turned—until I became heartless, and Lysander, humane.

"Coral," Lysander's voice was deathly quiet, like the calm before a storm. "Can we talk about what just happened?"

"What's there to talk about?" I breathed, finally turning to face him. I met his gaze and found that I could hold it. "You got what you wanted—"

"I didn't want this," he said firmly. "I didn't want you to be trapped here with me. I didn't want..." He ran a hand through his thick black locks. "I didn't want it like *this...*"

His eyes were filled with regret, and my chest caved.

"Lysander, it's fine," I said softly, and took two steps toward him. He reached out and traced my cheek, and I leaned into it with a shudder. His eyes darkened, and I noticed how he stiffened—like he was practicing a great deal of restraint in his movements.

"I've wanted to do this for days," he confessed, his voice raw. "But I kept stopping myself..."

I reached up to grip his wrist. I didn't want to talk anymore. Without another thought, I leaned forward and pressed my lips to his.

261

He startled at first, then let out a groan and leaned into the kiss. His hands immediately cupped my face, kissing me softly and deeply. He tasted like salt and sea berries.

I tugged on his collar to bring him closer and he obliged. Our lips melded together slowly. Taking the lead, I reached up to run my fingers through his lush black curls. He made a soft noise, and I felt a thrill go through my body. As if instinctively, his hands trailed down to my waist, his touch sending shivers through my body.

Only when we began to stumble back toward the bed did I realize what was happening... and I found that I didn't care. I had already played my last card. There was nothing left for me to fight for.

If you knew what kind of thoughts are running through my head right now.

The memory sent an ache through me as he laid me down on the bed and crawled over my body. I tugged at the buttons of his shirt, needing more access to him.

You're everything I crave.

He paused to take in the sight of me under him—the sleeve of my dress slightly skewed, my cheeks, which were no doubt flushed as I finally undid the last of the shirt buttons.

"Tell me what kind of thoughts were running through your mind earlier," I breathed, meeting his gaze. A noise escaped the back of his throat, and he slowly pulled his shirt off, revealing his muscles and chest.

"If I do that, I don't know if I'll be able to stop," he admitted, his voice ragged, and he reached to grab my hand. He lifted it and pressed a kiss to my palm before adding, "Don't get me wrong—I *want* to keep going... but I'm not sure that we should."

Why did he have a moral compass all of a sudden? Why couldn't he just let me *have* this?

"Lysander," I whined, my voice ragged. "Please..."

I *couldn't* be alone with my thoughts. It was easier this way. If we kept going, I could just surrender to him, to the feeling of wanting him, to the feeling of *being* with him... without all the overthinking that came with it.

He leaned down to kiss me again—this time more urgently than before. I arched into him, and he groaned against me as I let my hands explore his chest, his waist, his back...

"I wanted to kiss you," he breathed against my lips, his gaze intense as it met mine. "For *days* now, I've wanted to."

He lowered his lips to my neck and continued kissing from my collarbone to my ear. I arched my neck to give him more access, and his hands skimmed my waist, my *stomach...*

"I wanted to feel every inch of you," he whispered in my ear, and my breath came out shaky as I became more aware of what his fingers were doing. They teased at the hem of my dress, brushing my thighs through the material.

I was acutely aware that I had no experience with this kind of thing, but I imagined Lysander didn't either. Still, the further we went, the harder it became to breathe. As much as I liked him touching me, and as much as I wanted to touch him... a small part of me was terrified.

He studied me for a moment, noticing my hesitation.

"Coral," he breathed. "We don't have to do this."

He was being so kind and considerate. Despite everything, despite his curse, all of his flaws, the clear lust he'd had for me earlier... he wasn't willing to make me uncomfortable.

Before I knew what was happening, I'd started sobbing, and he recoiled.

"Did I hurt you?" he asked quickly, and I shook my head. I wanted to climb under the bedsheets and disappear. I couldn't face the reality of this situation.

I buried my head in my hands, and a moment later, I felt his presence as he wrapped his arms around me.

"What is it?" he murmured into my hair, and I shook as I sobbed into his chest.

"I... I think I'm falling in love with you," I gasped between sobs. "And I don't know how long I have before I stop feeling it. Before I stop feeling *everything*. Before I stop caring that I'm trapped down here with you. I don't want to lose that part of me. I want to see my family again. I want..."

I was crying harder now, my body shaking as he held me.

I'd wanted my future... and now it was too late.

"You won't stop feeling it," he said, stroking my hair gently. "You won't lose *any* part of yourself, Coral."

My sobs slowed, and I looked up to meet his gaze. He brushed the tears from my eyes as he gazed back.

"Haven't you been listening to me? The curse ends with *you*. I couldn't just court a group of females until someone gave me their heart. It *had* to be you."

I didn't understand. He pressed a kiss to my forehead, but he didn't explain further.

"As for your family, I'll find a way to reunite you. You'll see them again—you have my word."

"Does that mean... you'll let me go back to the surface?" I asked, hope fluttering through me. He hesitated, and that hope died in an instant.

"I will see what I can do," he promised finally, but I shook my head.

"What does that even mean?" I pressed, and placed my hands against his chest as my sorrow seeped into anger. "You either let me go or you don't—there's nothing to *consider!"*

"It's more complicated than that," he replied, grabbing my hands and threading his fingers through mine. "Can you trust me, Coral? Have I let you down before now?"

I hesitated. He *hadn't* let me down yet. He'd always been there for me, and he was the most honest person I knew due to his curse. If there was anyone I could trust, it was him.

"I trust you," I said finally, and I felt all final resistance release from me. I felt *fully* surrendered to him. He held me for a while longer until my breathing had steadied once more.

Then, he leaned in and kissed me again—slow and gentle, and I reached up to cup his cheek. Before long, the kiss became more urgent again, and this time, I didn't hesitate as he laid me down against the soft kelp bed.

This time, I let him touch and explore to his heart's content.

I reveled in the feeling of his hands slipping under my dress to cup my breasts. I blushed deeper as he let out a low chuckle at my every reaction.

"You're so responsive," he murmured in my ear, as I tilted my head back into the pillows.

He touched and teased his way down my body, and when he brushed the sensitive place between my legs, my breath hitched.

"Shall I keep going?"

I whimpered in response, and what followed was bliss unlike anything I'd ever felt before. It left me panting and left him smirking as he indulged his own curiosity, marveling at the many noises that escaped me.

Each time, his voice became more guttural, his whispers more brazen, and I felt unhinged—like I couldn't think straight anymore. It was the distraction I'd wanted, but this time, I welcomed it fully.

In my dreams, I was standing on land once more. It was *glorious.* I could feel the cool wind and the warm sun, the sand between my toes, and smell the salty sea air. I indulged in the senses—I'd missed them more than I realized.

But then, I noticed a figure in the waves again—likely the reason I was here. My mother stood there again, watching me.

Could she only appear to me in the sea? Was it because of her heart magic and her ties to her true nature?

I took a few steps into the waves, waiting to see if she would speak. Her expression was solemn.

"You were never meant to know," she breathed, her voice a gentle whisper. Laced with sorrow, it filled every part of me with a deep regret. "The more you know, the stronger it gets."

"What does?" I asked, taking another step toward her.

"Your heart magic," she breathed. "You cannot allow it to awaken, Coral. You must leave the Undersea immediately."

I frowned at her.

"But why? What will happen if I unleash my magic?"

Her familiar eyes bore into mine with sadness.

"The spell you seek is the same—just reversed," she explained, and my heart skipped a beat. "If you unlock your magic and change into your mer-form, you will be trapped forever. You will never be able to return to the surface."

Horror slammed into me.

No...

But then... my plan. How would I ever save Kendra and Dad? I *couldn't* face Melody without my magic. Her songs would overpower me.

"But... then... what am I supposed to do?" I cried, my mind rushing with panic.

She didn't answer. Or rather, *couldn't*—she was already fading away.

I ran as fast as I could through the ocean, but the further out I got, the more the water pushed against me, slowing me down.

She was almost gone.

"Wait!" I shrieked desperately, and collapsed forward into the water in an attempt to swim to her.

I clawed at the water, the outline of her figure the only thing left visible. I reached out, stretching as far as I could.

I could almost reach her—almost *touch* her—

A cold wall slammed into my left side, throwing me backward and under the water.

267

A wave, I realized, as I floated there in the shallow depths for a few minutes. Somehow, it didn't bother me to be under the water for so long anymore.

I felt defeated. What was the point of going back to shore when I couldn't do anything to help those I loved?

I blinked slowly, and when my eyes opened again, I saw Lysander floating over me. He wore a white shirt completely seeped through with water, which drifted around his slender frame.

But his eyes were shut, like he was asleep.

Confused, I reached out to touch him—

I awoke suddenly, letting out a gasp. Bubbles escaped my mouth as I sat up in a strange bed. No... it was my bed in the Alta Palace, the one made of kelp and clam.

Lysander slept soundly beside me, and my face heated as I remembered what had happened earlier. Rattled from the dream, I carefully swung myself over to sit on the side of the bed, putting some distance between the two of us.

I sat there for a few minutes, thinking about what my mother had said. I didn't want to believe it. But if what she said was true... then all of my options really *did* result in me spending the rest of my life down here.

If I upheld my alliance with Lysander, he would keep me here, in human form I presumed, while the fate of my family rested with his men.

But if we found a way for me to go back to the surface, and I unleashed my heart magic... I would be forced to remain in the sea forever. I wouldn't get the chance to face Melody unless she herself returned to the Undersea. And I'd *never* see my family again.

Both options trapped me down here unless I chose the worst option of all—to run.

To abandon it all and never look back.

But I could never do that. Not after Maya. Not after what she'd sacrificed just so that I might live, and I'd already decided I would do good in her place. I couldn't go back on that now.

I drew in a ragged breath and brought my knees up to my chest. The floaty high from kissing Lysander hours ago was gone—and now there was uncertainty cloaking my thoughts of him again.

CHAPTER TWENTY-FOUR

Coral

I dressed and left for breakfast long before Lysander awoke that morning.

Today, I was in a similar dress to yesterday—this one wine-red. After some navigating and having to ask directions from guards and staff, I found my way to the dining hall. The long mother-of-pearl dining table was covered in dozens and dozens of mostly vegetarian dishes on large golden plates. There was kelp and berries, dried berries, dried seaweed, plankton, five variations of algae dip, and... more kelp.

Fantastic, I thought sarcastically, my stomach rumbling, and went straight for the dried berries.

Once I was finished eating, I explored more of the palace. Nobody bothered me, and I didn't worry about getting lost. I didn't want to be found.

After what felt like hours, I stumbled upon a ballroom—the ceiling glowing with jellyfish and preserved coral spiraling up the marble columns that lined the long, expansive room. It was clear that it hadn't been used in a long time from the mold growing on the walls and floor.

"Here you are," a voice sounded, making me jump. I spun around and came face-to-face with Nerissa. *"My lady,"* she added dryly, and smirked at me.

I breathed a sigh of relief that it hadn't been Lysander. Nerissa swam a little closer to me.

270

"I just had a rather interesting conversation with the king," she informed me. I didn't know how to respond, so I said nothing, and she folded her arms. "It seems that we will be going to war alongside Veranis—and that *I* am to journey to the Vera Palace to be at your side."

"That's... not necessary," I began. "I already have a handmaiden—"

"Not just as a handmaiden," Nerissa interrupted. "As a point of contact. *And* I will be teaching you magic."

My heart skipped a beat. The king was giving me all of my requests.

"Don't I need to be in my mermaid form to use magic?" I asked, and dread seeped through me as I remembered my mother's warning. Nerissa raised an eyebrow.

"Well, isn't that the plan?"

I frowned. I was torn on what to do. What if they needed my mermaid power to defeat Melody? What if they lured her into the Undersea so that I could help fight her? Would that be expected of me?

I didn't want to promise anything, so I kept my mouth shut. Nerissa frowned at me.

"I suppose that will be our first lesson," she decided finally, with a sigh. "But we will begin once you return. I will not be traveling with you as my form will draw too much attention. I'll take a more secluded route and meet you there in the days after."

I nodded, her reasoning making sense. I couldn't tell if Nerissa was pleased about this turn of events—she was hard to read. But before I had a chance to ask, she added, "It's about time someone stood up to the king."

My eyes widened with surprise, and she grinned at me fiercely.

"I can't tell you how happy I am to be doing something *other* than scouting and reporting. Their plan was to stay fortified in the palace for the rest of their lives... that is, until *you* came along."

I smiled back then, and a sense of pride washed over me. My actions were *already* having an impact, and it was reassuring.

"I should also mention that Lysander was looking for you," Nerissa said, her eyebrows waggling at me. "When I came to wake you and found *him* in your bed, I promptly kicked him out before he had a chance to explain what had *really* happened. Though I certainly have no regrets."

I burst out laughing. The thought of Lysander being booted from my bed, still drowsy—*damn,* I was disappointed that I'd missed that.

I wasn't ready to see Lysander yet, but I told Nerissa I'd seek him out when I was. She left me alone after that, and I continued to wander the palace in peace.

❧⌘❧

After lunch, I couldn't avoid Lysander any longer. I wasn't ready to bring up what my mother had told me with him. Still, after last night... I couldn't *not* see him. I didn't want things to be awkward between us.

My knocking at his door interrupted the sound of faint rustling papers, and I heard him call out a greeting. I squinted as I opened the door—the lights seemed brighter in here—and spotted a Lysander standing by a bookshelf.

His eyes lit up when he saw me.

"Coral," he breathed, and immediately dropped his book, crossing the room to me. Just the sight of him made any feelings of hesitation melt away, and I was secretly happy when he wrapped me in his familiar, warm embrace once more. "Where did you go? I've been looking for you."

"I just needed some space to think," I told him, pushing back on his chest to meet his gaze. "Sorry to disappear on you."

He tucked a loose strand of hair behind my ear, and a gentle smile appeared on his face.

"I'm glad you're here," he said finally. "There is something I want to show you."

"What is it?" I asked, as he stepped back and let his hand drop to entwine with mine.

"Come with me," he said, leading me across his room. I followed as he led me through a different set of doors, revealing a smaller sitting room. There were more bookshelves in here and two pearlescent armchairs, but the space was too small for much else.

However, on the opposing wall that we were heading toward, there was a large, clear set of balcony doors—and what I saw on the other side made my jaw drop.

A school of jellyfish was swimming by. There were *hundreds* of them, each one glowing a bright, luminescent blue, lighting up the ocean surrounds with hues of green and blue.

We couldn't open the balcony doors—not with the crystal protection keeping us inside—but I couldn't tear my eyes from them. They were so beautiful, like stars in the Undersea.

"They pass through our kingdoms once a year," Lysander said, and my hand slipped from his as I walked right up to the doors, as close as I could possibly get. Lysander remained standing behind me. "My mother used to like watching them too. I think they fascinated her somehow."

"I can see why. They are unlike anything I've ever seen," I said quietly, leaning my hands on the balcony doors, wishing I could step out for a closer look. We watched them in silence for a few minutes, captivated by the scene.

Eventually, I turned to glance at Lysander. He'd come to stand next to me and was beaming at my reaction. The moment was special—and I didn't want to ruin it. But my mind was still teeming with questions and curiosity about what would happen next between us. I didn't know what to expect... and I wanted to be clear on it.

"I need to ask you something," I said, and turned to face him head on. "What would solidifying this alliance look like?"

His expression dulled a little, but he reached out to take my hand again and squeezed it.

"My father will wish to commemorate it with some kind of ceremony," he replied. "A public show of strength between you and I before we march our troops."

"And in order for you to gain permission to attack Melody on land?" I pressed, raising an eyebrow. "Would you need my heart magic? Would you need me to..."

I couldn't bring myself to finish the sentence.

274

"No, of course not," he said quickly. "You are powerful enough as you are. Our alliance would unlock certain abilities—one of them being that we could request a binding change from the sea witch."

I nodded slowly.

"So... the more alliances you have, the more powerful you become?" I asked, and he nodded.

"In Melody's case, she thrives on brute force power. In our case, we thrive on allied power."

Interesting.

I hadn't thought much of the sea witch since being in Lysander's library and deciding it was a lost cause. But now that I was left with no options, I wondered if it would be worth pursuing that path again.

However, that thought quickly faded from my mind as Lysander leaned a little closer to me. It was as if he was caught in a trance, unable to take his eyes off of me.

My throat felt like sandpaper with his proximity, and my gaze fell upon the buttons of his shirt. I realized that I had a rather prominent urge to undo them all and throw the shirt to the floor. My thoughts went back to last night, and I must have blushed because Lysander flashed a grin at me.

"I don't think I'll ever stop being enthralled by you," he murmured, bringing my hand to his lips to kiss the back of my palm. "Especially when I make you react in such interesting ways."

Despite my hesitations and my uncertainty about what my future with Lysander might look like, I couldn't help wanting him.

Especially when his lips found mine, gentle at first, but then he deepened it, and I couldn't help the groan that escaped my throat. He began to kiss along my jawline, down my neck and collarbone. I tilted my neck to give him more access.

Without warning, he guided me back against the balcony doors. Heat pooled between my legs, and my lips crashed against his again. His hands tangled in my hair, and I craved more of him—craved his touch, wanted to feel him everywhere. I bit down on his bottom lip, and that snapped something in him.

In seconds, he'd scooped me up and carried me through the doors, over to his bed, where he set me down with a tender gentleness. And then he covered his body in mine, and we spent the rest of the afternoon tangled in each other's embrace.

CHAPTER TWENTY-FIVE

Coral

There were just seventeen days left until the wedding—and it was time for us to return to Veranis.

By mid-morning, we were ready to leave. We still had a lot to do—we needed to make news of Lysander and I's alliance official throughout his kingdom and then we needed to prepare for war with Melody.

King Malvin agreed to send us off through a secret passage—one the castle staff had been using to collect food. It came out on the other side of Atlantis, far from the patrolling soldiers.

"I had someone fetch three new seahorses for your journey back," the king added, as he walked us down to the kitchens where the passage began. I'd changed into a new sea-green dress and navy traveling cloak. Lysander donned a rather charming emerald-green cloak over his navy-blue attire. Leif was dressed in a lighter shade of blue with a brown cloak. Nerissa had already left and would arrive a few days later than us.

"Thank you for your kindness," Lysander said, flashing the king a charming smile. The king merely grunted in response before waving us through the dark passageway. It was similar to the tunnel we'd taken to enter Atlantis, but this one was much smaller, and I had to bow my head to stop it from bumping the ceiling.

The passage took almost half a day to complete, but we eventually came out among stalks of kelp, well hidden from any lurking soldiers or open roads. We found the seahorses waiting for us among the kelp, tethered to individual stalks.

Lysander offered me his hand as I climbed atop the first one, and I took it. His gaze was gentle as he watched to make sure I was settled on the seahorse. Then, we rode onward.

Despite everything, new burdens were twisting around my heart as I tried to decide what to do about my heart magic. I would need to decide—and soon—whether I would stay in the Undersea forever or hold on to my one chance of going back to the surface.

Lysander had told me it was complicated, but I trusted him. I held faith that I'd go back there someday. And that was keeping me tethered to my human form for the time being.

It didn't take long for Lysander to notice my simmering mood as we rode the seahorses out of the kelp and onto a backroad.

"Coral," he said finally, catching up to me and falling into a rhythm beside my seahorse. "Is everything alright?"

I forced a smile at him.

"Everything is fine," I told him, but he'd become perceptive enough to my moods that he didn't buy it. *Blasted curse.*

"I know that look. Tell me what's bothering you," he replied, and I let out a small sigh. I valued his honesty, but I wasn't in the right headspace to return it.

Instead, I opted for a slight change of topic.

"What did you mean, the other day, when you said the curse ends with me?" I asked, watching him curiously. "That I

278

would continue to feel emotions, and I wouldn't change? How do I even know that my heart has been *given* to you?"

"You'll know when the curse breaks because we'll both feel it," he explained slowly. "You'll feel it snap into place, like a bond."

"But how are you so certain that I'll be the one to end the curse?"

"I just know it," he said determinedly, and I noticed how he avoided my gaze. I frowned. He seemed far too confident for someone who presented no evidence.

What was so different this time around? In the past, undines would have picked partners—just like Lysander had picked me. They fall in love, the curse shifts, and the females go mad while the males are plagued with guilt.

I thought long and hard about why it would be any different this time. Was it because I was a mermaid?

No... nobody ever said undines were solely bound to other undines. Lysander used the term "being", meaning any being in the Undersea could be chosen.

Any being... within *reach*.

I remembered what Deandra had told me in the library, and a realization came over me like a slow wave.

"There is yet another way to break it, but it has not been discovered."

I was different because I was still *human*. And up until recently, no Undersea beings could travel to the surface. Lysander had chosen me—*obsessed* over me—meaning there had never been another human girl to endure the curse.

279

I felt numb all over and then another thought slammed into me. When I asked about using my heart magic against Melody, the king had said, *"If that were possible, we would all be saved. But that would be far too easy."*

And then, when I'd pressed about the sea witch, they'd forbidden me to ask about her again—for no apparent good reason.

Unless the sea witch does *know another way—and they're trying to keep me from unlocking my magic. Because if I do that, then—*

"You lied to me," I said, and I pulled my seahorse to a halt, studying him. He pulled his own to a stop and stared at me in confusion.

"What are you talking about—"

"The curse won't break unless I'm human, won't it?" I pressed, and his face paled. I narrowed my eyes at him. "And you were trying to keep me from learning the truth because you knew there's another way for me to save my family—a way that involves my heart magic. A way that results in me becoming a mermaid."

His bottom lip fell, and he could do nothing but stare, his expression one of slow horror. It sent a pang of anger and hurt spiraling into my gut.

"You *knew* this whole time—and you allowed me to venture across the sea kingdoms looking for answers?" I demanded, a surge of anger flooding through me as more things became clear to me regarding his behavior. "You let me agree to this alliance in front of the king, then had the *nerve* to tell me you didn't want it to be this way?"

Had he seriously been *so* selfish and so scared of losing me that he'd kept everything vague, thinking I wouldn't figure this out?

"No—that's not entirely true—"

"But it's *partially* true?" I confirmed. I'd felt a deep bond of trust forming between us until now. But it had been shattered in an instant.

He avoided my gaze again, and that was answer enough.

"You're *never* going to let me go, are you?" I breathed. "Even if the royals *had* revealed another way for me to save my family, you still would have forced me to stay here. Either way, I don't have a choice!"

If I stayed here as a human, I would break Lysander's curse. And that is all Lysander cared about—*himself.*

"I can't believe this... I can't believe *you!*" I growled at him, and briskly tugged again on the seahorse, urging it to ride on ahead.

I'd *trusted* him.

I'd trusted him, and I'd been stupid to trust him.

He was a creature of the sea. My own *grandfather* had told me that mermaids were the only beings capable of true love. Lysander could never love me—never *fully* love me. He would always be flawed, always let his own desires sabotage our relationship.

I couldn't be with someone like that. I just *couldn't.*

It hurt to even look at him, so I continued to ride ahead. I didn't want to speak another word to Lysander, and I intended not to for as long as I possibly could.

CHAPTER TWENTY-SIX

Coral

There was an awkwardness in the air over the next five days as we traveled back to Veranis. We rarely spoke to one an-other—even though Lysander tried many times, and I com-pletely ignored him.

We couldn't risk going through Coronis again, so we lost two days taking a back road around the seamounts. The cur-rents were harsh and icy during those days, and I could barely move my fingers and toes from how frigid they became.

I mostly minded to myself, but I did notice at one point, when we had stopped for a short break off the main road, that Lysander summoned a group of fish. They circled the length of his arm as he whispered to them, then he sent them on their way. A day later, another group of fish returned and nuzzled against his ear—as if whispering to *him*—before disappearing in all different directions. Lysander looked torn after the ex-change, but I didn't bother asking him about it. I was too an-gry at him and too prideful to entertain normal conversation.

I was thankful to finally see the stacking buildings of Veranis in the far distance by the fifth day. I couldn't stand Lysander's presence, and I was so exhausted, I felt I might sleep for a week. With five days gone, we didn't have much longer than a week left—the wedding was in eleven short days, and time was running out to stop Melody.

I still needed to figure out how I would sneak out and seek the sea witch's help on my own. And if that didn't work, how I'd ever tolerate a life with Lysander after everything that had come to pass.

We finally arrived at the stables, where Leif dismounted to tend to the seahorses. I was straight off my horse, heading for the city gates, when Lysander caught up to me and grabbed my shoulder. I shrugged him off violently, but he then caught my wrist and met my gaze.

"Coral, I must tell you something."

"Let me go!" I growled, and tried to shake off his grip on my wrist. He held firm, his gaze determined.

"Please—you said honesty was my best quality. Let me be honest with you now."

"Don't you think it's a little late for that?" I hissed back, and only then did I notice how his expression fell. It was enough to make me stop fighting—at least, for the moment.

"I haven't been entirely honest with you, but I vow to change that now," he said earnestly, slipping his fingers from my wrist to entwine in my hand. "There's something I should have told you the moment you got here."

Another secret. What a surprise.

"What is it?" I asked roughly, pulling my hand from his to fold my arms.

"It's... easier if I show you. Let's take a walk," he said, and this time I didn't miss the shakiness of his breath. I frowned.

"I don't wish to walk with you—"

"I'm taking you to the sea witch," he admitted abruptly, and I stared at him. Shock and confusion washed over me. I thought I would have to *fight* my way to her or sneak out at some ungodly hour. Now, he was taking me to her *willingly?*

"Why?" I asked finally. He swallowed hard.

"Because I realize that I might lose you... but this is more important. You deserve to see her... to know the *truth.* All of it."

I didn't understand what he meant, but as he gestured for me to follow him, I did.

He led me through the city streets, up slopes and down narrow walkways, in between houses and through markets, until we finally reached a small stone building with a single weathered wooden door. It looked exactly like all the other buildings—hidden in plain sight.

Only then did he finally turn to me. His face was pale, and he seemed shaken. It must have taken him a lot of courage to do this, but I still didn't fully understand why.

He let out a steady breath.

"I should have told you this earlier," he said, meeting my gaze. "And I understand if it changes everything between us. But I was wrong to try and hide it... and you have a right to know."

Hesitantly, he reached out to cup my cheek, and I fought the urge to lean into it. To savor it, to press my lips against his palm—to do all the things my traitorous body wanted to do that went against every moral he had broken.

"My sweet Coral," he breathed, a sadness in his eyes. "Please forgive me."

I opened my mouth to speak, but at that moment, the weathered door opened. I turned to look at the figure in the doorway, and my heart stopped.

Her familiar brown eyes had a strange green shimmer to them, and her caramel hair floated in the water around her face. She was dressed in a gown of green, trails of fabric snaking around her body like tentacles.

I couldn't breathe, my mouth falling open at the sight of my deceased best friend, Maya, standing before me.

She regarded me with a strange expression. The one thing that was notably off about her was that she was translucent—like a very thin, delicate fabric.

My mind was reeling.

"Maya," I finally choked out, air bubbles floating past my face. I desperately wished I could run to her, embrace her—but I was frozen in shock.

She didn't smile nor speak to me. Her gaze only lulled toward me blankly, like she was trying to place who I was.

"I wasn't keeping you from the sea witch because there was another way," he confessed. "I was keeping you because..."

Because he didn't want me to be reunited with my best friend?

"What's wrong with her?" I breathed, reaching out to touch her too-still, lifeless figure.

"Maya is no longer as you may have remembered her," Lysander explained gently, drawing my attention to him once more. "The day I first saw you, Coral... I *thought* you would become mine. But my men made a mistake that day. Instead of bringing me you, they brought me *her.*"

Could he be referring to the day the incident happened? Had he been there as I went under? Tears shone in my eyes as ˋ

285

he looked pleadingly at me, and I knew this story was headed in a bad direction.

"Unfortunately, when my men brought her to me, and I realized she was not you... I let her drown."

At first, I didn't understand—how could she be standing before me if she had drowned? But I realized her transparent appearance could only mean one thing...

She was a *ghost* of sorts.

"You let her drown?" I repeated numbly.

"Because I didn't feel that it was wrong," he explained, his voice trembling. "I didn't know remorse or regret or any of it. I... I didn't care, Coral. My emotions are only different when I'm around you or when they concern you."

I let out a strangled sob as my composure broke, and I fell to my knees. She'd died down here, alone, and nobody had *cared*. She must have been so scared, knowing she would never return to land, never see her family again or Matt or I. I felt it in that moment because it was how I felt now—trapped and forced in a corner where I would meet a similar fate.

"I didn't want to tell you because I thought you'd hate me," Lysander whispered. His words made everything worse, and I clenched my fists.

All thoughts I'd ever had about Lysander—about his charms and smiles and sparkling eyes—meant *nothing* in that split second. He was a murderer—*the* murderer of my best friend! I felt sick to my stomach that I'd ever even trusted him.

"I *do* hate you," I rasped, wiping hot tears from my eyes as I glared at him. "You let her *drown."*

"I did," he replied, his voice very quiet. "And then... magic restored her life from the inside. It happened so suddenly, out

286

of nowhere. But she awakened in a new state as our new sea witch."

He bowed his head.

"I couldn't even return the body. She's bound to the Undersea now."

"How could you?" I screamed at him, springing to my feet. I couldn't believe he had let such a thing happen to my best friend—someone I cared about so deeply! "You just let her *die* despite dragging her down here against her will, and she just *happened* to become a sea witch?" I snapped the last part. Maya was still staring at me blankly. It was unnerving to see her like this. She wasn't the Maya I remembered at all.

"If you want to hit me, go ahead," he said, his voice filled with remorse.

I wanted to—but I'd been raised better than that. Unlike Lysander, I *cared* about people. I *respected* them.

I could never stay here with him. He was a *monster.*

"Coral..."

"Shut up," I seethed at him, before turning to Maya. I took one tentative step toward her. She didn't react, so I walked up to her and gently wrapped my arms around her. She was solid enough that I could feel her, and I began to weep into her hair.

"I'm so sorry," I sobbed into the crook of her shoulder as I held her. "It should have been me, not you."

She didn't hug me back, and that made it all the more painful. She was really gone, even if she stood here before me.

Lysander said nothing, letting me grieve for some time. When I finally pulled away, sniffling, Maya was still staring blankly beyond us.

287

I couldn't stay here a moment longer. I didn't care what Lysander wanted or about his kingdom or anything else. I had to get back to land. I would face Melody myself, heart magic be *damned.*

I began to march down the narrow street, and I heard Lysander's footsteps follow.

"Coral, where are you going?"

"I'm leaving your pathetic kingdom," I snapped. I felt a hand tighten around my wrist, and Lysander pulled me back to him. I managed to dig my heels into the ground before I collided with his chest so that we wouldn't touch.

"You can't leave," he said, his voice gentle and remorseful. The words blew through me like a punch to the gut as he reminded me, "You're allied with me."

"I don't care what I declared!" I exploded. "You can't expect me to stay here knowing what I know now!"

"I know. And I won't ask you to. That's why I'm sorry."

"Wha—"

My eyes widened as he snapped his fingers, and seaweed lunged from the ground around us, wrapping me in dozens of loops until I was tangled and couldn't run.

I screamed in anguish, struggling to get free, and Lysander just watched me as I thrashed around. Minutes ticked by, but they felt like hours, and I didn't stop until I'd exhausted myself.

Panting heavily, I met his gaze with intense hatred.

"Don't do this," I warned Lysander. "Just let me *go.*"

"You know I can't do that," he whispered, cupping my cheek again. I flinched away from his touch, but I could barely move.

288

"What you feel for Maya right now, that's what you'll feel for me if you don't let me go," I warned. "How can you keep me here against my will knowing you did the same to her?"

"Believe me, it pains me more than you seem to think," he replied weakly. "But I *can't* let you go."

"Then know that you will *never* have my heart, Lysander," I seethed. "Not as long as I live—and I *hope* you suffer your curse for the rest of eternity."

He didn't reply, but I could see my words had hurt him. He refused to meet my gaze as the seaweed restraints snapped along the ground, leaving me bound. I stared him down anyway with as much loathing as I could as two guards came to escort me away.

CHAPTER TWENTY-SEVEN

Coral

The Vera Palace dungeons were cold and desolate. Barnacles and mold coated the walls of my cell, and my seaweed restraints had been traded for iron chains that shackled me to the wall. They felt hard against my wrists, forcing me to sit in an uncomfortable position so as not to cut myself on the razor-sharp barnacles nearby.

I wanted to scream, but my throat was already tired of screaming. And it would do me no good down here where nobody would hear it anyway.

More than anything, I wanted to cry. I grieved the loss of Lysander—whom I'd thought to be my friend. Who I'd hoped could be something more. Whom I'd thought I could *trust* before he turned around and stabbed me clean with betrayal after betrayal.

And I grieved Maya, who was dead *again*. Seeing her body hadn't given me the closure it needed—it had only confirmed that any sliver of hope I'd had that we might *recover* her body was impossible. She was trapped down here too, like me. A prisoner in this fatal world and more bound to it than even I was.

He'll only drag you down into depths you'll never escape from.

290

Melody's words rang in my ears again. How long ago had she said that to me now? How many times had it proven to be right?

I grieved the fact that I was never going to see my family again. I grieved my sister, my father, who would likely perish under Melody's rule. I grieved myself—the life I'd lost. The life I'd given up for them in hopes of saving them.

I wondered if Lysander had been lying about that too. I wondered if they would send any men at all to help my family.

I was alone with my thoughts for a day—I knew as much because I was brought two meals, hours and hours apart, and time seemed to stretch on forever. The meals were plain kelp, and I hadn't touched the first serving, but by the time they brought the second, my stomach was aching for food, so I'd forced the disgusting, slimy stuff down my throat.

My thoughts grew tiring, and my arms began to ache from the way I'd angled them. I was desperate to lean my back up against the wall properly, to relax my stiff arms, but I knew how much barnacles hurt, and I didn't want to risk a scrape.

Kendra and I had been sitting at the back of Dad's sailing boat once as kids, our feet swinging over the edge as we kicked in the water. When we decided to leave, and I kicked my foot up out of the water into the air, my heel was coated in blood. I'd cut it repeatedly on the bottom of the boat, not realizing it was covered in sharp barnacles, and the salt from the seawater had numbed the pain long before I'd realized.

I remembered not being able to walk properly for days.

The memory alone made me wince and convinced me to endure the ache in my shoulders and back.

So I continued to sit there until a jingle of keys sounded somewhere above, followed by the sound of a door creaking. Then, heavy footsteps echoed through the dungeon, and a figure emerged at the end of the long hallway ahead.

King Conrad.

He strode toward my cell, and I watched him approach. What was he doing here?

By the time he reached my cell, he towered above me, staring through the crusted cell bars. His gaze was cold.

"Afternoon, Princess Coral," he greeted. I frowned at him. So, he'd known who I was this entire time as well...

I said nothing, and he let himself into the cell, his cape sweeping the ground as he walked. His crown was similar to Lysander's—made of glittering silver coral—but his was embedded with raw bornite.

"I can't imagine that these cells are very comfortable. Would you be willing to negotiate for more comfortable quarters?" he asked lightly. I couldn't tell if he was being serious or taunting me.

"Do I even have anything left to bargain with?" I drawled, and he let out a single chuckle.

"I understand how things seem, but you might be surprised to learn that you still have *much* to offer us."

I waited for him to continue.

"My son *must* break his curse before he comes of age to rule. I myself ruled at a young age, back when I was heartless, and I did terrible, reckless things because of it."

His lips pulled thin as he reflected.

"Siding with Coronis in the war against Atlantis was one of those things. It should never have been done, and all I can do now is try to remedy my past mistakes. I won't allow my son to make the same mistakes that I did, but our ancient law states that Lysander *must* begin his rule within the next year."

My brow knotted.

"So... you want him to gain his humanity so that he will be a fairer ruler?" I realized, and the king nodded.

"Yes. And I ask that you be that person to break his curse. I ask that you oversee what he did to your friend, our sea witch. I ask that you forgive any secrets he kept from you. He did it so that you would give him a chance—because *I* knew you would never accept him if you knew what he'd done."

I held my breath, and things started to make more sense. Lysander had always been honest with me, or so it seemed. But in the past week, he'd appeared to go back on everything he'd ever said to me. I'd been too angry to realize how out of character it was for him.

"You asked him to keep these secrets," I realized, remembering how the king reacted at the mere *mention* of the sea witch, how Lysander had swiftly changed topics when I mentioned her.

"Yes. And I know I ask a lot of you—but I urge you to see where I am coming from. This kingdom is all I have left. After my late wife passed..." he trailed off, his eyes going distant, and swallowed hard. He straightened his stance. "I won't lose anyone or anything else. I won't risk this curse continuing."

Had Lysander *really* been the one to throw me in here? Had he really been so heartless? Or had he been ordered to do it by his father?

"You did this, didn't you? *You're* the one who's never going to let me leave," I accused quietly.

I'd asked Lysander this same question before, *plenty* of times, but he'd always responded by saying he wouldn't endanger me. *It's complicated*, he'd told me, that night we spent together. But not because of anything *he* felt—because of what he was bound to do. Lysander hadn't turned on me at all. He'd been *forced* to trap me because of his father.

I wondered if he'd have let me go had it not been for King Conrad.

"I am offering you your own suite. I am willing to give you staff, books—whatever your heart desires. You will be treated like family here, Coral."

The king knew nothing about me. He knew nothing of what I wanted—and his attempt to bribe me into his "family" was an insult, given what my family was currently suffering through.

"Go to *hell*," I seethed, my nostrils flaring. The king's eyes turned cold again.

"What he did to your friend, that is *nothing*—only the beginning of what horrors could come to pass should he rule with his curse intact. Think of what that will do to him—to this *kingdom*—"

"I don't care about any of this!" I snapped, turning my gaze from his.

"But you care about Maya, don't you?"

My blood froze, and I barely dared to breathe. He chuckled lowly.

"You could save her, you know," he added softly. "Bring her back from her all-knowing, comatose-like state. Restore the life within her."

Slowly, I met his gaze again.

"How?"

He took a leisurely step toward the cell.

"Do this, and I'll tell you," he promised. "You owe her that much, don't you?"

I did. Her being trapped down here... it was all my fault. Not only had she gone under the waves to save me, but Lysander's men never would have snatched her up if he hadn't been trying to grab me. She didn't deserve any of what had happened to her.

I owed her for her life. I owed her family for their pain. And most importantly... I owed her because she was my best friend. Because I'd let this happen to someone I loved so dearly.

"If you want me to help your family, and Maya, you will do this. You *will* attend a ceremony announcing your alliance with my son. And you *will* give him your heart."

I couldn't argue—couldn't say no to that. He had exactly what I wanted, and he knew it.

I let out a steady breath. I felt like I was in more chains than the ones present on my wrists.

"And what if I were to transform, right here and now, into my mermaid form?" I challenged, raising an eyebrow at him. "So that the curse *doesn't* break properly, and it continues to pass? Will you cease your line of succession? Or shall I do that for you too?"

The king let out a low laugh.

"As long as those shackles hold you, you shall *never* transform, *never* access your heart magic, and so the curse *will* finally break for good. Your children won't suffer the same fate. And you will be known as a hero—Coral the Cursebreaker."

The way he said it made me feel sick to my stomach.

"Fine," I gritted out finally. "For the people I love—*not* for you or your kingdom. I will do as you ask. I will do all of it."

I tried to focus on the positive instead of the idea of me being forced into life as a prisoner. Lysander would come out of this a better person for it. His *kingdom* would thrive for it. My family would be safe... and Maya would finally be free.

"Good. Then we're in agreement," the king said, and he turned to leave. "I'll send someone to prepare you for the ceremony in the coming days. After that, we can discuss alternative accommodations."

He clicked the cell door shut behind him, and I glowered at his retreating figure until it disappeared from sight.

CHAPTER TWENTY-EIGHT

Lysander

I stood beside the tall windows of my quarters, my gaze fixed outside. Before me was a grand view of the coral gardens and the many colorful schools of fish passing through. My focus was skewed though, as my mind kept drifting back to Coral.

It had only been a day since our fight, but it felt like an eternity. My heart still ached when I thought of how she'd looked at me, how she'd *screamed* at me when I'd sent her off with the guards. I already knew that she was never going to forgive me.

I'd stormed straight to my father to demand her release, but I knew it would be hopeless. He'd already refused my request to free her when I sent my messenger fish on our journey back to Veranis. I hadn't been able to bring myself to tell her he'd threatened not to send men to rescue her family if I refused him. She'd already been so angry with me when she found out about Maya...

A tiger shark swam past, pulling me out of my thoughts, and I remembered how Coral had reacted to the baby shark nuzzling her. Even the damn *sharks* reminded me of her now.

There had been many arguments between my father and I over the years. After each one, I had left the palace for days, following the marine life through the lands of the Undersea simply because I had never cared enough to appease my father. I'd always felt more at ease around sea creatures.

But for the first time in my life, I didn't wish to run. Every muscle in my body yearned to fix the damage I'd done.

The doors to my quarters opened suddenly. I knew it was my father before I turned to face him—he was the only person who never bothered to knock first.

My father strode inside, only pausing when he reached the center of the room.

"The ceremony will take place tomorrow," he informed me by way of greeting. I ignored him, turning my gaze back to the fish outside the window. He let out a disgruntled noise.

"Son," he insisted, and I heard him take another step toward me. "I told you not to tell her."

About Maya. He'd warned me long before she ever got here to keep it a secret, told me Coral wouldn't react well. And I'd been so afraid to lose her that I'd heeded his words... until the guilt started to eat at me. Guilt brought about by Coral's presence.

She blamed herself, but it had not been her fault. If it hadn't been for *my* men, Maya would have made it out of those waves alive that day.

They *both* deserved better.

"She had a right to know," I said finally, holding my head high as I finally faced him. The king's gaze soured.

"And now, she will despise you for the rest of her life— which she will spend trapped down here for *your* sake. You could have spared her the truth. She would have been happier."

Again, my gut twisted at the thought of her staying against her will. I had never wanted her to despise me.

"There is a way to restore Maya's soul," I said finally. "A spell to undo what has been done to her. But it requires the caster to venture to the Sea of Souls."

My father's gaze softened slightly, and he shook his head.

"You know that I cannot allow that, Lysander," he said firmly. "You will never return."

I swallowed hard, my gaze hardening.

"It's *my* fault that Maya is suffering. It's *my* fault that Coral hates me. Helping Maya is the *least* that I could do."

"But Son, you are to be *king*," my father warned. "You cannot leave this kingdom without a ruler. And even if you *did* return successfully, Maya will *always* be our sea witch. That is ancient magic that can never be undone."

But at least she'd have her soul again, I thought. *It would be like she never died.*

My father sighed and offered me a sympathetic look.

"Everything that I am doing is for *your* sake, Lysander," he said softly. "I know that you don't see it now, but you will. That is why I am hereby binding you from ever seeking the Sea of Souls—if you attempt to set foot there, you shall turn to sea-foam."

My eyes widened, but as soon as he'd spoken the words, a current swept through the room—icy and foreboding as it caressed every inch of my skin. My father's eyes glowed green, the way they only did when a True Ruler used ancient magic.

I snarled at him, shaking the current off of me. I felt violated by his actions. But my father simply stepped back, a cool expression masking his features.

"When I am king," I said slowly, taking a step toward him as I fought to control my heated breathing, "*you* will not be able to stop me."

"Then you'd best show up tomorrow," he said with a raised eyebrow, before turning and exiting the room. I watched him go—but I knew before the door had fully shut that I wasn't about to let him get away with this.

Leif and I kept to the shadows as we knocked on the weathered door of the sea witch's home. Every moment that passed while I waited was distressing, and I kept feeling as if I should be looking over my shoulder to make sure no guards had tailed us—or worse, my father himself.

At least I didn't have to worry about any fish reporting back to him. The fish here were loyal to me, and I knew they'd keep my secret.

There was no answer, so I knocked a second and then third time. There was a good chance Maya was ignoring us as a result of her lifeless state, but Leif eventually cracked the door open, spilling silvery light onto the pebble path. One scan of the room told us nobody was here.

"Let's be quick," Leif muttered, and we both stepped inside her tiny abode and shut the door.

As I looked around, I noted the ancient texts on stone bookshelves, herbs and plants in collections opposite, and a wide array of other strange objects, vials, potions, and substances chaotically jumbled around the room in various cabinets. There was no bed, no other appliances—I supposed the sea witch didn't need such things.

"What exactly are we looking for?" I asked Leif, as I began to rummage through the many texts on the shelves. He was scanning the cabinets opposite the room.

"A spell—something to send Coral back to the surface," he replied. "I spoke to my men earlier today. They're moving into position, and Nerissa's scouting a route—I got a response from her yesterday. Good thing our warning reached her before she arrived in Veranis."

I nodded. As soon as my father had left, I'd sought out Leif to tell him what my father had done—and begged him to help me break Coral out of the dungeons. If I couldn't save both Coral *and* Maya, I had to at least try to save one of them.

Leif had obliged, saying it would be pointless to break her out unless we were able to get her far away from my father. So, we'd come here, hoping the sea witch would help, and Leif had sent his men to the surface to keep watch when she returned.

"I think I found something," Leif said finally, pulling a scroll from under a stack of books, and I crossed the room to look. Indeed, scribbled in Latin was a one-way travel spell.

I opened my mouth to speak when the door opened, and both our heads whirled. Maya stood in the doorway and bore her distant eyes at me. Her hair drifted in the water, and her wispy dress floated gently.

"Our apologies," Leif said quickly, straightening. "You weren't home, and we are short on time."

She didn't respond but drifted into the room. The door eased shut behind her as she made her way past us, toward a cauldron that was centered on a small slate table in the middle of the room. The chairs around it were filled with shimmering scrolls and tomes.

Leif and I exchanged a weary glance, and he indicated toward the door with his head, tucking the spell into his pocket.

But I looked back at Maya and swallowed hard.

"Just a moment," I said finally, and crossed over to Maya. She didn't look at me, but I sat in one of the chairs beside her cauldron and forced myself to look at her. I felt like I was going to be sick, my fingers trembling.

"It's my fault that you're here," I said finally, my voice shaky. "My men never should have taken you. I never should have let you drown. And I should have tried to find a way to restore your soul long before Coral arrived."

I'd never bothered to speak to her, to take the time to even apologize before now. I simply hadn't cared before I met Coral, and her presence had altered my emotions. I felt vulnerable to say the words, but I knew I needed to.

"I'm so, so sorry for what I did to you."

She slowly turned to look at me, a haunting look in her eyes.

"And it's true—I did only try to find a way to help you because I was afraid of Coral's reaction if I didn't. But I realize now how wrong that was too."

She looked away and continued to stir her cauldron with the mere wave of her hand—she didn't even need to touch the liquid for it to swirl and bubble. I watched wearily as she glided around the room in her floaty dress, grabbing various substances and herbs and throwing them in the mixture.

"Lysander," Leif prompted quietly from behind me. "We need to leave."

"I did find a way to undo what's been done to you," I insisted, ignoring Leif. "But my father has prevented me from venturing to the location. If you were to undo the binding he placed on me, I could help you."

Maya looked at me once more, her voice an empty drawl as she spoke.

"Only a Reigning Queen can reach the Sea of Souls."

I didn't ask how she knew about the sea. She returned to her stirring, and I glanced over my shoulder as Leif approached behind me. He met my gaze.

"A Reigning Queen..." he repeated, frowning. "But we haven't had one of those in thousands of millennia."

It was true. We only had True Rulers, who were granted certain powers to rule their home territories. But never a Reigning Queen. Though Melody had come close to gaining the title through her dominating war tactics.

"Only a Reigning Queen can undo what has been done to me," Maya drawled softly, and met my gaze. "That is why *she* must live."

Realization came over me, and I shook my head.

"No," I insisted, getting to my feet. "If Coral transforms, she'll be stuck here forever. It *has* to be me who ventures to the Sea of Souls."

"It is not possible," Maya said sadly, and the way her eyes shimmered seemed to suggest that she was seeing all possible pathways at once—with only one clear route.

I stepped back, shaking my head. I was being forced to choose between them. I could only save one...

The water shifted around us suddenly, turning brisker, and Maya stiffened.

"They are coming," she warned suddenly, her void devoid of emotion. A chill went down my spine.

"Who's coming?" I asked. I whipped my gaze to the door, then back to her. "My father? His guards?"

"They are coming," she repeated, her eyes blank. "Only a Reigning Queen can undo what has been done to me. *She must live."*

I opened my mouth to ask again what she meant, but she was already off again in her own world—like the conversation had never happened. She drifted over to the bookshelves and started rummaging absently through them, her pace slow, like she had all the time in the world.

"Lysander," Leif said urgently, grabbing my arm now to drag me away. "Come on!"

We made for the door, but just as Leif's hand grabbed the handle, Maya's voice called out one last time, "The debt must be paid, *prince."*

I stopped in my tracks and looked back at her. She inclined her head at me, her gaze drifting down to my chest.

It took a moment for her words to click, but once they did, realization swept over me.

At that moment, I knew what I had to do.

"Thank you," I breathed, hope flickering through me like a light.

The waters seemed to rustle around me in response, but I didn't wait a moment longer. Someone was coming, and we didn't know who it was, but we couldn't stay any longer. So, I followed Leif through the door and disappeared into the shadowy night once more.

CHAPTER TWENTY-NINE

Coral

Early the next morning, the jingling of keys woke me. My neck was twice as stiff and aching, and I could barely move it as two guards stepped into my cell. They undid the chains from my cuffs—leaving the cuffs themselves on my wrists—before pulling me to my feet.

I remembered what the king had said about the cuffs preventing me from transforming, and I scowled as the guards dragged me out of the cell and marched me down the cold, forbidding corridor.

The first flight of stairs brought us back into the charm and splendor of the main palace, but we didn't stop there. They kept marching me up staircases until we'd reached a third floor, and I was brought into an unfamiliar room.

A figure was bustling with dresses near a bed, and when she spun, I recognized her by her long dark hair and kind eyes.

"*Rue,*" I breathed, and she beamed at me.

"My lady," she greeted softly, but eyed the guards warily. "I'm to prepare you for today's ceremony," she added, and waved me toward her. I was only too eager to escape the guards' grasp and cross the room to stand by her.

The guards took up position next to the doors. Unlike before, when they would station themselves outside, they remained inside the room with us. I guessed that the king no longer trusted me to have privacy.

306

I didn't have any idea what to expect today, and when I asked Rue, she didn't let on anything. She simply sat me down on a stool and told me to stay still while she threaded pearls and shells into my hair and braided it. Tendrils of curled fringe framed my face by the time she was done. Then, she swept me up so that she could fit me into a sleeveless gown of navy and silver with pearls adorning the neckline.

The pampering felt strange after spending days in a dirty cell. It felt like she fussed over me for hours, until finally, one of the guards cleared his throat, and Rue stiffened.

"Time to go, my lady," she urged me, and I felt my stomach twist as I turned toward the door. Rue placed a gentle reassuring hand on my back as we walked through the doors, and the guards flanked us. Rue walked with me as far as the stairs before turning to face me.

"Everything will be okay," she told me, fixing the tendrils of my hair one last time and patting down my dress. "Off you go now."

The guards were moving before I could say anything, and they urged me down the staircase. My heart began to thud in my chest, and I scanned the palace. It was a maze of hallways and doors, and I'd never been on these higher levels before. If I tried to run, my chances of getting lost were high, and I'd probably never make it. Plus, I was weaponless.

And running won't save the people I love, I thought. So I kept walking, letting the guards guide me down two more flights, then through the many halls until we came to a set of heavy double doors.

307

I stared at those doors, and I didn't feel ready to face what waited for me inside. But I had no choice—the guards pushed the doors open, and their proximity kept me moving forward.

The room was filled with seated people, all of which turned to look at me. It was a huge, sprawling space with an aisle leading down the middle and up a flight of curved stairs toward some kind of altar.

I spotted Lysander, standing directly opposite me at the other end. He wore a navy jacket very similar to the one he'd been wearing when I first arrived here and his silver coral crown. I realized our attire matched perfectly, and my stomach flipped.

I felt like I couldn't breathe as our eyes met. I remembered all the things I'd screamed at him days ago. I remembered the intense anger that had flooded me, but now, guilt washed those feelings away. Looking at him now, I *knew* he'd been innocent in all of this.

He was waiting for me, his eyes revealing nothing to me yet.

I walked because I couldn't not walk. The attendees stared, and I felt every hair stand at attention on my neck. My eyes continued to scan the room—I didn't want to focus on one thing too long. As my gaze skimmed, they fell upon King Conrad. His cold gaze followed me across the room, and I couldn't hide the anger that curled through me at the sight of him. I held his gaze and made sure he knew it.

He lifted his chin as if challenging me to do something about it. But we both knew I'd do nothing because this wasn't about me. This was about Maya, Kendra, and my dad.

I finally reached the stairs and began to ascend them toward Lysander. He stood with his back to his father, but his expression still betrayed nothing. Still, once I passed the final stair, and I was close enough to touch him...

His gaze bore into mine, and that sense of safety filled me once more.

It became easier to breathe, but now, I was grappling with trying not to break down in tears in front of him. There were so many things I wanted to say to him and too many people watching us.

Someone I didn't know walked up to us—an older male with greying hair and wrinkles across his forehead. He held a tome, which he opened, and flicked to a particular page.

"Please join hands in the alliance union," he commanded, and I didn't know what that meant. But Lysander offered me his hand, showing me how his fingers curled around my wrist, and I did the same.

I stole a quick glance back to the crowd and spotted Leif next to the doors I'd entered from. He appeared to be in an official position, standing among his men, but his eyes were locked onto us.

"We are here today to commemorate an alliance between Princess Coral Klassan-Quarte, representing Atlantis and the land, and Prince Lysander Myronas, representing Veranis," the officiant continued. "This alliance will fortify our lands and strengthen our power."

He turned to the king and said, "I shall now read the terms of this alliance."

The king gave a single nod, and the male flipped a page.

"The terms are as follows, as recorded by Princess Coral: *in return for allowing me to travel to Atlantis and to ask the royals about my heart magic, I will accept Lysander's alliance proposal—but only on the condition that the royals reveal no other way to save my family.*"

My heart stilled. I hadn't realized my words had been recorded—or understood *how* exactly that had come to pass. Perhaps it was some form of magic.

"Princess Coral, do you confirm these terms?" the officiant asked me, and my heart was in my throat.

"Yes," I spoke, my voice barely a whisper.

"And do you, Prince Lysander, agree to these terms?" the officiant asked him. Lysander's eyes found mine, and they seemed to ask *do you trust me?*

I gave a slight nod of my head, and he smiled gently at the officiant.

"I do not."

A collective gasp sounded from the audience, and the king took a step toward us. Lysander broke our hold, striding out to face the audience.

"I would like to propose *new* terms," he said, glancing at me over his shoulder with a twinkle in his eye. "As I feel our old terms have become outdated with all that has come to pass."

"Son," the king warned, but Lysander waved him off as he strode around the altar.

"First of all, we must speak of Princess Coral's heart becoming mine," he said, crossing to a chair that had been placed on the right-hand side of the altar. He lifted his leg to rest his foot on it and leaned on his knee. "The terms I propose

310

are this: that her heart shall be mine at her own discretion. That her heart will *not* be a requirement for our allied strength to be reflected. That our kingdoms can work together simply through a spoken agreement."

"Your Grace," the officiant said weakly, turning to the king for guidance. The king was glowering at Lysander.

"Stop this at once!" he commanded, but Lysander sprung up to continue pacing the altar.

"I would also like to propose that in this alliance, we are bound to protect all inhabitants of the kingdoms being represented—including that of Coral's family, regardless of what comes to pass afterward."

"You will proceed with the old terms or no terms at *all,*" the king hissed, and I felt the currents sway with heated anger around us.

"The old terms are outdated, Father," Lysander insisted, facing him head on and straightening his lapeled jacket. "And as it stands, I owe a debt to the sea."

He pulled something out from under his jacket. The *conch shell.* I remembered Leif saying something about Lysander owing a debt for summoning a manta ray in Coronis to help us escape.

"Whatever it is, it can wait," the king pressed, taking another step forward. But Lysander turned to the crowd, and I watched as Leif pulled the ceremony hall doors open. A hush fell over the murmuring crowd as a figure entered—one that made my muscles tense up.

Maya.

"I'm ready to repay my debt," Lysander called to her, his voice loud and echoing through the hall. Maya strode all the way down the aisle until she was standing at the foot of the stairs. The king did nothing, watching with a torn expression as the events unfolded.

"What will you exchange?" Maya asked finally, her voice empty. It was the first time I'd heard her speak since she died, and she sounded *nothing* like she had when she'd been alive.

"My heart," Lysander stated. My eyes widened, and my heart skipped a beat.

"You don't have a heart," Maya reminded him, her voice a long, empty drawl as her dress floated slowly in the current.

"I realize this. I am exchanging my right to *gain* a heart—so that Coral can have her freedom. So that she can return to the surface and live the life she pleases."

My stomach turned. If he did this, the king wouldn't tell me how to save Maya.

"No!" the king snarled, storming forward to cut in between Lysander and Maya. "Son, if you do this, you can never break the curse!"

"You're wrong, Father," Lysander replied slowly. "If I do this, the curse will end with *me*—not Coral. I will die heart-less."

"But you *cannot!*" he bellowed, his face going red. "Lysander, you are not thinking straight—"

"Isn't this what you wanted, Father?" Lysander pressed, narrowing his gaze. "You want my curse to end? Then I will end it. *Me alone.*"

Lysander caught my gaze once more, his eyes full of affection, and I was at a loss for words.

He was giving up his chance of humanity for me.

He was giving up *everything* for me.

312

Tears welled in my eyes.

He turned back to the officiant and added, "those are my terms."

The officiant seemed at a loss for what to do. He looked between the king, who I feared might rip his head off, and Lysander, whose gaze was so fierce it would scare anybody, and let out something between a wince and a whimper.

"The terms shall be," Maya called out from the bottom of the stairs, her voice carrying ten times the weight and power than anyone standing at the altar. "The debt will be paid."

The king stiffened and whirled to face Maya. But there was nothing he could do—the sea witch's word was law. Her magic bound the Undersea.

I stole a quick glance at Lysander, whose' eyes shone with relief. Despite my own relief, a feeling of disappointment had settled in my stomach. How was I going to help Maya now? Was there another way to learn what the king knew? Would Lysander be able to coax the information from him?

"I hereby declare that the alliance is official," the officiant said faintly, and snapped his book shut. The king's shoulders dropped slowly, and the officiant eyed the steps at the back of the altar, looking as if he wanted to run for his life. But the king didn't turn around.

"Lysander," he said quietly, his voice terse. "What you have just *done*—"

Glass shattered around us, and screams erupted as the currents rippled. I ducked, but no sooner than I had, something grabbed me by the arms and yanked me back hard. I looked up just in time to see a siren sail through the broken windows toward us.

He swooped down and stabbed the king clean in the heart with a sword.

My jaw fell open, watching as the king went limp. Watching as Lysander's eyes widened. As the king's body sagged forward, as it tumbled down the stairs until it lay lifeless at the foot of the stairs with blood clotting the water around him.

And then he was dead.

CHAPTER THIRTY

Coral

By the time the guards reacted, the siren that had grabbed me had me in a chokehold—her clawed hand firm around my neck, grasping my pearl necklace as she pinned me to her chest. I didn't dare struggle, in fear that the pearls might rip free again and I'd start drowning.

Maya had barely reacted, even though the king lay dead at her feet. Lysander had barely reacted too, but I couldn't tell if that was shock or his heartlessness. He eyed Maya, not his murdered father, with a frown on his face.

"They are coming," he muttered, eyes fixated on her. "You meant—"

"Everyone stay *calm,"* the siren that had stabbed the king sang, and I felt a familiar heavy dizziness come over me. Around us, the undine guards' expressions went blank, their limbs limp, and they lowered their spears. Across from me, just out of reach, Lysander struggled against the spell, his shoulders slacking as he finally turned to me.

I was dragged back two paces by the siren who gripped me, and a dagger appeared in her free hand, pointed directly toward my chest. I realized my chest wasn't glowing and re-membered the iron cuffs around my wrists. Maybe that had something to do with it.

"Stand down, little prince," the siren hissed at him, and he eyed the dagger with wide eyes. After a moment, he slowly dropped to his knees, holding up his hands to show he was un-armed. The siren let out a melodic chuckle, and I winced as the point of the dagger dug into my skin lightly.

The ceremony hall doors swung open, and heavy footsteps sounded as a man strode in with an entourage of sirens. His cape was made of a vibrant green silk, and he wore a white dress shirt and black pants. His golden crown was adorned in vibrant green emeralds.

"Sorry I'm late," the man purred like a lullaby, and I felt his power resonating on every inch of my skin. He paused to flash the room a lazy grin before his eyes fell upon Lysander, who scowled back at him.

"Alas, I should have known it would be *you*," Lysander drawled back. "I don't recall sending you an invite, Eugene Pryor."

I stiffened against the siren's hold. *Pryor...*

I noted how the male constantly flicked his golden-blond locks. It was so similar to how Melody would constantly check her nails—

I sucked in a breath. This was Melody's *brother*.

Eugene's eyes then fell upon me.

"Ah—and it seems you *indeed* have the little mermaid," he sang, an amused smile creeping onto his face. "How delight-ful. I've been chasing down her heart."

"You will *not* touch her," Lysander growled quickly. He was panting, like the effort to speak was overwhelming. I watched on carefully, not even sure if Lysander could fight back with this many sirens influencing us.

Eugene simply laughed at him—it was a roaring laugh that reverberated off the walls.

"You are a fool," he snarled finally. "My dear sister has staked a claim on her heart for *weeks* now. You *will* hand her to me as I have promised her a wedding gift *befitting* a queen."

"Melody never has, and never *will* own any piece of me," I shot back. His eyes flicked to me, a slow smile spreading.

"She said you were stubborn," he replied, a hint of amusement in his voice as he took a few slow, leisurely steps toward me. "I imagine ripping that heart from your chest will be *immensely* satisfying for us both."

He motioned for me to approach him, and the siren shoved me forward. I found I had no choice as waves of compulsion rippled through me, pushing my legs into action.

I made it two steps down the stairs when Lysander came out of nowhere, shoving an arm out to stop me from progressing further.

"You will *not* take her," he snapped, rounding on Eugene. "She is with *me.*"

A stormy current swept through the room as if carrying the promise of his words. I struggled against Lysander's arm, but he held me firm in his grasp, wrapping me in a protective hold.

"Let the poor thing *go,* you silly prince," Eugene drawled, his eyes cold, and such a strong wave of dizziness came over me that I stumbled forward. Lysander had released me instantly, and I nearly tumbled down the remaining steps. I walked straight past Maya and the dead king's body, and my heart pounded as I neared Eugene's broad, towering figure.

I stopped only a few feet in front of him, and he examined my features—my face, my chest, my figure. My face burned under his scrutinizing gaze, and he frowned, as if dissatisfied with what he was seeing.

"You're only a *weak* little thing," he taunted finally, and he reached out his hand. I was rooted to the spot, unable to move an inch as his fingers brushed against my chest, where my heart was pounding beneath my rib cage. He tilted his head slightly as if debating whether to rip it out right there and then.

I could barely breathe. I wanted to shut my eyes, but I couldn't even do that. I didn't want to think about how much his claws would hurt—but I couldn't stop the thoughts from running through my mind.

He noticed my quickened breathing, my pale face, and chuckled lightly.

"Don't fret, little mermaid—my sister wants you alive. She wants to take your heart herself," he mused softly, his voice strangely calming, and I felt sick to my stomach. "But that doesn't mean I can't have a little fun first."

He reached up and gripped my neck, and I gasped. I tried to push away, but I couldn't move, couldn't break free of the compulsion. Eyes flaring, he flung me across the room. I plummeted through the water before hitting the wall hard. A crashing pain traveled from my temple to my eyes and ears, and stars danced in my eyes. I slumped to the floor and found I couldn't get up again.

He was at my side again in an instant, dragging me back up by my shoulder to meet his gaze.

"You've caused me so much trouble these past few weeks, evading my men. *Escaping* my city," he hissed at me. *"Stubborn human."*

Out of nowhere, Lysander appeared and punched Eugene in the face. I heard the resounding smack. Eugene let me go as he stumbled backward.

I stared at Lysander with wide eyes, unable to comprehend how he was able to move against the siren spell. Eugene clutched his cheek, which had gone red, and his nostrils flared. Lysander grabbed a spear from under his jacket, but within seconds, Eugene had reacted. With a single kick clean to the stomach, Lysander was sent flying back across the room, the spear clattering to the ground.

Eugene let out a terrible roar that nearly burst my eardrums as he bared his razor-sharp teeth. Then, his hands were on me again, claws digging deep into my shoulders as if he could meld me into them and drag me away. Pain erupted, and I tried to twist out of his grip but failed. Lysander was still struggling to stand from across the room, and the entire royal guard was still under the siren spell, their eyes glazed over. Even Leif was frozen in place near the entry doors of the room.

Eugene started to drag me across the ceremony hall, but I reached out and grabbed the spear, the sound of it ringing as it scraped along the floor. I lifted it and stabbed at Eugene, my aim skewed by his claws in my shoulders. The sharp spear grazed his upper arm, and he ripped his clawed hand out of my right shoulder. I let out a yelp of pain but stabbed again. This time, I got his forearm.

Then, Lysander was there again, knocking Eugene down with another clean punch. The second set of claws released me, and blood appeared in the water around us as my shoulders throbbed.

I took shaky breaths, clambering to my feet and gripping Lysander's spear for protection as Eugene eyed the two of us with wide eyes.

Lysander backed up a couple of steps toward his dead father while I held the spear firm to keep Eugene down. Lysander reached down and plucked the silver and bornite crown from his father's head, then placed it on his own. His eyes glowed green for a moment.

"Get out of my house," Lysander snarled at him, the order resounding off the ceremony hall walls. The command was laced in ancient magic—I could tell just from the *feel* of the words on my skin. "You and all of your sirens are not welcome here."

It was like the magic was stripping the siren spell from the guards, who slowly began to regain movement and immediately drew their spears to angle at the sirens surrounding us. Leif sprung into action, sprinting toward us to point his own spear at Eugene's unguarded back.

Eugene simmered quietly for a moment, then held his hands up in surrender.

"Fine," he insisted, eying me once more. "But I'm not leaving without her."

"Yes, you *are,*" Leif snarled, digging his spear tip into Eugene's back, and he grunted.

Before Eugene could react, a strong current erupted between us, dragging Eugene away from us and back to the entry doors. Screeches sounded as the other sirens near the doors were also snatched up by the ocean's powerful grip and sent hurtling through them. Only myself and the undines were left untouched by it.

What was happening? I thought. It was eerily similar to what had happened to me back at Melody's dinner party, with the random freak storm that had saved me from drinking the poisoned cider.

My eyes swept the room and then I noticed her.

Maya, still standing by the steps, had a single hand stretched out as if she was pushing the sirens out the door with her own force. Her eyes were deadly and glowing pale green, and her hair flew wildly in the current with her dress.

"The king has spoken," she rasped.

My gaze flew to Eugene, who was now gripping the door-frame so hard his knuckles had turned white. Claw marks scratched into the door as he lost hold, and he was flung back-ward, carried by the current.

Within minutes, every siren in the room had been vacu-umed out. Maya dropped her arm, and the doors flung shut with a resounding bang. Her lifeless gaze drifted to meet mine, and I let out a breath.

There were clots of blood in the water drifting around me, and when I reached up to touch the back of my throbbing head, my hand came back red and sticky. It wasn't a good sign, but I chose to ignore it, breaking into a run toward Maya.

I crossed the room in seconds, and without thinking, I en-tangled her into a hug. She didn't hug me back, but she didn't stop me either. I pulled back and studied her expression, which had returned to that blank, empty face she now wore as a sea witch.

"Why did you do that?" I asked her, my eyes stinging. Maya had saved us. In fact, now that I thought about it, Maya must have caused that storm that night. She'd saved me *before* too. "You've done so much for me already—why do you keep using your magic to save me?"

Lysander and Leif had followed me across the room, coming to stand behind me now.

"Because... there's a way to undo what's been done to her," Lysander revealed finally, and I glanced over my shoulder at him. He met my gaze with uncertainty, and my stomach twisted.

"Only a Reigning Queen can venture to the Sea of Souls," Maya drawled softly, drawing my attention back.

"She means you," Leif added from behind me, and I shook my head.

"But... I'm not a queen..." I trailed off. "I don't even know what that means."

Gentle hands appeared on my upper arms, careful to avoid my wounds, which spun me around. Lysander wrapped me in a tight hug, and his warmth seeped into me. It felt good to hold him in my arms, and I melted into his embrace.

Then he held me at arm's length and said, "It means... that if you were to come back once you've saved your family... you could restore Maya's soul. I think she's keeping you alive because you can help her."

I blinked in shock, letting the info sink in.

"You're letting me go?" I whispered finally, and he nodded, tucking a loose strand of hair behind my ear. Then, his gaze narrowed in on the wound on my head.

"Let's sit and talk for a moment," he said, and waved someone over as he took my hand and guided me to the staircase. To my surprise, Maya followed us. Someone had moved the king's body while we'd been distracted.

Lysander sat me down on the steps and instructed the healer that approached us to tend to my injury. Then, he refocused his attention on me as he knelt in front of me.

"How bad does it hurt?" he asked me, as the healer began dabbing at my forehead and cheeks to clear the blood with a cloth.

"A lot," I admitted. The wound felt warm, and my entire head throbbed through a splitting headache. At least I didn't feel dizzy or woozy. "How did you break free of Eugene's spell?" I was still replaying Lysander's punches in my head.

"I don't know," he admitted, running a hand through his hair. "It was like... I couldn't think straight from the dizziness of their compulsion, except when the conversation concerned you. As soon as he hurt you, I somehow recovered my free will, and I ran before I knew what I was doing."

The healer was dressing the wound now, and she handed me a vial of green liquid.

"This will speed up the healing process," she told me, her voice light and airy. I wrinkled my nose at the look of it but quickly uncorked it and swallowed it before the liquid escaped into the seawater around us. It tasted bitter, and I nearly gagged.

"That's foul," I coughed, handing the empty vial back. "I like the ointments you've been giving me more."

"An ointment would just get caught in all of your hair," the healer told me, finishing up the dressing and stepping back. She bowed before excusing herself, and I turned my attention back to Lysander.

"Thank you," I said, and I meant it about a lot of things. His eyes sparkled, and he offered me a gentle smile as he reached up to cup my cheek, stroking his thumb along my jawline.

"For you, anything," he vowed—and he'd truly proven it. He hesitated before speaking his next words. "The truth is, I'm not ready to let you go... but there are just six days left until the wedding—and by the time you adjust to being on land again, there will only be four."

My bottom lip began to tremble against my will, and he pressed his thumb against it. Tears formed in my eyes.

"I was prepared to go with you, but now that my father is dead, I can't leave the kingdom without someone in charge. And if you choose not to return... someone will need to go to the Sea of Souls and help Maya. I will find a way."

"Do you trust me to come back?" I whispered, and he nodded.

"And I understand if you have no desire to," he added softly, and then it was his turn to get glassy eyed. "I don't deserve you at all, Coral. Not after all I've done to you and everything I've put you through. If you came back, I would question your sanity and whether you really are of capable mind to face Melody alone."

That made me laugh, and he chuckled with me.

"But you've proven yourself capable more than once," he added, and he pulled something else out from under his jacket. *My dagger.* He handed it to me, along with the sheath, and I took it gently from his warm hands. "I cleaned it, by the way—Leif advised me to do so."

I laughed again, and this time I leaned in and pressed my lips to kiss. He leaned into the kiss as if savoring it, and carefully wrapped a hand around my neck. His kiss was addictive, and I didn't want it to ever end.

But my family was waiting for me. I didn't have any more time to waste.

Lysander pulled another thing out from under his jacket—I was starting to think the jacket was enchanted to hold an entire satchel's worth of items—and handed me a scroll.

"This is a spell, which will take you to the surface," he told me. "And when you're ready to return... *if* you return... Leif's men will be nearby and waiting for you."

I nodded, tucking the scroll safely into the folds of my dress. A voice cleared from beside us, and I glanced to my left to see Leif standing there.

"Sorry to interrupt," he said, "but do you want me to remove those cuffs for you before you go?"

I glanced down at the shackles that were still on my wrists.

"Oh... yes, please," I said, extending my arms to him. He pulled out a smaller dagger and got to work picking the locks on each one.

"I will send our forces to assist you as well, if you need them. You only need to ask—your voice will carry on the wind, and they'll be close enough to hear it," Leif told me. He finally cracked the shackles, and they dropped to the floor. I rubbed my wrists thankfully and nodded.

Turning my gaze back to Lysander, I wrapped my arms around him one last time. He squeezed me back.

"I'm sorry about your father," I murmured gently in his ear.

"It's fine," he replied, and I leaned back to study him.
"I'm... a little bothered by it, I'll admit... but I suppose our relationship wasn't the best, so it doesn't appear to be affecting
me very much." His gaze darkened, and he added, "What's
important is that *your* father doesn't meet the same fate.
Which is why you need to go now."

I swallowed hard and nodded again. I didn't think it would
be this difficult to leave him, but standing was one of the hard-
est things I did. Feeling his hands leave mine, and walking
away from him, was even harder.

I looked over my shoulder and saw him standing there by
the stairs—with Leif and Maya in tow.

When I'd run from Melody, I'd vowed to return to save
my sister and dad.

Now, as I read from the shimmering scroll, and a bubble
formed around me to float me back to the surface, I vowed to
return to the Undersea someday.

To help Maya, who had already sacrificed so much for me.

And to be with Lysander again.

CHAPTER THIRTY-ONE

Coral

When I opened my eyes, I felt drained, and something rough was pressed against my cheek. I moved and instantly my stomach rolled with nausea—every single limb in my body feeling ten times heavier than before.

I pushed against rough, wet sand and rolled onto my back, taking steady breaths to try and calm my stomach. It was dark—the stars twinkled above me, and I smelled salt and fresh air. Sand coated my cheek, my palms, and my arms, and waves rolled and sloshed against my legs.

I finally sat up and thought back to what had happened. The last thing I remembered was feeling light-headed in the bubble and then I must have passed out and washed up on land, but I couldn't tell how long I'd been lying here. When I looked down, I saw my pearl necklace lying in the sand beside me, the pearls scattered and undone.

I was finally back on land, finally able to face Melody. And after all this time, I realized I still had no plan. I had no power—only my dagger. Then I remembered that Leif's unit was waiting below the ocean surface and that I could call on them if I needed to. Relief swept through me, but it was short lived. It would mean nothing if I couldn't hold my own against her. I would need to be smart about this.

I slowly got up from where the waves were still lapping at my legs, not bothering to brush the sand off of me. Being back on land was surreal. My experience in the Undersea felt like a fevered dream now that I had returned to my more familiar surroundings.

I didn't know where I was on the island, so I started walking. I was heading around the bend, past a rocky cliffside, when another figure in the darkness made me freeze. The figure hadn't noticed me. They stayed close to the rocks and kept looking up the face of the cliffside.

I held my breath. I didn't know how much time had passed on land or who was loyal to Melody and who wasn't. I debated turning back—even getting straight back into the ocean and swimming instead.

I went to step back and my foot slid on a bunch of shells. They clinked and scraped, and the figure looked toward me.

"Who's there?" they called out. Their voice was low and deep. In fact, it seemed familiar.

I didn't dare respond—barely dared to *breathe*—as the figure inspected me through the darkness. I remembered my dagger, tucked under the bodice of my dress, and slowly began to back my hand toward it.

"No way," the figure said finally. They started racing toward me, and I grabbed the dagger.

"Stay away from me!" I warned, pointing the dagger at them. The figure froze a few paces from me, letting out a yelp. In the moonlight, I could finally make out their face, and my guard dropped.

"Matt!" I cried, and I dropped the dagger, then raced forward to tackle him into a hug. "Oh my God—you're *okay*. You're alive! What are you *doing* here—?"

He hugged me back tightly for a brief moment, then shoved me back.

"What the hell—where have you *been,* Coral?" he demanded, staring at me with wide eyes. "I've been looking everywhere for you for *weeks.* I thought Melody had murdered you! And what are you *wearing?"*

He wrinkled his nose at my sodden gown, and I let out a weak laugh.

"You wouldn't believe me if I told you," I replied. He folded his arms.

"Are you sure about that?" he pressed, glaring at me. "Because since you went radio silent on me, your evil-siren-stepmother has been taking over the entire island. Just about everyone is following her orders, and I've had to pretend like I'm under her crazy-ass spell for weeks!"

Maybe it wouldn't be so crazy for Matt to hear my story, then.

"I'll tell you, but first, I need to know what's happened to my family. *And* how you've been able to evade Melody's siren spell!" I replied quickly.

"Come with me," Matt said, and gestured for me to follow him. I grabbed my dagger and stumbled to keep up in my gown, which felt like a heavy weight around me. "I came here on foot, so I don't have my car. And Melody's sirens are everywhere, so we'd stand out if we were to drive around anyway. But I'm taking you to Maya's grandmother's place—it's the only place we'll be safe."

We hiked up the slope of the beach toward the road.

"What were you doing here anyway?" I asked.

329

"I was trying to find another way into your house. I've been trying to get inside for weeks—trying to find *you,* actually. But Melody has it completely surrounded with guards."

My eyes widened, and I looked back at the rocky cliffside. I knew where we were now—it was the cove on the furthest side of our house. There was no direct access to this cove from the house. Not unless you were prepared to scale the cliff, and even I wouldn't attempt it without some proper rock-climbing gear.

"Do you know if Kendra's inside?" I asked him, and he shook his head.

"I don't know *what's* going on, or what she's done to the place. To be quite honest, I thought Kendra was dead too. The both of you have been missing for a *long* time." He glanced at me and added, "How come she wasn't with you? Did you get separated?"

I let out a steady breath, and as we continued to walk along the dark, deserted road to Ms. Mugo's home, I began explaining everything that had happened to him.

A couple of hours later, I'd changed into a spare blouse and a pair of jeans at Ms. Mugo's house. I'd told Matt about everything... *except* for Maya. I didn't know how to tell him that part, or if I even should.

He'd told me about Melody taking over the island, influencing all the inhabitants with her siren spell, and how Ms.

Mugo had woven him a bracelet to keep him from being affected.

We sat around her kitchen table now, and I was studying
the bracelet. It was made of brown tassels, and it seemed ordinary enough.

"How did you make this?" I asked Ms. Mugo—who had
one of her own.

"Our ancestors *were* witches," she reminded me. "Maya
refused to believe me, insisting that they were just stories, but
my own mother passed down many spells and charms to me.
This is just a simple protection charm—I wasn't even sure if it
would work, but it seems to have."

"But we still have to be careful—the two of us are outnum-
bered by Melody's army, and if she found out we're clear-
headed..," Matt added.

It seemed too easy. A simple charmed bracelet was enough
to prevent Melody's influence? There had to be more to it than
that. But I decided not to dwell on it—I had to get to Kendra
and my dad. And though I didn't want to involve Matt and
Ms. Mugo, I could really use their help.

"I need to get inside my house," I told the two of them. I
didn't know if I'd find either of them there, but it was the first
place worth checking. Especially if Melody was keeping it
well guarded. "I'm the only one who can break Kendra out of
that crystal she's trapped in. And maybe we can get one of
those bracelets onto my dad—"

"I'm sorry," Ms. Mugo said quickly. "The charm I used requires a special material to weave the bracelets—and I don't
have any more of it left. I can't make another one."

331

I grimaced. *Damn it.* I'd have to find another way to snap my dad out of Melody's spell then. I sat for a few more minutes, trying to come up with ideas, but nothing came to me.

Fine, I decided. *I'll figure it out as I go.*

I stood, and added, "I'm going there now. If there's one thing you could do for me, you could create some kind of distraction to lure the guards away. Anything would work, so long as I can sneak in somehow—perhaps through the back, like I used to."

Matt exchanged a look with Ms. Mugo, then nodded.

"We could light a bonfire down on the beach. That would definitely attract attention, at least as far as your house."

I nodded in agreement.

"And I could make sure Lysander's men are nearby, in case you get into any trouble."

They still seemed to be having a hard time wrapping their heads around everything I'd told them—so at the mention of Lysander's men waiting in the ocean, they both blinked a couple of times.

"Right...," Matt said slowly, as he processed. I guess they hadn't been prepared to accept that more magical and mythical beings existed.

"Never mind—just trust me, I've got your back," I promised him. It would be easier if they saw it anyway.

I headed for the front door, double-checking that I had my dagger and the vial Lysander had given me. Matt was right behind me, but Ms. Mugo took a little longer to catch up to us.

"I'll try to be quick," I said to both of them as we walked out of Ms. Mugo's house and down the rickety front steps of her house. "And for the love of God—let's not get caught."

CHAPTER THIRTY-TWO

Coral

By the time we'd made it back to the beach—this time on the side that had the direct trail leading to our house—the sky was starting to lighten. We didn't have a lot of time before the sun would rise, and it would be riskier to be sneaking around the island.

I stayed hidden in the shrubbery while Matt and Ms. Mugo piled the last of the firewood onto a giant bonfire on the beach. Matt had brought a lighter, and he looked to me for confirmation. I nodded, and he flicked the lighter, then began to set the logs afire.

Within minutes, the logs were burning, smoke gathering toward the top of the pile. Matt offered Ms. Mugo his arm as they took off to hide down on the boardwalk—they wanted to be nearby in case they needed to offer additional distractions while I was gone.

I waited among the shrubs and bushes, twitching constantly as I tried to peer up the sloped path for any sign of guards coming down. My thoughts began to stockpile—what if this didn't work? What if they didn't come down? What if I couldn't get past them at all?

Minutes and minutes ticked by, but it felt like an eternity. Then finally, I heard heavy footsteps on the dirt path, and I kept very still as I peered out from my hiding spot.

There, on the path, were three men finally coming down to investigate. I didn't recognize them, but that didn't mean they were sirens. They could have just been ordinary residents that Melody had recruited. Either way, I didn't desire to fight them, so I waited for them to pass me and continue down the path toward the bonfire.

Once they were gone, I snuck from my hiding spot and hurried up the path, doing my best to keep to the shrubs in case I ran into any more guards. The path seemed so much longer than I remembered, and my heart was racing as I continued up and up the slope.

Then finally, at long last, I reached the cliffside rock once more and pulled myself up.

I'd made it, and I did a quick sweep to make sure there were no more guards nearby. I didn't see anyone, so I hurried to the back gate of my house.

Then I stared at the gate code, and horror slammed into me.

What if Melody changed the gate code?

I quickly punched in the old code, and it flashed red with a beep. I felt as if ice water had washed down my back as I stared at the locked gate, my heart beating in a panic.

What now? I thought, looking over my shoulder again to make sure I was still alone.

I looked up at the towering stone walls that circled our house and grimaced. I was going to have to climb over. But I needed a boost to reach the top of the wall.

Looking at the gate, there weren't enough slats for me to climb up. But there was one toward the bottom that would boost me high enough to grasp the top of the stone wall.

335

So I hooked my foot onto the slat and used all the upper body strength I could manage to pull myself upward on the gate. I reached desperately for the top of the wall, stretching my fingers as far as I could.

And then my fingers grasped it. I grunted, trying to shimmy just enough that I could get a firm grip. My hand clutched the stone, and I managed to heave myself up and over the wall. I was sweating by the time I made it, my abdomen aching from the effort. Looking down into our ever-blooming garden, I knew the drop would hurt and braced myself as I jumped down.

My feet slammed into the ground, and even though I'd kept my knees bent, they still went numb with white hot pain for a moment. I winced, trying to wriggle the pain out of my toes and stumbled forward a few steps.

I couldn't take the back stairs this time—it would be way too risky. Instead, my eyes fell upon the trellis leading to Kendra and I's bedroom windows. It was thick from the pink bougainvillea that grew on it, but I saw places where I'd be able to grasp the trellis and climb up. I quickly crept over and reached up to grab hold. Then I began to climb, my feet scraping a little as I kicked away the bougainvillea to gain footing.

It took me a few minutes to climb the entire thing, and I shimmied over so that I was under Kendra's bedroom window. I tried to ignore the way my hands were shaking from the height.

Now, I just needed to get the window open. It was locked from the inside, the curtains drawn, and I hadn't thought to bring a rock up with me.

Then, I remembered my dagger, and I very carefully reached down to unsheathe it from my side, my fingers grasping the trellis tightly.

I twisted the dagger in my hand so that the hilt was aimed at the window, then shut my eyes tight. I lunged, and I heard the window crack. Opening my eyes, there was a huge spiderweb crack in the center of the glass.

One more hit, I thought, and I lunged again. The glass shattered, and fragments flew everywhere, falling down around me and into the curtains. I shook the curtains to try and clear the way, then sheathed my dagger again and carefully climbed through.

As I pulled the curtains aside and stepped through, I spotted Kendra's encased body lying on her bed. Relief sagged through me, nearly causing me to collapse on the spot at the sight of her.

I rushed forward toward her bed, holding back a sob, and placed my hands against the crystal.

"Kendra," I breathed, staring at her peaceful sleeping form frozen within the crystal. Our mother's necklace still sat around her neck—protecting her. The crystal glimmered under my touch in hues of vibrant blue and lilac. I pressed my hands more firmly to the crystal, trying to figure out how to break the crystal. I needed to get her out of here.

I remembered what Nerissa had said about me passing through the Alta Palace. *The magic recognizes pure intentions.*

I closed my eyes and visualized embracing Kendra—keeping her safe. Escorting her out of here. Taking her far, far away from Melody.

The crystal moved under my fingers, and my eyes snapped open. It was melting under my touch. My eyes widened, and I watched as it shrunk and flickered away, leaving Kendra's sleeping form perfectly intact in front of me.

Slowly, Kendra's eyes fluttered open.

The sob finally escaped my throat.

I wrapped my arms around her tightly, pulling her toward me, and blinked back tears as I held her. *She was okay.*

After all this time, I had her.

"Coral?" she asked, her voice croaky. "What... happened...?"

I felt her hands lightly touch my shoulders, like she wasn't sure whether to hug me back. I leaned back, and she looked around slowly.

"How did I get here? Weren't we just at Melody's party?"

"There's no time to explain," I replied quickly, grabbing her hand to pull her to her feet. "Can you walk? We need to hurry."

She frowned at me, but I dragged her toward the door. Now, all I needed to do was find my dad, and we could get the hell out of here!

I pulled her into the hallway, scanning both ways quickly, then crept down the hall. It had started to rain outside, the sound echoing on the roof. Kendra crept behind me, but her footsteps weren't as quiet as mine.

"What is going *on?*" she demanded in a hiss, and I whipped around to face her and pressed a finger to my lips. We finally reached the staircase, and I descended first to scan the foyer over the railing. When I saw that it was clear, I waved Kendra down, and she hesitantly crept after me. Her eyes were scanning the room too now, trying to piece the situation together.

"Where's Dad?" I whispered finally, but I felt stupid for asking. Of *course* Kendra didn't know where he was—she'd been asleep this entire time. Frustration bubbled in me as we continued to search the house.

As we entered the kitchen, Kendra eyed the pale sky outside and then the digital clock above the fridge that spelled out the date and time.

"Wait... how long have I been out?" she asked, her face going pale.

I turned to face her fully. "It's a long story—but it's been three weeks," I said quickly, and her bottom lip fell.

"What the *hell?*" she asked, her voice trembling. "Coral, *what is going on?*"

I shook my head at her. "Not now—we *need* to find Dad. Where did Melody say they were getting married again?"

"Why does that even matter right now—?"

"Kendra!" I cried finally, everything in me snapping. "Melody is going to *kill him.*"

Kendra backed up two steps, eyes wide with horror. Her throat bobbed, and her hands began to shake.

"She... uh..." she stammered, shaking her head like she was trying to think. "I think she said they were going to marry at the sailing club."

I grabbed Kendra's hand.

"Let's go," I ordered, and tugged her back through the kitchen toward the back stairs.

I made it about five steps before my heart began to glow, and I ran straight into someone.

The first thing I noticed was the heavy scent of jasmine and white rose. I looked up, and a pair of narrowed green eyes bore back at me under thick, full lashes.

Melody smiled sweetly at us, planting her hands on her hips and then purred, "Welcome back, *Coral.*"

CHAPTER THIRTY-THREE

Coral

I shoved Kendra behind me and drew my dagger in an instant, pointing it straight at Melody. She chuckled at me, her voice sweet like a lullaby.

"Oh, you won't be needing that, my dear," she sang at me, and her power hit me—*ten* times stronger than I'd ever felt it. I dropped the dagger instantly, and it clattered to the ground.

My heart began to thud in my chest, but I refused to show my fear, squaring my shoulders at her.

She'd done enough damage—I wouldn't let her harm Kendra.

"How was your time away?" she asked, her eyes glittering with amusement. "Did you enjoy the company of the undines? Was Lysander as *charming* as you'd hoped he'd be?"

"More charming than you've ever been," I shot back, and Melody's smile fell slightly.

"Well, I'm sorry I didn't live up to your expectations, my dear daughter," she drawled back. "Won't you give me another chance to prove myself?"

Her words were heavy, and my head began to spin. I clutched my temple, wincing, and Melody's smug laugh echoed again.

"Step... daughter..." I ground out through gritted teeth.

"Stepdaughter or not," she whispered back, grabbing my arm with her clawed hand and bringing me close so that I was eye to eye with her. "You're *mine.*"

She walked me back into the wall, and I smacked into it. A gasp ripped through my throat, and my spine throbbed in protest. Melody's eyes gleamed with hunger and greed as her gaze trailed to my chest.

To my *heart,* which continued to glow brightly like a beacon, showing her exactly where to rip into me.

Something between a scream and cry sounded, and my gaze snapped to Kendra—who lunged forward at Melody and plunged something into her gut. The necklace around Kendra's neck shimmered brightly. My gaze flicked down to whatever Kendra had stabbed Melody with.

My dagger, I realized, and my eyes widened as Melody staggered back from me, gasping. She clutched where the wound was as blood began to seep through her cream designer dress. Melody's eyes narrowed to slits as she looked up at us.

I sprung into action, grabbing Kendra, and we sprinted for the back door. If Melody followed, she wasn't fast enough.

"Grab that chair!" I shouted to Kendra, as we tore across the stone terrace. Kendra paused beside the iron outdoor dining set that sat under our lemon tree and began dragging the chair toward the gate. I shoved it against the wall and urged Kendra to use it as a boost and climb over first. My gaze tore to the back door, watching for Melody.

She appeared a moment later—the dagger gone from her abdomen and now clutched in her hand—and she stormed toward us, her eyes glittering with rage.

I scrambled after Kendra, hoisting myself up and over the wall. My foot only just escaped Melody's clawed hand as I tumbled over, and this time I rolled and fell. I landed hard in the dirt and I felt something pop. White hot pain erupted from my shoulder, and I cried out.

"Coral!" Kendra cried, but I pushed myself upright with my good hand and we kept moving. The pain in my shoulder throbbed, and my entire right arm had gone limp. I tried to hold it steady with my good hand as we ran, so as not to cause more pain than necessary, but it continued to ache regardless.

"We need to get to the beach," I said through gritted teeth, trying to hold it together as hot tears welled in my eyes. We scaled down the path as fast as we could, knowing Melody was right behind us.

"You need a doctor!" Kendra cried as we ran. I let out a dry laugh.

"There are no doctors—everyone is enslaved to *Melody!"* I growled back, as we sprinted down the slope.

We made it to the beach quickly, but we couldn't keep running. I ran to the edge of the rolling waves and looked out into the sea, but I couldn't leave without my dad. Then I looked to the boardwalk, but by the time I'd done that, Melody had finally caught up to us.

"Stop!" she growled, and I was instantly frozen in position on the sand. She was panting, her breath ragged and her dress bloody, clutching a hand to her gut. It clearly wasn't a fatal wound, but if she kept bleeding, maybe we'd have a better chance of stopping her. Her other hand grasped my dagger so tightly her knuckles turned white.

"You have meddled for the *last* time, dear daughter," she seethed at me, baring her perfect white teeth.

Three guards were approaching us from the boardwalk now—with two other people in tow. I recognized Matt, who was sporting a ginormous gash on his forehead, in the grasp of a guard. But the second...

"Dad!" Kendra cried, and I wanted to cry tears of joy at the sight of him. Dad's eyes brightened at the sight of us, but then he saw the blood on Melody's dress.

"Oh my God—*Darling!"* he cried, and raced across the sand to her side. "What happened to you?"

Melody brushed him off with a cold sweep of her hand, still shaking with rage.

"Stand aside, Christopher," she snapped at him, then turned to one of the guards and pointed a slender, manicured finger at him. "You—go get an officiant. We're doing this wedding *right now."*

She turned to glare at me and added, "Before this one slips away again."

The guard raced off across the sand, leaving Matt in the other guard's clutches. He spoke up.

"We found this one and an older woman—both appear immune to your spell," he informed Melody. "But the older one got away."

Matt snarled at the guard, blood dripping down his face, and something told me he'd been the reason Ms. Mugo had escaped with her life.

Melody was still breathing heavily and swallowed hard.

"Kill him," she rasped, barely looking at him.

"No!" I cried, my heart rate quickening, and Melody glared up at me.

"Make it long and painful," she added, her lips curving as she stared at me.

My gaze flew back to Matt, and one of the guards already had a dagger drawn. But Matt roared in outrage, thrashing against the other guard. He was fit—he hadn't stopped surfing, like I had—and managed to yank one arm free and started clawing at the guard who had him. I struggled against Melody's spell, screaming as well, but I couldn't get to him

Kendra was shaking, her eyes wide as she stared at the horror unfolding. The guard with the knife lunged for Matt, but Kendra sprung into action and barreled into the two of them.

"Kendra!" I screamed, my heart pounding as I watched. Matt tumbled free of his guard, and Kendra helped as they tackled him to the ground. Matt then turned fast, tripping the armed guard with his foot before the dagger could plunge into his back. He wrestled the dagger from him and threw it out into the sea before either guards could take it from him.

"Enough!" Melody roared, her throat hoarse. The guards grabbed Matt and Kendra and hoisted them to their feet, but they continued to struggle—immune to Melody's spell due to their protective charms.

Melody strode toward me and grabbed my hand. I held my breath, my entire body tense, as she placed the hilt of my dagger into my good palm and curled my fingers around it.

"Dear daughter," she whispered, her voice feathery and light. "I order you to carve out your sister's heart."

Immediately, the compulsion took hold of me, and my blood turned to ice. I couldn't stop my legs as they moved toward my sister.

No...

I gripped the dagger tightly, holding it ready, my eyes locked onto her. My dislocated shoulder had eased to a dull, almost numb ache.

Stop.

Kendra struggled against the guard that held her, and Matt was yelling for me to stop. But I couldn't stop. I inched closer and closer.

Please...

Her eyes were filled with fear, and tears streaked her face. She trembled, eyeing the deadly sharp blade of my dagger.

I lifted my hand, preparing to lunge at her. Matt's roar was so loud it nearly burst my eardrums.

And then something moved between us as I brought my hand down. The dagger connected, plunging through his chest.

My entire body went numb.

My dad stood there, staring blankly at me.

The compulsion broke, and my hand instantly let go of the dagger. I let out a choked cry, and my dad stumbled a little.

"No..." I said, my voice breaking.

My dad's eyes crinkled slightly—almost kindly. He'd stopped me... he'd protected *Kendra*...

How had he broken free of the spell? It was so unexpected, so *similar* to how Lysander had broken free to protect me from Eugene Pryor...

"I'm sorry," my dad croaked at me. Then, he collapsed.

346

I began to pant heavily, my breaths ragged, and tears formed in my eyes.

"Someone do something!" I cried, staring in horror as he lay still in the sand. *"Someone do something!"*

Kendra was bawling. Matt had gone quiet. I couldn't breathe. But nobody did anything because it was too late.

He was already gone.

CHAPTER THIRTY-FOUR

Coral

In that moment, a screech tore through the air, piercing my eardrums so bad, I had to clutch my ears. I turned to Melody, who was shaking and looking at me with pure murder intent.

"No!" she wailed, her screech unbearable. I wanted to rip my ears off, it was so bad. *"Christopher!"*

I didn't understand why she was screaming—she hadn't even *loved* him!

She took a shaky step toward me, nostrils flaring at me.

"I will *kill* you, Coral Klassan! You're just as treacherous as your wretched *mother!"*

I spotted a guard racing down the beach, accompanied by another man, and I remembered how Melody had sent for an officiant. It hit me all of a sudden.

I was the living heir to the land and sea.

My father had passed before Melody could marry. Now, Melody had no way to inherit the island's power and leverage ancient law.

I stepped toward her.

"If you kill me and Kendra, then there will be nobody left to grant you power over the land," I replied plainly. *Not that we ever would.* "I would advise you to consider your next moves carefully."

"My next move is to *carve your heart from your chest,*" Melody snarled, taking another step. I backed against my father's body, and my gut heaved as I reached down with my good arm and pulled the dagger free from his chest. I leaped back just as Melody swiped at me with her vicious claws, her eyes feral.

My eyes flickered to my father's body as Melody backed me toward the swelling ocean waves. My grandfather's words echoed in my head all of a sudden.

No creatures of the Undersea, except for merpeople, are capable of true, unconditional love and kindness.

I felt the cold ocean water slosh against my ankles.

That is what makes mer-hearts so powerful... and what makes Melody so vicious. If you seek to use your own power, you will find it in that one strength.

I held the dagger steady as Melody stalked toward me, predatory and snarling. Lysander's words replaced my grandfather's.

As soon as he hurt you, I somehow recovered my free will, and I ran before I knew what I was doing.

I'd been about to hurt Kendra... and my dad snapped out of Melody's spell.

Love.

Love was more powerful than a siren spell.

"You may have controlled our father for months, but he loved us, fully and unconditionally," I said slowly to Melody. "There's nothing you could have done to break that bond. He would have saved us a thousand times over."

Melody let out a low, humorless laugh.

"Your father was *blind* to my terrorizations for *months,*" she seethed. "Can you really be so sure?"

I blinked hot tears out of my eyes.

"You'll never know what it's like to be loved unconditionally—because your kind is *truly* heartless and incapable of love. I pity you, Melody. I pity the miserable existence you live, where only power can satisfy your needs... and even then, it's not enough."

She screeched and swiped her claws at my face. I ducked and stepped back even further into the waves, which now sloshed around my knees. My dislocated arm still ached dully, and I panted as adrenaline pumped through me. Kendra and Matt were calling out to me from the shore, but I couldn't hear their words over the waves.

If love was more powerful than a siren spell, then just how powerful *was* it? Was it more powerful than curses and bindings? Was it more powerful than ancient magic?

If I unleashed my heart magic right now, I wouldn't have to kill Melody.

I could do far *worse* to her—and she deserved to suffer after all she'd done to us. I could curse her, like Ms. Mugo had originally told me to. I could—

She swiped again, and this time, she got my dislocated arm. I barely registered the scratch as she clawed my upper arm, leaving three long lines of blood there. I stumbled back so far that the waves came up around my waist, and I thought of Lysander.

Lysander...

I thought of all he'd done for me. All he'd given up for me. And I knew I *couldn't* unleash my heart magic. Not unless...

Not unless...

My mind was reeling, and I was only half focused on Melody. Maybe it could work. Maybe it would be enough. I prayed it would be—if this didn't work, I would never forgive myself.

"Maya," I whispered, but the waves and wind were drowning out my voice. *"Maya!"* I shouted, and I closed my eyes as I felt into it.

I give my heart.

I thought of Lysander, and I longed for him to have my heart. It was his—it always had been. And it was my deepest desire for him to accept it.

"Maya, please," I breathed and opened my eyes—just in time to see Melody tackle me into the waves.

Pain flashed through me. Her claws dug into my arms as she grappled with me, trying to reach my chest. Salt water went up my nose and burned. I struggled against her, trying to shove her off of me. My chest ached from the lack of oxygen.

The current intensified around me, and Melody's claws dislodged as she was swept aside. It was only a moment of reprieve, but I acted fast—slashing at her torso with the dagger. She recoiled, red blood staining the water, and I tried to push up to the surface. My lungs were burning—I had one last huff of air in me before I'd run out.

Then, I felt a warm presence wrap around me, and somehow, I knew without looking that it was my mother's spirit. *She was here.*

She whispered something in my ear, and I used my last breath of air to repeat them, the words soundless and dull underwater.

351

And then I felt something snap into place in my chest.

I inhaled involuntarily, my lungs desperate for oxygen. Everything burned as I swallowed water. My limbs began to ache, and I felt a strange tingling throughout my body. The dagger slipped from my fingers.

And then my heart began to shine, and my chest bubbled with power, and I felt the waters swirl around my fingers long-ingly—twirling along my fingertips and traveling up my wrists and arms. It was as if the ocean itself was wrapping around me, as if I could hold it in both hands and bend it to my will.

Melody was cutting through the current, fiercely swim-ming back toward me. But I took one look at her, and it was as if the ocean itself could feel my will.

It erupted around me, like a tornado, the sound roaring as the waves spun and swept her up. I threw her back toward the land and let the current carry me through the waves.

My head emerged, inhaling oxygen again, and I spotted her body lying in the sand—her dress sodden, her hair matted. She shakily pushed herself upright and twisted around to face me.

I held out my good hand, palm facing Melody, just as Maya had done with the sirens, and my voice echoed on the wind.

"I bind you, Melody Pryor. I bind you from doing harm. I bind you from using your power. I bind you for the rest of time."

Melody went slack, and she let out a screech of anguish. But it no longer pierced my ears—and she looked like a wail-ing child throwing a tantrum on the shore. Kendra and Matt were looking on with eyes wide open—staring at the waves rippling and swirling powerfully around my body... and staring at *me*.

And then the power left my body. The waves settled back into a calm rhythm around me. A strange tingling came over my body—along with an overwhelming wave of exhaustion.

Then, the usually gentle breeze began to rip into my skin, piercing me like a thousand needles, and I stiffened as pain shot over every inch of my body.

If you unlock your magic and change into your mer-form, you will be trapped forever. You will never be able to return to the surface.

I tried to inhale the air, but I couldn't breathe. It was like air refused to enter my lungs. Black spots danced in my vision.

Kendra and Matt were calling out to me again, but their voices sounded distant and far. I sank into the waves, my body going numb, my vision going black.

And then there was nothing.

EPILOGUE

Lysander

I'd never known that being king would require so much paper-work, so much *planning* and *strategizing.*

I didn't know how Leif could stand to do this every day. Even now, I wanted to disappear to my chambers or escape into the gardens to be alone with the fish. Instead, I had dozens of requests to approve, war plans to familiarize myself with, and... certain thoughts of Coral to block out of my mind.

My heart ached at the thought of her. I longed for her to return, and every time she came to mind, my stomach turned with worry.

There was a knock at my study door, and Leif entered, carrying half a dozen more scrolls under his arm. I groaned out loud at the sight of them.

"*How* are there more of these?" I protested, but Leif only smirked.

"Perhaps you were onto something when you fantasized about *not* becoming king," he replied. "My men just reported that Eugene Pryor is planning another attack, and *soon.* I've put these reports together for you to look over."

I leaned back in my chair, my hair floating around my face, and closed my eyes. Maybe if I continued like this, I would simply disappear, and all duty would forsake me.

Something snapped into place in my chest all of a sudden, and all at once, a plethora of emotions hit me—*pain, anger, fear, joy.*

I jerked so fast I fell from my chair, gasping so hard I felt I might choke.

"What is it?" Leif demanded, rushing forward. I clutched my chest, my *heart...*

Frowning, I felt into the new feelings. What was this?

It couldn't be.

It shouldn't have been possible. I'd given up my heart to save Coral. How was this possible?

"Lysander?" Leif urged, staring wildly at me. Slowly, I gripped the desk and pulled myself upright, steadying myself as ripples of emotion flooded through me. I was shaking and crying and on the verge of laughing all at once.

What had she done?

"Your unit," I rasped, meeting his gaze. "Send your men to Coral. *Do it now!*"

Leif's eyes widened, then he nodded and rushed from the room. I collapsed back into my chair, burying my head in my hands—just as a *second* bond snapped into place. This time, I felt it resonate throughout every bone in my body, and I inhaled sharply.

Awareness settled over me.

Coral had become the most powerful being of the Undersea—heir to the land and sea, and... my *queen.* A Reigning Queen.

Of course, I realized. *Because she gave me her heart.*

I was king, which made her queen, because now I was hers... *and she was mine.*

355

ACKNOWLEDGEMENTS

Let's start by thanking my haters.

Without them, I wouldn't have been motivated to write this book the way I have, nor record the entire publishing process (which I know is going to benefit SO many authors out there.)

Secondly, I want to thank my community, for always supporting me and motivating me to do the work I do. Writing might seem easy on the outside, but I endure demotivation and self-doubt too. It's you guys that always remind me how far I've come and how much I still have to give the world.

Thirdly, I want to thank those who contributed to this book: Sam, for beta reading, Kayla, for sensitivity reading, Susan, for proofreading, and Bianca, for cover design. Without all of you, this book wouldn't be anywhere near as good as it is today.

And finally, if you're new around here, I want to thank you for picking up this book and reading it.

ABOUT THE AUTHOR

Pagan Alexandria is a fairy tale retelling author best known for her dual retelling of Snow White and The Little Mermaid, KINGDOM OF SIRENS AND MONSTERS.

She grew up in Proserpine, Queensland— a small, Australian country town on the edge of the Great Barrier Reef— when she gained the inspiration for her debut contemporary novel, STUCK ON VACATION WITH RYAN RUPERT (published under P.S.Malcolm).

Pagan quickly realised she had a love of blending contemporary worlds with fantasy, and went on to write a seven book fantasy series, THE STARLIGHT CHRONICLES (signed by Lycaon Press in 2015 and The Parliament House Press in 2017) before walking away from traditional publishing to go completely independent.

Today, Pagan writes dual retellings of beloved fairy tales— filled with star-crossed romance, morally grey characters, supernatural twists and a sprinkle of spice. When isn't writing, she's making charcuterie boards, playing cosy video games, and recording her podcast, Bestseller Energy.

Follow Pagan on Instagram for updates: @PaganAlexandriaCreative

THE STORY CONTINUES...

KINGDOM OF SONGS AND CURSES (BOOK TWO)

The kingdom is crumbling, her reign forthcoming.

The Undersea has a new queen—but Coral Klassan has far more than mere court duties to worry about. Between retrieving her best friend's lost soul, navigating King Lysander's newfound emotions, defending the kingdom from the ruthless Eugene Pryor, and uncovering a dark secret about a terrible curse, the highly anticipated conclusion to this duology will test Coral's strength and reveal whether she truly has the grit to rule the Undersea, and all the monsters within it.

HEART OF STONE AND SEA-FOAM (NOVELLA)

A mermaid and a siren—an unlikely friendship, and one that will tear the land and the sea apart. The Little Mermaid meets The Evil Queen in this stunning prequel novella, where the story of Coral Klassan's mother and step-mother will finally be told.

Continue to the next pages for a free preview…

ONE

Melody

I lounged in the courtyard of our manor, watching my brother and mother bicker with our handmaidens. Usually, the courtyard was a peaceful and inviting space—with red potted seagrass lining the towering set of double doors on all four sides of us and a fountain at the center of the squared space releasing a fast, consistent stream of air bubbles that spiraled up and up and *up*.

But today, it was chaos and mayhem as my mother commanded the space. I averted my gaze for the umpteenth time as she snarled at our handmaidens, baring her teeth, and listened as they scurried to rifle through the arrangement of fine gowns and coats on a long rack. It had taken two dozen servants to lug the rack down to the courtyard.

It was always such a *pain* when Mother got like this. Mother loved the spaciousness and light in the courtyard cast by the red crystal lights, and it was closed off to the public eye, so she always insisted that we did our fittings here. But I could have *sworn* she did it just to spite us... simply because she could.

"Don't you think the green matches my dazzling eyes, Mother?" Eugene cooed, and I looked up again as he snatched a lush green coat from the rack. The emblazoned sapphires along the cuffs and collar glittered under the golden glow crystals lining every intricate pillar of our home. I turned up my nose at him as he threw the coat over his shoulders and admired himself in a nearby standing mirror. The handmaidens nodded meekly with approval, but their shoulders were tense, and they practically skittered away as my mother strode toward Eugene.

Scowling, she ripped the coat from his shoulders and threw it to the ground, and Eugene gaped at her in shock.

"Don't be ridiculous, Eugene," she replied, her voice low. "You will never attract anybody worth marrying in a coat like that. You are a prize to be won, and you must dress like such!"

Her words burned in my gut, and I shifted my gaze away once more as Eugene's shoulders slackened. How many times had she aimed that same condescending tone at me and told me I was only good for my status?

As my gaze drifted, I noticed a tray sitting at the end of the marble bench I lounged on. It was filled with stacks of oysters and a large, alluring bowl of caviar, and had most likely been left by the servants.

My mouth watered, but I stayed put as I eyed my mother again. She had her back to me and was now ordering the handmaidens to find something bold and red for Eugene. Eyeing the display of food again, my stomach rumbled quietly, and I longed to devour all of it. I hadn't eaten all morning, but the thought alone made my gut twist in guilt, yet it simultaneously increased the urge to shove all the food down my throat.

Finally, after many agonizingly slow minutes had ticked by, I couldn't stand it. Quickly and quietly, I slid across the bench and seized the opportunity to gulp down a spoonful of the caviar. I nearly moaned at the taste. It was soft and fresh, with a mild saltiness that I relished. Addicted, I swallowed another quick mouthful, then *another*, before skirting back across the bench and resuming my bored reclining as if I'd never moved.

By the time I felt my mother's gaze return to me, I had my eyes fixed on the regal red tiled floor and was twirling my golden hair in my fingers—the same golden curls we both shared that earned us envious looks at the market from other sirens.

"Melody," she drawled, and her tone made me tense. I met her gaze with a cool expression—the kind I'd plastered on my face a million times and had mastered years ago. This entire routine was like clockwork to me.

"What is it, sweet Mother?" I asked innocently, and she narrowed her gaze at me, planting her hands on her hips.

"I asked for you to come—I've found you a gown," she replied. Her words burned in my gut again—the feeling full of dread and despair and resentment. But I obeyed, gracefully rising from the bench, and walked toward my mother with my shoulders squared. I expected her to hand me some ridiculous, extravagant gown in the same shade of red as the coat the handmaidens were now fitting on Eugene. Or something outrageously gold.

But she surprised me when she handed me a long sleeveless gown of deep royal blue. It lacked the puffy sleeves, gems, and ruffles my mother favored. But the material was shiny and metallic—like armor. *Powerful yet simple.*

I frowned at it, then at her.

"What is this?" I blurted finally. "Did you not just scold Eugene for wanting to wear green?"

My mother's eyes gleamed.

"Your *brother* is not trying to impress Nikolai Galanis."

The dread in my gut coiled tighter, and it felt like the walls of the courtyard were closing in on me. Sometimes, I envied Eugene; being male, all he had to do was look good, wait on a female siren who wanted to claim him, and produce a ring to the lucky siren who deemed him worthy. But being female, it was different for me. The options were limited... and the stakes were too high...

"Who says I am trying to impress Nikolai?" I shot back carefully, stepping away from my mother. She let out a long breath, and I knew she wasn't going to let this go.

"Melody, darling, you've had *months* to decide. So now, I am deciding for you. And the ball is just three short days away—"

"—I will *not* attend the ball with Nikolai," I said firmly, and my mother's gaze darkened with displeasure. The hairs rose on my arms and neck. I knew I was playing a dangerous game, talking back to her like this. Even Eugene sensed the tension, and he stepped in between us.

"Mother, she has three days left. Perhaps Melody has already decided on another suitor?" Eugene said calmly, his eyes flicking between both of us. When he met mine, they communicated a silent question:

Tell me you've picked someone.

I scowled, that suffocating feeling increasing, and I wanted to laugh. A long, hysterical laugh. If only they knew what I really wanted... they would exile me instantly. What I desired was impossible and so far from my mother's wishes, it would never stand.

Nikolai was the son of Alastair and Elenora Galanis—and they were the second most powerful siren clan in all of Coronis. We were the third, and my mother reveled in the knowledge of us being *so* close to overthrowing Queen Chora and ruling Coronis for ourselves.

But the only way for us to gain enough power would be for me to raise my status, and that meant I had to marry up, not down. Only females could raise their status on behalf of their clan, and in order to do that, I had to claim a husband from a higher clan than ours.

Not to mention that succession was different here to all other kingdoms, and when a new clan was recognized to be most powerful, the Undersea would crown them. If we could not beat the Galanis clan in the race to overthrow Queen Chora, the next best thing would be to have married directly into their family, raising our status to the second level... and I was my mother's most valuable asset. More powerful than Eugene, whose masculinity was a weakness. Because males only existed to be claimed, to be showcased and paraded like trophies, and the song of a female siren was the most dangerous and alluring of all.

I knew my mother had her sights set on Sloane Drakos for Eugene—she was in the fifth highest clan—but he'd be lucky to attract her attention at all. A female like her had the entire kingdom of Coronis to pick from, with hundreds of males falling at her feet for the chance to be considered. In fact, she was probably aiming for Nikolai's attention too.

Eugene and I both knew we were puppets in my mother's game of power, and I was helpless to stop her. Even if I ran away, if I entertained my own desires... if I married for love or didn't marry at all... I would be exiled. My status gone; my power weakened. It was worse to be unmarried and "independent" in Coronis than it was to marry into a lower clan. And my brother... he would be alone. I couldn't leave him all alone to endure my parents and their constant demands.

I let my shoulders drop and slowly reached out to take the dress from my mother. A dress to keep me small—that wouldn't upstage my potential suitor.

A slow, satisfied smile grew on Mother's lips, and her eyes glimmered again as she said,

"Nikolai favors blue—you'd do well to remember that, *Melody darling.*"

Continue reading this companion novella by ordering your copy of HEART OF STONE AND SEA-FORM.

Links to order are available on Pagan's Instagram: @PaganAlexandriaCreative

www.ingramcontent.com/pod-product-compliance
Lightning Source LLC
Chambersburg PA
CBHW020255120726
47904CB00001B/206